ACCIDENTAL HEROES

Danielle Steel has been hailed as one of the world's
most popular authors, with nearly a billion copies of her
novels sold. Her recent international bestsellers include
Fairytale, Past Perfect and *Fall From Grace*. She is also the
author of *His Bright Light*, the story of her son Nick Traina's
life and death; *A Gift of Hope*, a memoir of her work with
the homeless; and the children's books *Pretty Minnie in Paris*
and *Pretty Minnie in Hollywood*. Danielle divides her time
between Paris and her home in northern California.

By Danielle Steel

Accidental Heroes • Fall From Grace • Past Perfect • Fairytale
The Right Time • The Duchess • Against All Odds • Dangerous Games
The Mistress • The Award • Rushing Waters • Magic • The Apartment
Property Of A Noblewoman • Blue • Precious Gifts • Undercover • Country
Prodigal Son • Pegasus • A Perfect Life • Power Play • Winners • First Sight
Until The End Of Time • The Sins Of The Mother • Friends Forever
Betrayal • Hotel Vendôme • Happy Birthday • 44 Charles Street • Legacy
Family Ties • Big Girl • Southern Lights • Matters Of The Heart
One Day At A Time • A Good Woman • Rogue • Honor Thyself
Amazing Grace • Bungalow 2 • Sisters • H.R.H. • Coming Out • The House
Toxic Bachelors • Miracle • Impossible • Echoes • Second Chance
Ransom • Safe Harbour • Johnny Angel • Dating Game • Answered Prayers
Sunset In St. Tropez • The Cottage • The Kiss • Leap Of Faith • Lone Eagle
Journey • The House On Hope Street • The Wedding • Irresistible Forces
Granny Dan • Bittersweet • Mirror Image • The Klone And I
The Long Road Home • The Ghost • Special Delivery • The Ranch
Silent Honor • Malice • Five Days In Paris • Lightning • Wings • The Gift
Accident • Vanished • Mixed Blessings • Jewels • No Greater Love
Heartbeat • Message From Nam • Daddy • Star • Zoya • Kaleidoscope
Fine Things • Wanderlust • Secrets • Family Album • Full Circle • Changes
Thurston House • Crossings • Once In A Lifetime • A Perfect Stranger
Remembrance • Palomino • Love: *Poems* • The Ring • Loving • To Love Again
Summer's End • Season Of Passion • The Promise • Now And Forever
Passion's Promise • Going Home

Nonfiction
Pure Joy: *The Dogs We Love*
A Gift Of Hope: *Helping the Homeless*
His Bright Light: *The Story of Nick Traina*

For Children
Pretty Minnie In Paris
Pretty Minnie In Hollywood

Danielle Steel

ACCIDENTAL HEROES

MACMILLAN

First published 2018 by Delacorte Press,
an imprint of Random House,
a division of Penguin Random House LLC, New York.

First published in the UK 2018 by Macmillan
an imprint of Pan Macmillan
20 New Wharf Road, London N1 9RR
Associated companies throughout the world
www.panmacmillan.com

ISBN 978-1-5098-0046-9

1 3 5 7 9 8 6 4 2

A CIP catalogue record for this book is available from the British Library.

Printed and bound in Australia by McPhersons Printing Group

Visit **www.panmacmillan.com** to read more about all our books
and to buy them. You will also find features, author interviews and
news of any author events, and you can sign up for e-newsletters
so that you're always first to hear about our new releases.

To my wonderful, very special children,
Beatie, Trevor, Todd, Nick, Sam,
Victoria, Vanessa, Maxx, and Zara,

You are *my* heroes, and always will be,
bravely facing the challenges
that have confronted us,
with poise and dignity,
courage and grace.

You have my love and admiration,
always! And forever!

I love you so much,

Mom/d.s.

Foreword

Dear Reader,

Accidental Heroes was an exciting and challenging book to write because the action and interactions happen on so many levels. It is inspired by, and reminiscent of, some of the challenges of traveling today, and at the same time it is reassuring, because it reminds us of how *many* agencies are involved to safeguard us when we travel. Mishaps can happen anywhere (you can slip in the bathtub at home too, or trip over your dog when you take him for a walk). But from the time we enter the security lines at any airport—which seem so annoying as we take off our shoes, get slowed down as we wrestle other passengers for plastic bins to put our belongings in—we forget that those security measures are there for our safety (not just to annoy us), and that they *do* protect us from untoward things happening. And beyond that, there is airport security watching what goes on in the entire airport, Homeland Security and all the federal agencies, and highly trained people under that umbrella who are actually like guardian angels, unseen by us, watching over us even before we take off, during our flights, and until we leave the airport when we reach our destination. It really is reassuring.

And in the case of something unexpected happening, or even suspected, it is fascinating to know how many agencies and skilled people are involved to solve the mystery and the problem *before* something happens. That's good to remember too.

I was fascinated by the different personalities involved, with the characters in the book. The very, very capable senior Homeland Security agent, at JFK Airport, whose confidence has been shaken by a recent incident, so he has to get it right this time. The psychiatrist who helps evaluate situations. The young female agent with multiple degrees but little experience. The young TSA agent, a single mother, who follows her instincts and is smart enough and brave enough to do so. Passengers, police, federal agents, the fantastic female–Air Force pilot, the crew, and passengers on the plane.

I also wanted to honor the fact that we never know how we will react to unusual situations. The meekest among us can turn out to have the courage of a lion, and in the toughest of times, we draw on resources we didn't even know we had. Many of us turn out to be accidental heroes when we least expect it. I hope you'll enjoy the people you meet in this book, and the events that unfold as a network of people do their jobs with remarkable skill.

Have a great time reading!

Love, Danielle

ACCIDENTAL HEROES

Chapter One

Bernice Adams woke up, as she usually did, just before the alarm went off, so she didn't wake her six-year-old son, Toby. Some maternal instinct pulled her out of her dreams before the buzzer sounded. She smiled as she looked at him sleeping next to her in the queen-sized bed that had been a lucky find in a secondhand furniture store. She'd bought a new mattress for it that they had tried out together, and Toby said it felt like a cloud. It was a stretch for their budget, but she decided it was worth it. Toby needed to get to school rested so he could pay attention and do well. She wanted him to have every advantage she could give him.

She had managed to furnish the small one-bedroom apartment with hand-me-down furniture and what she found on the sidewalk on Tuesday nights, when people left out big furniture items they didn't want, for garbage pickup the next morning. It was always a treasure hunt. She had found her night tables that way, a blue dresser, and the kitchen table they ate on every day. The Formica was chipped around the edges, but the bright red looked cheerful in their tiny kitchen, barely big enough for her to cook in. She had painted the walls and some of the furnishings herself, and found the living room rug at Goodwill. All put together, it looked homey and cozy, and she had framed the Spider-Man posters Toby loved for their bedroom, and there was one of Batman and Robin over their bed.

Bernice was a single mother. Toby's father had taken off when she got pregnant at nineteen. She'd been working as a waitress by day, and going to City College of New York by night. She hadn't seen him since, although she'd heard that he was married now and had three other children. She wanted no contact with him. He'd been a smooth talker, she'd fallen for him, and the pregnancy was an accident. He had disappeared as fast as he could. She'd had Toby when she was twenty, and had managed parenthood on her own ever since.

Bernice was a survivor. More than that, she wanted to make something of herself, and set an example for her son, to show him that he didn't have to be limited by the world he was born into, and with an education, he could have a good job and a good life one day. It was what she aspired to herself.

She'd been raised in foster homes after her parents died when she was in her early teens. Some of the homes were awful, and some of them were okay, but she was determined that nothing like it would ever happen to her boy. Bernice's only relative, her brother, Clive, had been in and out of prison for a dozen years since he turned eighteen, for credit card fraud, grand theft auto, and drug dealing, all the means of making a living he had learned on the streets. She hadn't seen him since she was sixteen and he was twenty, fresh out of prison on parole. She didn't want to see him again, and he knew nothing about his nephew. Clive wasn't an evil man, and he'd been nice to her, to the best of his ability. He just didn't know how to get out of the trap he had grown up in. She wanted her life and her son's to be different.

The building they lived in was clean, and lived in by respectable families, on 125th Street. It had been built in the 1930s and must have been beautiful then. What had once been spacious, handsome apartments had been broken into small ones for low rents. Now it was shabby, and the people who had lived there, and could, had moved downtown. Other buildings near her had been renovated, and parts of her neighborhood were slowly becoming gentrified. She'd been fortunate to find an apartment she could afford on her salary. She managed to get by and take care of her son.

After graduating from City College, she had worked for TSA security at JFK International Airport for the past five years, checking passengers as they came through the lines, observing them keenly, directing them to the body-scan machines, and doing pat-downs when instructed to do so. She was also enrolled in law school online. In Bernice's mind, the secret to everything was education and hard work, and no one was going to cheat her of that. She reminded Toby of it every day, whenever she could.

She hated to leave his small, warm body, curled up against her back as she got out of bed and headed to the shower to get ready for work. When she left at four o'clock, she would leave him with her neighbor, who would take him to school with her own children. Bernice worked a 5:30 A.M. to 1:30 P.M. shift, which gave her just enough time to pick Toby up at school herself, and be with him for the rest of the day. She taught him the extra lessons he didn't have at school yet, and then did her own homework for law school after she made dinner and put him to bed. She tried to be asleep by nine-thirty or ten, since she had to get up at three-thirty to get ready for work. She ate breakfast on the train to save time. She didn't go out with friends and hadn't been to a movie in years. Her whole life was her son, her job, and her studies so that one day they'd have more than that, and he would have a real future. They talked about it a lot, even though he was only six. She talked to him like an adult and told him she was going to be a lawyer and work in a law firm down-town when she graduated. That was her dream. And dreams be-came realities if you worked hard enough to achieve them. She said it to Toby almost like a mantra.

She showered, had a cup of coffee, and put on her uniform. Ber-nice was African American. She was a pretty woman and wore her hair in neat braids tied at the nape of her neck. She had a slim figure and watched her weight, and looked nice in the TSA uniform. Sev-eral men she worked with had asked her on dates, many of them married, and she always turned them down. She'd gone out briefly with one of her single male colleagues right after she started work-ing for TSA. It hadn't turned out well, and she hadn't made that mistake again. She hadn't had a serious date in years, or even a casual one in the last two. There would be plenty of time for that, she told herself, when she had a better job after law school. She didn't love working for TSA, but it paid the rent and bought their food, and gave her the time she needed to study for her law classes. Her schedule was good for her.

When she was dressed, she rolled Toby, still asleep, into his Spider-Man sleeping bag, carried him to the neighbor's, and knocked. She didn't ring the bell, so she wouldn't wake the other children. They didn't have to be in school until eight o'clock. Toby woke up in his mother's arms just before the door opened.

"Why do we have to get up so early?" he complained, burrowing against her and closing his eyes again. It was still dark outside and would be for several hours.

"Because I have to go to work and do my job," she said, kissing his forehead, "and you have to go to school so that one day you can have a good job too, like a doctor or a lawyer," she added, programming him early.

"I want to be a policeman," he grumbled as the door opened, and their neighbor took him in her arms and smiled at Bernice. She knew what a good mother she was and admired her for it. Toby was almost back to sleep as Bernice handed him off. He had a few more hours to doze before he had to get up, have breakfast, and get dressed for school.

"Have a nice day," their neighbor whispered and gently closed the door. She took Toby in every morning for free, as a favor to Toby's mother. On weekend nights, Bernice often babysat her two children in exchange, and let them sleep on her couch or in the bed with Toby, and slept on the couch herself, if their mother had a big date. They did what they could to help each other, two women alone with their children. The neighbor had a son and a daughter close to Toby's age, and the three children were best friends, which worked well too.

It was a beautiful May morning as Bernice left the building, and she thought of the church day camp she had enrolled Toby in for the summer. There would be lots of things for him to do there. She had saved enough money to pay for it by skipping lunch for five months. The money was in her bank account now, and they had already accepted him.

Bernice rushed to catch the first train she took to work every day, and arrived at the airport right on time. She put her purse in her locker, and reported for duty at JFK airport on the dot at 5:30 A.M. She didn't love her job, but it was a good means to an end, and she reminded herself daily that it wouldn't be forever. Once she graduated from law school, she'd have better opportunities and could look for a job in a law firm, even as a paralegal until she passed the bar.

But for now, her daily work life was rife with petty jealousies, unpleasant supervisors, and angry passengers who didn't want to take their shoes off and complained when Bernice had to go through their bags, looking for computers or liquids, or because of something they'd seen on the X-ray, like a can of dog food, or a suspicious object, which in most cases turned out to be nothing when they checked. They were trained to look for weapons, materials that could be combined to create explosives, or whatever seemed suspicious on the X-ray screen.

Her current supervisor, Denise Washington, was particularly disagreeable, and it was obvious that she disliked Bernice and everything she stood for. Bernice was too clean-cut and too straight-arrow, and had made the mistake of casually saying one day that she was going through law school online. Denise had been scornful and angry toward her ever since. She hated girls like Bernice, who talked about their bright future as though it were something they could just pluck off a tree. Denise knew better. She had been passed over for promotions for years and she didn't even care why anymore. In her mind, she was always getting screwed over by some ambitious young woman like Bernice, desperate to get ahead, whatever it took. She was fed up with women like her, had singled Bernice out years before, and treated her with contempt. Bernice had thought of complaining to Denise's superior but knew it wouldn't do any good, and she was sure it would make things worse. Denise was an angry, bitter woman. She talked about Bernice behind her back, just loud enough for her to hear. She hated her job, and had never done anything to try to change it. She took out her resentment and frustrations on the people she supervised. Bernice was used to the snide remarks and overt insults, and Denise's obvious disapproval of her. She was jealous of Bernice, although she could have done the same things herself if she had any interest.

Bernice took her assigned spot in the security area, while Denise glared at her, as usual. Bernice turned her attention to the early passengers heading for their flights, putting their belongings into plastic bins to pass them through the X-ray machine, and then going through the metal detectors and full-body scan in stockings or bare feet.

She saw the first flight crew roll through in uniform minutes after she got there, and noticed that, judging by the stripes on her uniform, a woman in the group was the pilot, which made Bernice smile. She liked to see that.

She thought she got a glimpse of a famous movie star, Susan Far-row, but she might have been mistaken. The woman was older than Bernice would have expected, with oversized dark glasses, which made her hard to recognize. She was pleasant to everyone, and was dressed simply in blue jeans and a sweater. She wasn't glamorous, but seemed like a nice person, as Bernice watched her. It was one of the things she liked about her job. You never knew who you would see or what to expect on any given day. It was a pleasant distraction and made putting up with her nasty supervisor easier to bear.

Helen Smith woke up at four-thirty, to give herself time to shower and dress, have coffee, and be fully awake by the time she and the others left the midtown hotel where the flight crews of their airline stayed in New York. There was no traffic at that hour so they could leave the hotel at five-thirty in the van that came to get them, and be at the airport at six-thirty. And there would be little for Helen to attend to once they got there. The airline planned the routes for them and checked the weather. All she and the rest of the flight crew had to do was make sure that everything was mechanically in order once they were on the plane before they took off.

Helen had had a distinguished career as a pilot, and after years as an Air Force fighter pilot, she had been flying for the airline for two years. They had been the hardest years of her life.

She had a text when she woke up informing her of an equipment change, the second one relating to this flight back to San Francisco. The day before, she had been notified that she'd be flying an Airbus A380 they had on the ground in New York after a flight from London, because it needed to get to San Francisco for a flight to Tokyo. The largest Airbus, the A380 didn't normally fly between San Francisco and New York. But she was checked out for it, and was looking forward to flying it.

During the night, they had discovered a mechanical problem on the A380, and couldn't use it for the San Francisco flight after all. They had almost three hundred passengers booked for the flight, and had decided to use a new, smaller Airbus A321 for the 8 A.M. to San Francisco, and a Boeing 757 they had available for the overflow, which would take off at 8:20, so the passengers would be happy, could stick to their schedules, and no one would get bumped due to the change of equipment. It meant they needed a second crew for the 757, Helen had been assigned the A321, which was a plane she liked to fly. It was small and easy to maneuver, and the crews liked the aircraft too. The text message she received said that she would be flying with the San Francisco crew returning to home base as planned. The only change was of the copilot, to Jason Andrews, whom she didn't know.

They informed her that Captain Connor Gray would be flying deadhead, which meant he would be flying as a courtesy passenger. He would be traveling in the cockpit with her since the flight was full and every passenger seat was sold. The text said only that he had been deactivated and retired due to a medical incident on the ground after his flight to New York two days before. The formalities of his retirement would happen in the coming days. But he was no longer cleared to fly, and after the incident wouldn't be again. The airline and FAA were strict about grave medical issues. She'd heard of him, as one of the airline's senior pilots, but they had never met.

He was close to retirement age, though maybe not quite there yet, and whatever had occurred must have been serious for them to deactivate and retire him summarily halfway through a trip. She thought about it, and hoped to make his return to home base as pleasant as possible under the circumstances.

Flying with an unfamiliar copilot was standard fare for any commercial pilot, since the crews were varied and interchangeable. It made no difference to her. Some were easy to get along with, others were less pleasant, but all were skilled pilots on the first-rate airline she worked for. She flew the plane she was given to fly, just like in the military. And after years of training and experience, she could fly anything they handed her with her eyes closed. She loved her job. Flying was in her blood. Her father had been an Air Force pilot and retired as a full colonel.

Helen had been a fighter pilot for the Air Force in Iraq for several years. She and her husband had both served there, and they had decided that she would leave the Air Force and return to civilian life before his last tour ended. They both had offers from commercial airlines and, for the sake of their children, thought it was time to muster out.

It had been a big adjustment for her. She had grown up in the military, and everything about civilian life was unfamiliar to her. It was difficult at first with her husband still in the Air Force. He had been killed four months after she left, eight weeks before he was due to fly home.

She wasn't bitter about what had happened to him. He'd been shot down and taken prisoner, and he and all of his crew were killed in an incident that had received press and cries of outrage from around the world. He had been decorated posthumously by the president, and the medal he'd been given was on their mantelpiece in Petaluma where she and her children lived, less than an hour outside San Francisco, in a small, slightly dilapidated house. She had been in shock over her husband's death at first, and it had an unreal quality to it. They both knew the risks, but she never expected it to happen to him, and she had no idea how to manage civilian life without him. She had thought about reenlisting after he died, and going back to the only life she knew in the Air Force, but it wouldn't be fair to the children. They had wanted them to experience life outside the military, but not without their father. That had never been the plan. Her own father had done everything he could to help her, and stayed with the kids when she was away. A year and a half later, she was still adjusting to civilian life without Jack. It hadn't been easy for her or the kids. It was much harder than she expected, and infinitely more so as a widow.

She was forty-two years old, and the Air Force and military life were second nature to her. There was some resistance to her being a female pilot with the airline, but others had broken that barrier before her, and most of the men she flew with respected her for her flying record, particularly those who knew of her tours of duty in Iraq. Flying Airbuses between San Francisco and New York, or internationally, was a piece of cake. She had five days off coming to her when she got back to San Francisco, and had promised to take all three of her children camping. They were just a regular family now, or tried to be, with two sons in middle school and a seven-year-old daughter, even though their father had been a war hero and their mother had been a fighter pilot.

Helen hadn't made many friends in the community yet. She had little in common with the other mothers she'd met at school, and she kept to herself or spent her time off with her children. She had to be mother and father to them now, which was double the work with two boys in Little League, and a daughter in Girl Scouts and taking hip-hop dance lessons after school. Helen questioned her decision often, about leaving the military. There were times when she missed it desperately. It had been like leaving the womb. Everything about civilian life had been a shock at first.

She had found that the only time she was comfortable in her own skin, and felt like she knew what she was doing, was when she was flying. The rest of the time, she felt like a fish out of water. She hadn't learned to be a civilian yet, but she was trying. She was living day by day. What had happened to Jack had taught her that you couldn't count on the future, or on anything. Life was a game of chance. She had nothing and no one to believe in now, except herself. And there were times when she felt like she wasn't enough for her kids—the boys especially needed their father, and all she could do now was her best, which wasn't always enough.

Nancy Williams lay awake long before the alarm went off, trying to force herself to stay in bed until five. She had gone to sleep knowing what she was going to do the minute she woke up. It had only dawned on her the day before that she might be pregnant. After twelve years of infertility treatments and eight attempts at IVF, she and her husband had finally given up and had filed papers to adopt a little girl in China. She was two years old, and they were going to Beijing soon to pick her up. They could hardly wait.

And suddenly, the day before, on the flight from San Francisco, it had occurred to her that she might be pregnant, without hormone shots or harvesting her eggs this time. It seemed too good to be true. She had gone to a drugstore near the hotel that night to pick up a test kit. It was sitting on the bathroom sink, waiting for her to use it. She was afraid to be disappointed again. At thirty-eight she had been down this path too many times, and crushing disappointment had become a way of life.

At five A.M. she couldn't stand it anymore. Wide awake, she threw back the covers, headed to the bathroom, and told herself she didn't care. Soon they would have an adopted daughter, so it didn't matter. Except it did. If humanly possible, they still wanted a baby of their own. She hadn't even told her husband her suspicions, not wanting to get his hopes up. He was a pilot for the same airline, had flown to Miami the day before, and was coming back to San Francisco that day too.

She used the test and left it on the sink to work its magic, hopped into the shower, let the hot water run down her face, and got out of the shower faster than she would have otherwise. She had to know, one more time, and when she looked, she let out a scream and held the test in her shaking hand. Two pink lines. She was pregnant, without assistance. It had just happened. All their earlier attempts had been futile. And what were they going to do now about the little girl in China? A thousand thoughts ran through her mind as she sat down on the floor, feeling dizzy, still holding the test kit. She was pregnant at last! Their dream had finally come true.

Joel McCarthy was just getting out of the shower when his cell-phone rang. He was rushing, and had overslept by a few minutes. He recognized the number immediately, and his face broke into a broad smile. He was a tall, dark-haired, handsome man, had done some modeling in his youth, and loved his job as a flight attendant.

"What are you doing up at this hour?" he asked his partner, Kevin. "It's two in the morning for you." Kevin was at the apartment in San Francisco.

"I can't sleep. All I can think about is Friday."

"I know. Me too." Both men smiled and there was a moment of silence between them. Joel was thirty-four, and his partner was forty, and a doctor. They had met on one of Joel's flights two years ago and had been together ever since. They were getting married in two days, with a small circle of friends around them, and Kevin's parents, who were coming up from Los Angeles. Joel hadn't told his ultraconservative parents in Utah, nor his five brothers and sisters, even his one brother who was gay and had never told their parents either. None of them had ever been willing to face the reality of Joel's life, and expecting them to celebrate his marriage to a man would be too much for them. Kevin would be his family now. Joel loved his own family, but they were unable to accept him. He had spent years in therapy dealing with it, and he was finally at ease in his own life. Marrying Kevin was the most wonderful thing that had ever happened to him.

"My parents arrived tonight," Kevin told him, sounding euphoric. "My mother is even more excited than we are." Both Kevin's parents had welcomed Joel into their family, and his sister and her husband were just as warm. They were the family Joel had always dreamed of.

They were going to Tahiti on their honeymoon. Kevin was a successful plastic surgeon, and had asked Joel to consider giving up his job, but Joel didn't want to be dependent on him and was going to continue flying, at least for a while, maybe until they adopted a child or found a surrogate for their own. Joel was already living in Kevin's apartment, and they were going to start looking for a house to buy when they got back from Tahiti. And they had just gotten a dog. Joel loved all the evidence of domestic life.

"I've got to go, I'm going to be late," Joel told him when he saw the time. "I love you. I'll see you tonight. I'll have dinner ready when you get home."

"My parents want to take us out," Kevin told him quickly.

"Go back to bed and get some sleep, or you'll be exhausted on Friday," Joel said, smiling. All either of them could think of was their wedding. They'd had fun planning it for months.

"Have a safe flight," Kevin said before he hung up. He always said that, which touched Joel. He'd never been on a flight that had a problem, but Kevin was nervous about him flying, and was a fearful flier himself.

Joel was smiling as he put on his steward's uniform, thinking about Kevin and how lucky he felt to be marrying him. And he was in a great mood when he got in the van with the crew. There were muted greetings of good morning, as everyone kept to themselves at that hour. Joel didn't know them all, though he had seen most of them on the flight two days before.

"They've switched us to an A321 and added a 757 to make up the difference," the captain, Helen Smith, said in a matter-of-fact tone, which caused some comment in the group about the equipment change and breaking it into two flights. Most of them were sorry not to be flying the A380, which they all liked, although they would have had more passengers to deal with on the bigger plane, and the A321 would be easier for the flight attendants. "They're using a New-York-based crew for the 757," Captain Smith added, as they waited for the copilot to come out of the hotel. She glanced at her watch. He was late.

Joel and Nancy chatted quietly while they waited. Nancy was elated after what she'd discovered, but tried not to show it. She didn't want to share the news with anyone until she told her husband. And Joel had been excited all week. This was his last scheduled flight before the wedding.

There were two very senior female flight attendants in the van, who'd been assigned to first class on the trip out. And Joel assumed they would be again. One of them, Jennifer, was the chief purser. They were competent and experienced at tending to demanding first-class passengers, but made it obvious that they didn't enjoy it. Nancy had commented on it to Joel on the flight to New York. She could never see the point of staying in the job once you felt that way, and a number of their older colleagues were visibly tired and bitter. They'd done it for too long, and the vagaries of the passengers they dealt with annoyed them. There was an edge to how they spoke to people and an attitude you could sense the moment you saw them. Nancy hated working with women like that. They fulfilled the passengers' requests, but only to the degree they had to. And she hoped she wouldn't be working with either of them today. They were conferring quietly about their trips to Hong Kong and Beijing the following month, while the two younger members of the crew, Bobbie and Annette, had been assigned to coach before and probably would be again. Annette was whispering to Bobbie about a date she'd had the night before, and they both laughed as Helen looked at her watch again with a stern expression.

She glanced over then and noticed the older pilot in the van, and realized it was Connor Gray, the newly retired pilot due to fly home with them. She waited until he looked her way, and then smiled at him. He nodded in response with a somber expression. He had recognized her too, and knew her military history. Helen thought Captain Gray looked subdued and somewhat pale, and whatever his medical issue had been after the flight out, Helen got the feeling that he was depressed about it, which wouldn't have been surprising with an immediate forced retirement after the incident.

He said nothing to the rest of the crew, nor to her. And then, finally, the copilot they'd been waiting for jumped into the van with no apology for the delay. He was strikingly handsome with blond movie-star looks, and acted as though he were playing a part. He introduced himself as Jason Andrews and immediately complained about the equipment change, and said he'd been looking forward to flying the A380 since he had recently qualified for it. And then he looked at Helen with a sarcastic expression as the van took off for the airport. "Girls' flight today?" he commented as Connor Gray glared at him with blatant disapproval for his lack of respect for Captain Smith.

As the van threaded its way between several trucks, Jason Andrews made it clear that he thought female pilots were second-rate at best. The rest of the crew members were shocked into silence. Helen said nothing and didn't care. She had met many men like him in the Air Force, who disliked female pilots, and it didn't faze her at all. He was obviously a smart aleck, full of himself, and was wearing his uniform hat at a rakish angle. When they got out at JFK he made a comment about how "hot" Bobbie was. Bobbie heard him say it and told him she was married as they collected their bags out of the van, and he looked at her with a roguish smile.

"And the problem is?" he countered to Bobbie, and then focused on Nancy, who was a tall, attractive blonde with a good figure. He seemed to think that all women were easy prey for him, and his for the picking.

Nancy ignored him and chatted quietly with Joel as they rolled their bags into the airport. The copilot had made no friends on the trip out. The two older flight attendants looked right through him, and Bobbie whispered to Annette that he was a jerk. He had managed to rub everyone the wrong way with his snide comments on the drive to the airport.

He made another remark Helen didn't like as they moved to the head of the security line and put their computers, cellphones, and minor belongings in the plastic bins and their rolling bags on the moving belt to be X-rayed.

"Welcome to the heart of Africa," Jason said under his breath just loud enough for the others to hear, and anyone standing nearby, as he glanced at the TSA agents around them, most of whom were African Americans.

"Watch that!" Captain Helen Smith said in a sharp tone that reminded them all of her military background. She was wide awake and quick to call him on it, although she'd been quiet in the van. "You're part of my crew now, Andrews, until we land at SFO. I can write you up for that remark, or suspend you," she said bluntly, as a particularly pretty young TSA agent watched the exchange, and had heard the comment. The copilot seemed like a jerk to her too. Bobbie's assessment of him seemed apt.

"You must have heard me wrong, Captain," he said with mock respect.

"I hope I did. Make sure I don't hear you wrong again." He didn't respond, and followed the rest of the crew as they walked toward their gate. The two planes for the flights to San Francisco, leaving twenty minutes apart, were parked next to each other. The San Francisco crew members were joined by a full crew from New York who had been added for the 757. They were separated quickly, and went to their respective planes. On the A321, the flight attendants met with Jennifer, the chief purser, once they were on board, to get their cabin assignments, which, as Joel had guessed, were the same as the flight out. Helen, Jason, and the now retired Connor Gray headed for the cockpit to settle in. Jason gave Joel a contemptuous look as he walked past, but he didn't say a word. He didn't need to. His scorn for Joel was in his eyes.

Helen sat down in the captain's seat and turned to talk to Connor

Gray for a few minutes. She seemed to relax and warm up once she was in the cockpit. It was home to her. Nothing ever felt as good to her as flying a plane. She had all-American looks, with light brown hair, an intelligent face, and bright blue eyes that took in everything. And Connor looked more at ease and brightened while they talked. He explained to her in a low voice that he'd had a brief cerebral incident, a TIA. The doctors had said it might never happen again but it could. It lasted only a few seconds, during which he didn't recognize his surroundings, but his career had ended on the spot. If it had happened while he was flying the plane, it could have been disastrous.

"I'm really sorry," she said sympathetically and he thanked her. He had enormous respect for her not just professionally, but personally. Like most of the world, he had seen her husband murdered by his captors on TV. It had been horrifying, and something no one could forget. Connor didn't refer to it, but told her it was an honor to fly with her on his final flight in uniform. She said the same about him and he could see that she was sincere. She seemed like a kind woman in addition to her reputation as a highly skilled pilot.

Jason took the copilot's seat while they were talking, and paid no attention to either of them. He checked some of the equipment and gauges, and then started texting. As she watched him, Helen had the feeling that she was flying with a giant spoiled brat for their flight home. He was young and cocky, and his arrogance annoyed her, although she didn't show it.

After chatting with Connor, she made her initial checks, called the tower about their flight plan, and was satisfied that everything was in order. She thought it was a good thing that they had accommodated the passengers with two flights, instead of leaving half of them stranded when the A380 couldn't fly. The second flight was boarding at the same time. Helen was pleased to have the A321. It was a recent model and enjoyable to fly. The 757 was an older plane, and not as comfortable for the passengers. And she'd been told by air traffic control that the weather looked good all the way across the country.

She looked at both men with a broad smile. She was in her element. "Well, gentlemen, it looks like we're going to have a nice, easy ride home." Connor nodded, and she could see the sadness in his eyes. Jason looked straight at her and held her gaze for a long moment as though challenging her, shrugged, and went back to texting. Helen started the engines then, made an announcement to the passengers that they'd be pushing back from the gate shortly, and assured them of a smooth flight to San Francisco and possibly an early arrival. She had a feeling it was going to be a very nice day. It was off to a good start.

Chapter Two

Bernice watched the passengers for both San Francisco flights file through security after the crew. There were flights leaving for all over the country, and she noticed the last passengers in a hurry to get to their planes.

There was a young father with a baby who looked totally disorganized. He was juggling a diaper bag that had clothes pouring out of it, several bottles and sippy cups, a teddy bear, disposable diapers, and a pacifier in his hand. He had another bag with his computer. He dropped his cellphone twice. And he looked as though he wasn't used to managing a baby on his own.

There was a couple arguing while they put their sweaters and shoes in plastic bins and made nasty comments to each other. And a well-dressed, somewhat uptight-looking businesswoman with a large briefcase, who appeared to be about forty years old and seemed as though she could run the world. Bernice could see that she was anxious, despite her competent corporate look. She had well-cut blond hair and was wearing an expensive beige suit and high heels. Bernice could easily imagine her going straight to a meeting of some kind. She snapped at two of the TSA agents that they were going to make her miss her flight if they didn't hurry up when they checked her briefcase. Bernice smiled to her only friend at work as the woman went through and headed toward the gates for San Francisco.

"That one's a nervous flier for sure!" Bernice said in a whisper.

"How do you know?" Della asked her. She'd only worked there for a year. She was small and round, and passengers like the businesswoman always intimidated her. Bernice had seen it all a thousand times in the last five years.

"The nervous fliers always act like that," she said coolly, "then they get on the flight and get drunk or take a Xanax." Both young women laughed, after they had watched the well-dressed blonde grab her briefcase, shove her computer into it, grab her cellphone, put on her shoes, and hurry toward the gate for her flight. It was early in the morning and she already looked stressed.

There were a large number of businessmen who were obviously experienced travelers, and went through security without a problem. As they watched them head for the San Francisco gate, Della commented to Bernice that it would be a good flight to catch a man. She had been looking to meet someone for a while, after breaking up with her boyfriend. But the men she was talking about were all too old for her, as Bernice pointed out, and shook her head.

"Look at their left hands," Bernice said. "Wedding rings. They're all married." She was a pro at assessing passengers.

"Maybe they cheat," Della said hopefully.

"Oh, there's a dream come true, a married guy cheating on his wife. I'll pass on that," Bernice said without regret.

"Maybe they'd divorce their wives," she commented naïvely.

"No, thank you." Bernice turned away to find herself in the direct field of vision of their supervisor, who was scowling at them, as usual.

"Now, there's a woman who desperately needs to get laid," Della whispered, and the two of them tried not to laugh.

Five minutes after the nervous woman in the expensive suit and high heels, Bernice noticed a Middle-Eastern-looking couple taking off their shoes and putting them in the bins, with their computers. They were a pleasant, quiet man and a simply dressed young woman, somewhere in their twenties, and Bernice watched them, as she had everyone else. The woman was wearing a head scarf with a long gray cotton coat covering her clothes. He was in jeans, they both had on running shoes like most travelers their age, and he was carrying a leather backpack. She noticed Bernice looking at them and smiled at her, and the man seemed in a hurry to catch their flight then and was rushing his wife along. Bernice was still watching hand luggage pass through the X-ray when they collected their belongings on the other side, and sped off toward the first San Francisco gate.

Earlier, there had been a group of about fourteen girls who were part of a girls' chorus from Queens, and their heavyset blond chaperone kept shrieking their names in a high-pitched voice and threatening to call their parents. They said they were going to San Francisco for a performance and had won a competition, and the girls looked to be a range of ages from about nine to fifteen. They were all wearing sweatshirts that identified them as from their chorus. They were far better behaved than their chaperone, who got in an argument with a TSA agent about cosmetics she had brought with her that were in bottles over the size limit, and had to be taken from her. She wrote down the agent's name and said she would report her. There was always someone like that. But the girls were having fun, laughing and squealing and teasing each other.

They watched two children with their tearful mother then, handing them over to a ground agent to fly unaccompanied on the flight. She put ribbons around their necks with badges on them, which identified them as unaccompanied minors. The ground agent looked desperate to get away from the mother before she fell apart completely, after she had kissed them ten times. The little boy and girl were much less upset than she was, and they waved as they went through security, and then disappeared toward the gate as their mother sobbed, and Bernice said a kind word to her.

"I know that must be hard," she said gently. "But they'll be fine. They'll have a great time on the flight. They can watch movies."

"They're only six and eight and this is the first time I've ever sent them anywhere alone. They're going to see my parents, I just got divorced," she said and lost it. "My husband left me." Bernice handed her some tissues, and the woman thanked her.

"I have a six-year-old son too," Bernice volunteered as though it gave her credibility.

"Then you know how tough this is." The woman couldn't stop crying, and Bernice felt sorry for her.

"They'll be fine," Bernice repeated gently, and the woman finally left. As soon as she did, Denise, her supervisor, sidled up to her with a look of displeasure.

"Always kissing ass on someone, aren't you, Adams?" she said nastily, and Bernice shrugged and walked away. She had long since given up trying to reason with her, or win her over, or get a fair shake from her. She never did. The woman hated her and there was nothing she could do about it.

There was a lull then, after the early flights took off, that would get people to other cities in time for lunch or meetings that day. The two San Francisco flights were due to land at 11 A.M. and 11:20 A.M. Pacific time. Bernice had nothing to do, so she went to stack the empty plastic bins on a cart, where the next wave of passengers could grab them easily, and the whole process would start again. Although the people were always different, the routine was still the same. She was stacking the containers, thinking about the home-work she had to do that night, when she noticed a large postcard, a photo of the Golden Gate Bridge, that had been left in one of the bins. She picked it up, and when she turned it over, someone had scrawled across the whole back of the card, "You will remember me *forever*!" It sounded more like an order than a statement. It didn't sound romantic, like a message from a lover, but there was nothing unusual about the card. She assumed it had slipped out of some-one's coat or purse or briefcase going through the X-ray machine, and it had been forgotten in the bin. She picked it up to throw it away and walked over to the trash can, and something stopped her as she looked at it again, and noticed that the word "forever" was heavily underlined. There was something so emphatic about it, but maybe it was a love note of some kind, after a particularly memorable night or weekend. She was going to put it in the trash, and then slipped it into a drawer instead. She didn't know why, but she felt as though she should save it, although that didn't make much sense. There was nothing remarkable about it, and it wasn't a threat. She got busy doing other things then and forgot about it.

She pushed the cart of empty bins to the head of the line, and the postcard slipped her mind as things got busy again, and she stood there telling people to take off their shoes and take their computers out of their bags and place them in the bins. One thing she didn't like about her job was having to repeat herself all day long, and how annoyed people got when they didn't like what she said.

When the Muslim couple handed in their boarding cards at the gate, they were told to step aside and wait for a moment. The young man looked surprised and displeased, and the woman said something to calm him down, while he grumbled that they would miss their flight.

"They're singling us out!" he said unhappily, as the agent walked away.

"You don't know that, Ahmad," his wife, Sadaf, told him calmly. "And can you blame them? It's safer for all of us if they're careful and check everyone out." He looked seriously annoyed to have to wait as a ground agent returned.

"I have good news," the ground agent announced to them, with a smile that nothing could dampen, even the dissatisfied-looking customer. "Coach is oversold on your flight, because of the change of aircraft. We're moving some people up to business class, and we've upgraded you, free of charge." She beamed as though she were telling them they'd won the lottery. The man looked hesitant and conferred in a whisper with his wife, who appeared to scold him in response, and then she turned to the ground agent politely.

"Thank you, we accept." She took the two new boarding passes they were offered, and they walked down the jetway to the plane, still speaking quietly to each other. They had been polite during the entire exchange, but he continued to look ill at ease once they found their seats, and sat down looking as though he was sulking. They noticed that the door to the cockpit was open, and glanced past first class with interest, as the woman across the aisle from them in the beige business suit suddenly noticed them, Catherine James was the woman who Bernice had guessed correctly was a nervous flier, and they both could read on her face that she was now convinced there were terrorists on the plane. At that exact moment, a flight attendant walked past them with a tray of orange juice and glasses of champagne. Catherine James grabbed two of the champagnes and drained them both with a look of panic. The young couple politely declined both juice and wine, as the husband finally began to relax. The seats were comfortable, they were seated together, and there was a movie screen in front of each of them. The woman looked delighted at their good luck to be upgraded, and he smiled too.

Catherine James stopped staring at them then, and noticed that the man seated next to her was scrutinizing her, and she looked embarrassed.

"I don't normally drink at this hour," she said uncomfortably. "I'm a nervous flier," she explained. The man observing her was wearing a business suit and a tie, had paid for a WiFi connection, and was already sending emails, which encouraged her to take her computer out too. The champagne had made her feel calm enough to think about work. Her seatmate didn't say a word to her in response, and he wondered if he was going to be next to a hysterical drunk for the entire flight. It wasn't a cheering prospect, he had work to do.

She glanced at him repeatedly, and he finally said something to her.

"This is one of the safest planes in the sky," he assured her, and she looked unconvinced.

And with that, a steward came by with more champagne, and Catherine took another glass and drained that one too. The man in the business suit decided to ignore her then, and assumed she'd fall asleep. He went back to his emails, and she did the same. She concentrated on her computer, and looked a little less panicked after the glasses of champagne.

The flight attendants were all setting up their galleys and getting organized to serve breakfast while the passengers put away their hand luggage and settled into their seats. Every seat on the flight was taken, and a number of people from coach had been upgraded into business class. Not just the young couple across from Catherine, but several businessmen, and the two unaccompanied children as well.

The captain came on the PA system then, introduced herself, thanked them for their patience with the equipment changes, and wished them a good flight. She said they would be ready to leave as soon as everyone had taken their seats. And with that, Catherine looked panicked again and commented to her seatmate.

"Oh God, the pilot is a woman," she said anxiously, and he smiled.

"Some of the best pilots are women. I saw her when the crew came on. She looks very competent to me," he said, and they both went back to work. Catherine tried to focus on her emails. She was going to San Francisco for a big meeting and interview in Silicon Valley, and she had to get to work, whether the pilot was a woman or not. But by then, the three glasses of champagne had worked their magic, and she nodded over her computer and fell asleep. The man next to her shook his head and rolled his eyes, as he went back to work. The plane moved away from the gate and headed for the runway and ten minutes later, with Catherine still sound asleep, they were in the air, heading for San Francisco.

On the ground, there was another momentary lull in security, and the TSA agents stood around and chatted and waited for the next wave of passengers. It reminded Bernice of the postcard she'd found in the plastic bin. She took it out of the drawer and studied it again. Was it a message from a lover? A reminder of a great weekend? A warning of some kind? She couldn't decide as she looked at it, but the tone of it seemed harsh, as though ordering the recipient to remember the person who had written the card "forever." It lacked tenderness and romance, or was she making too much of it? And feeling foolish for doing it, she walked over to her supervisor, Denise, and handed it to her. She was standing alone and looking bored as Bernice approached.

"What do you think of this?" Bernice asked in an innocent voice. Denise looked at it and shrugged.

"It's a postcard. Why?"

"I know it's a postcard," Bernice said, trying to be pleasant with her. "I found it in a bin for the X-ray machine. Does it seem ominous to you?"

"'Ominous'?" Denise looked at Bernice as though she were stupid. "What's ominous about it? It just says, 'You'll remember me forever.' The guy who wrote this probably has a two-foot dick," she said and laughed, but Bernice didn't.

"I thought that too at first. But if you read it again, it sounds weird to me. It gives me a creepy feeling."

"Maybe you need to meet this guy," Denise said rudely. "Don't take yourself so seriously. You'll get your next promotion when you're supposed to. You don't need to invent shit to try and get it early. Throw the card away, it's just crap. If we jumped on everything we found, the planes would be grounded here ninety-nine percent of the time." Bernice nodded, and went to throw the card in the trash, but as her hand hovered over the garbage, she pulled it back, still holding the card. She didn't know why, but something about it was worrying her. She slipped it into her pocket instead and went back to work, as a new wave of passengers began to arrive.

Chapter Three

The takeoff of the A321 bound for San Francisco went smoothly in Helen's capable hands. She looked totally at ease, and it was a beautiful morning with cameo blue skies all around them. Once they reached their cruising altitude, she set the plane on auto-pilot and turned to smile at Jason Andrews and Connor Gray in the cockpit with her. Captain Gray was very somber and hadn't said anything since their brief initial conversation. Helen wondered if he was feeling unwell, but he didn't look ill. He seemed sad. She was about to say something to him when Joel knocked and was buzzed into the cockpit with coffee for all three of them and cinnamon rolls that smelled delicious. Jason took one and didn't thank him, and gave Joel an ugly look. Joel was courteous and pleasant and said before he left that their breakfast would be ready soon.

"I can't stand guys like that," Jason said as soon as the door closed behind him, and Helen gave him a disapproving look. "They think they own the world now. They make me sick."

"You seem to have a problem with a number of groups," she said sternly. "Female pilots, African Americans, homosexuals. That's a pretty limited view of the world. I take it you've never been in the military, Andrews. You have to learn to live with a lot of different people there. Or anywhere these days. It must be hard for you, with all these people you don't like to deal with." He didn't respond to what she said, but had a smirk on his face. Connor Gray was watching him closely, and admired how unruffled the captain remained. "What's your beef with female pilots?" she asked Jason, curious whether his prejudices were based on a negative experience or his own bad attitude. The latter seemed more likely.

"Depends on how you fly the plane," Jason said boldly. "But the fools who run our precious airline wouldn't let you fly if you weren't good at what you do, I guess," he conceded grudgingly. He wasn't afraid to offend her, but it didn't bother her. She looked calm and easygoing as she listened. He had eyes that were filled with resentment despite his boyish good looks. "Generally, I think men make better pilots, but I guess some women are okay," he admitted. "Your takeoff was pretty smooth just now." He was incredibly arrogant, had a superior attitude, and seemed to have an ax to grind against everyone. "But this plane is a breeze to fly," he said, mitigating his earlier praise.

"Yes, it is," she said in a friendly tone. "I'll let you land at SFO if you want." It was her prerogative to decide which of them would land. And she could always take over if she didn't like his approach, and the passengers would be safe. She wouldn't have let him land the big Airbus. He didn't have enough hours on it yet, but he was more than adequately qualified for the plane they were flying. There were always some flyboys in aviation who thought that men should own the skies. Fortunately, neither the Air Force nor the airline they worked for agreed with him. And she had long since earned her flawless reputation.

"Do you know who you're flying with?" Connor suddenly spoke up in a deep, angry voice, and startled both of them. There was emotion trembling through his words. "She was one of the most decorated fighter pilots in the Middle East. How does that stack up against your experience, sonny? I don't see you in the captain's seat." Jason bridled instantly at his words.

"Yeah, I know who she is. I saw her husband get his head cut off on TV."

What Jason said squeezed Helen's heart like a vise and took her breath away. Nothing showed in her expression, but both men could sense how shocked she was. Jason had hit her hard and done it intentionally, which Connor thought was despicable. He could see tears in Helen's eyes.

"I think that's enough of that for today," she said, wanting to stop the exchange between the two men before it got out of hand. Despite the words, which hurt her personally, she was the senior officer and in command here, and both men fell silent. Nancy knocked and was buzzed into the cockpit then, with Joel right behind her, carrying their breakfast trays. The cockpit door closed and locked automatically behind them after they walked in. They always served the pilots first, and the stewards in business class took care of them. The first-class flight attendants were always too busy, providing additional service to their passengers, although they helped out occasionally. And premium economy and coach had their hands full by sheer numbers. The flight crew had omelets, fruit salad, warm biscuits, and an assortment of breakfast pastries on their trays. There was no conversation in the cockpit, after what Jason had said, as Joel and Nancy set down their trays.

"Call us when you want to get rid of the trays," Nancy said pleasantly, as Jason eyed her again, and she ignored him. He acted as though any woman on the planet would be lucky to sleep with him. She had more important things on her mind after the positive pregnancy test that morning. She could hardly wait to see her husband and tell him. She and Helen exchanged a warm look of female solidarity, and both Nancy and Joel noticed that the other captain looked angry about something.

"Wow," Joel whispered as the cockpit door closed and locked behind them again. "You can cut the atmosphere in there with a knife today. That's the only thing I hate about our job," he said as they walked back into the galley in business class. "You never know how the chemistry is going to work out. I love flying with new people all the time, but when you get a lemon, it can sure turn your day to shit in a hurry." They both laughed at what he said. "And the flight deck does not look like fun today," he added, as he started putting the garnish on the trays.

They were offering three choices of breakfast to the passengers, which kept them busy working the ovens to heat the biscuits and the quiche they were serving. They also had scrambled eggs with sausages, smoked salmon and bagels, and oatmeal with fruit salad. They served a hearty breakfast on the early flight. With the time difference in their favor flying west, the passengers had a long day ahead of them, many of them with meetings to attend for the rest of the day, as soon as they arrived.

Joel and Nancy headed down the aisle with the cart loaded up with trays a few minutes later. They had handed out headphones for the entertainment system immediately after takeoff, and several people were already watching movies, including the two unaccompanied children, Nicole and Mark, who'd been upgraded and had been no trouble so far. Nicole was adorable, and Mark took good care of her.

Other passengers were working on their computers, getting ready for work, or keeping up with what was happening in their offices in New York by email. People who took the early flight were rarely demanding, which was why Nancy liked it. By the end of the day, passengers were tired, cranky, and stressed by whatever had gone wrong in their day, and took it out on the flight attendants. They were more likely to wind up with delayed flights, and often drank too much. Everyone was still fresh and in a better mood in the morning.

Catherine James was awake again by then, after her heavy dose of champagne before takeoff, and was working on her computer, as was the man sitting next to her. The couple across the aisle were conferring quietly, although he still didn't look happy. He took vegetarian quiche and his female companion smiled at Nancy, as though in collusion with her and silently apologizing for her somewhat grumpy husband. Nancy mentioned to Joel how serious and unsmiling he was compared to his very friendly wife, who seemed open and happy and excited about the trip and their upgrade.

"He didn't seem to approve when I offered them earphones," Joel added. "And he wouldn't let the woman take them. He told her not to in Arabic, I think. I'm sure they're fine, but I assume someone checked them against the no-fly list before they boarded," he said, and Nancy reassured him. Neither the crew nor the public knew exactly how the no-fly list worked, only that there was one that listed anyone suspected of terrorist ties or activities, and that Homeland Security was diligent about their job.

"I don't think he's a terrorist. He's just a crabby guy. She seems very sweet, though." She smiled at Joel.

In the course of their work, they had occasionally seen passengers refused entry to the plane, or removed before a flight took off, if their names were on any of the sensitive lists. And they knew that there was an armed air marshal somewhere on the plane, usually in first class, sometimes with a second one elsewhere on the flight. Some were harder to detect than others, and no one was supposed to be able to recognize them. They were on board to protect the passengers and crew, in case someone got violent or tried to take over the plane. There was a rumor that they were cutting back on air marshals, but the crew doubted that it was true. There had been air marshals on the flights as long as they'd both been flying, and it was comforting to know.

"The woman in 2C looked like she was going to have a heart attack when that couple boarded," Joel commented, meaning Catherine James.

"You mean the champagne guzzler?" Nancy said and both laughed. "She looks sober now," Nancy defended her. They had a lot of passengers who used alcohol to calm their nerves, even on morning flights. It always amazed Nancy how they could drink at such an early hour.

Joel cleaned up the galley, while Nancy picked up the trays one by one and brought them back. She offered coloring books with crayons to the two unaccompanied children, but only Nicole took one. Her brother, Mark, was engrossed in watching a movie, the latest Disney film about dragons, and they both looked happy.

Joel served another round of coffee in the cockpit, and the atmosphere had eased up a little after breakfast. The captain was quiet, and Jason was complaining about the airline when Connor let Joel in. Jason was grousing about how high-handed management was with younger pilots, and kept them in the copilot seat forever.

"You have to earn your position here," Connor was saying coldly, as Joel poured his coffee, and the retired captain smiled up at him and nodded. "You can't expect to just walk in and take over."

"I'll bet she did," Jason said, nodding toward Helen.

"I had a lot more flying hours than most people because of the Air Force," Helen said modestly, not wanting to make an issue of it, or get into an argument with her copilot.

"I flew in your seat for a long time. You've got years ahead of you. I'm sure you'll be in the captain's seat soon," Connor said to Jason. He wanted to add "If you clean up your attitude and stop shooting your mouth off," but he didn't. He knew better. The handsome young pilot was a hothead, and Connor was sure he'd been just as brash with top management, which hadn't done him any good. They wanted to see pilots who were calm and in control, could face any situation, both mechanical or with passengers and crew, and maintain a level head. Jason Andrews didn't fit that description, and had a lot to learn about how to treat people and behave with his superiors. Part of his problem was that he was young and felt entitled. It was an attitude and a generation of pilots Connor didn't like. Helen was much more the profile of who the airline wanted in the pilot's seat, whatever her sex. She looked like nothing would upset her. Jason's mention of her husband's murder on worldwide media had been an intentional heavy blow below the belt to upset her gratuitously, but she had handled it with grace. She was watching conditions and checking dials, even though the aircraft was on autopilot. She was ever vigilant, but the weather conditions were perfect an hour into the flight, and were expected to stay that way.

Connor left the cockpit then, and stopped to chat for a minute with the flight attendants. He said hello to both women in the first-class cabin and then chatted with Nancy and Joel in the galley in business, and they smiled when they saw the retired captain. They'd been talking about Susan Farrow, the actress, being on the flight in first. The purser had confirmed that she was on board before take-off, and Jennifer had come back for a minute to visit them, and said the famous movie star was a remarkably nice, unassuming person, and was traveling with a little dog she had registered with the airline as an "emotional support animal" so she could keep it in her seat with her. When he heard them, Connor said he had met her once when she was on one of his flights, and she had been a beautiful woman then, and extremely gracious.

"She still looks pretty good. She must be at least seventy by now," Joel volunteered. "I've seen every movie she's ever been in." She had won three Academy Awards in the course of an extraordinary career. "I think she's been married three or four times. I think her last husband died last year. She was married to a famous director. He directed her in her last movie. He was already sick and died right after that. I read about it in *People*," he said, looking mildly embarrassed to be gossiping about her, and for an instant, Connor Gray seemed sad again, and then he went to the restroom, and afterward nodded at them and headed back to the cockpit.

"They said management retired him in New York," Nancy whispered to Joel after he had left. "I don't know what happened, but it must have been something serious. The poor guy looks very down about something.

"A friend of mine was on the flight," Nancy added. "I don't know all the details. I think he had a heart attack or something after they landed. Or maybe a stroke. It was supposedly minor, but the next thing I heard was that they retired him. I think he was only a year or two away from retirement anyway, but whatever it was, he can't fly anymore. That must be tough for a guy like him, to have them force him into retirement from one day to the next, with no time to prepare for it or adjust. This is their whole life, but you can't have pilots whose health puts everyone at risk," she said sensibly, and Joel didn't disagree, although he felt sorry for him.

"Mentally and physically," Joel added, which was obvious, and justified the rigorous psychological and physical testing the flight crews underwent every year, and no one objected to. On the contrary, it was reassuring to know that the airline's standards were kept high to reduce the chance of any problems or even disasters that could occur while in the air. "He's a good guy. I've heard great things about him over the years."

"I like Helen Smith," Nancy commented. "She's got a fantastic flying record. I don't know how she survived what happened to her husband. I would be a basket case after that," Nancy added sympathetically. "How do you live through seeing your husband beheaded on TV? Bad enough to lose him in those circumstances, but to see it . . ." It brought tears to her eyes thinking about it, and Joel nodded. It had been gruesome, and the United States had objected vigorously and retaliated on the ground. "She must have kids too. But she looks sane in spite of everything. And she seems very personable. She's pretty quiet."

"You never know how things like that affect people. It's hard for the rest of us to imagine. I'm sure she's had a lot of counseling to help her get past it," Joel said quietly.

"I don't think you ever do get past it," Nancy said sadly, thinking about Helen's husband. "How could you? She doesn't seem like an angry person, though. A little sad maybe, or introverted."

"A lot of pilots are like that," Joel said. "Some of them aren't big talkers. And then you get the Chatty Cathys who schmooze their way through the whole flight, and drive everyone nuts on the PA system. Or our charming copilot today. I hate to say it, but he seems like an asshole. He's so full of himself. He's nice-looking, but no one is hot enough to get away with that. He's a racist, and I can tell he's homophobic. I was beaten up by guys like him in Utah when I was a kid. That's why I moved to San Francisco as soon as I got out of college. My parents made me go to BYU, Brigham Young University, and after that I got the hell out of Dodge. I left two weeks after graduation. My parents weren't happy about it, but I couldn't take it anymore. I have a brother who's gay and still lives there. He's totally in the closet and tells everyone he has a girlfriend. His girlfriend's name is Henry," Joel said. "It makes me sad for him every time I hear him lie about it. That's no way to live." And then he decided to share his good news with her, although he didn't know her well, but he was too happy and excited to keep his secret and was desperate to share it. "My partner and I are getting married on Friday." He beamed after he said it, and Nancy congratulated him.

"I had some good news today myself," she said, smiling too, but didn't say what it was. "Sounds like this is our lucky day," she said, and Joel laughed.

"Mine will be on Friday. We've been together for two years, and he's the nicest man in the world. I met him on a flight to Miami I switched for, to do a friend a favor, who wanted my Boston flight to see her boyfriend, and I got a husband out of it. Good trade for me." They were still talking when Bobbie, one of the flight attendants from coach, showed up during her break with a harried expression. She was young and full of energy, but she looked stressed as she joined them.

"We've got a girls' chorus of fourteen girls and they're running all over the place, with a chaperone who's driving us nuts and letting them do whatever they want. We've got a guy with a baby that hasn't stopped screaming since we took off, and one of our toilets just broke. You people have the good life up here. I'm not signing up for coach again." They laughed at her description of it, and had all been there too. It was luck of the draw as to where they got assigned, but they all agreed that business class was their preference. There were too many entitled people in first who demanded constant attention and the meals were more elaborate, but coach was a zoo. Business was mostly adults and often businesspeople on a flight like this, except for the two unaccompanied children who'd been upgraded but had been easy so far. After venting to them for a few minutes, Bobbie went back to "hell class," as she called it, and Nancy and Joel sat down to chat and read magazines until someone called them. Joel continued talking about his wedding. He was excited to land and see his future husband, and leave for their honeymoon in Tahiti. And Nancy was desperate to share her news with her husband. They were both in a good mood, and couldn't wait to land in San Francisco in a little less than five hours. And the sky was as smooth as silk. No turbulence, no problems. Inside the plane or out.

The first flight to San Francisco, the A321, had been in the air for an hour by then, and the 757 for forty minutes. Bernice felt the postcard of the Golden Gate Bridge burning a hole in her pocket. What if the message was serious or dangerous and she did nothing about it, and something happened to one of the planes? So many crazy things happened on airplanes these days. Ever since 9/11 you couldn't rule out any possibility, even if it seemed far-fetched. She knew she had to say something, even if they thought she was overly dramatic for her concerns, and there was no point talking to her supervisor about it. She would just blow her off again.

Bernice went into an office and picked up the phone. She knew the number to call, and wondered if she'd be reprimanded if she was wrong. But something in her gut told her she had to do it, no matter what the consequences for her. She called for airport security, and told them it wasn't a full-on alert of a bomb threat or an abandoned suitcase, but she had found something in an X-ray bin that concerned her, and she thought someone on the security team should come and see it, for risk assessment.

Maybe they would think she was ridiculous. But at least then she would have done what she could. And maybe it was nothing after all. But she also knew that if the airport security team was worried about it too, all hell was about to break loose. And she had started it. The postcard was in her pocket, and she was shaking while she waited for them to show up. She told no one she had called them, not even Della.

Bernice hoped she was just being cautious. But her instincts had been right before, about people carrying drugs, and once the components for a bomb. It had been a college kid who wanted to see if he could get away with it, but had gotten three years in prison nonetheless, and she had received a citation and mention on her record from Homeland Security. But this felt different. Even though she realized it could be absolutely nothing, she didn't want to take the chance of staying quiet about it. And if she was wrong, she'd accept responsibility for her mistake, and endure Denise's ridicule for sure. It might even jeopardize her job, but she felt she had no choice. She had people's lives in her hands.

Bernice had never hesitated to act on what she believed in and stand up for what she thought was right. She wondered how long it would take security to show up and talk to her. Her stomach was in a knot as she waited. It felt like it was taking them forever. Her heart was pounding in her chest, her palms were sweaty, and her uniform was damp under the arms. She felt like something bad was about to happen, and all she could do was pray that she was wrong.

Chapter Four

When Bernice called the office of airport security, a secretary took the call and jotted down what she said: that it was not a bomb threat, but something suspicious had been found in an X-ray bin. It wasn't a high priority, the way she had described it, but they had to check it out if a TSA agent called it in. The secretary walked into Dave Lee's office and handed him the slip of paper. He groaned when he saw her coming, and took the note from her hand reluctantly. He knew he couldn't dodge it, but he'd had a busy morning.

Two Indonesian men had been caught with more money than they were allowed to bring in. He'd been called, but turned it over to Homeland Security immediately for them to deal with. A college student was caught selling marijuana and cocaine in one of the restrooms, a passenger had reported her, and he had called in the Port Authority police and had to fill out a report. An abandoned rolling bag had turned up in Terminal 4, and he had called the bomb squad to handle it. They X-rayed it before taking it away to blow it up, and it was filled with pharmaceutical samples and a box of condoms. Some tired salesman had forgotten his samples, and they sent it to lost and found. Dave just wanted five minutes to himself for a cup of coffee before the next round, but he could see that wasn't going to happen. He tried to address each situation as quickly as he could, and rarely got a break during the day.

Even if some of the reports sounded ridiculous, they had to check out every call that came in, and if there was merit to it, he had to call the right authorities to handle it. His job was one of constant triage. He had wanted to be a chemical engineer, and his brother was a nuclear scientist. His parents were from mainland China, and he had been born in the States, and they still didn't understand what he did at the airport, and sometimes neither did he. He had taken a summer job he thought would be fun and exciting, and ten years later, he was still there as a senior security officer. Some days he loved what he did, and felt useful to humanity. Other days he hated it, and it felt like a bad joke or a reality show. Once he'd been called in for a pet alligator a man had smuggled in a carrying case, claiming it was a dog. A flight attendant had spotted it before take-off.

"Is this Bernice Adams a supervisor?" he asked the secretary, not that it made a difference, he would have to go either way. But the suspicious report was more likely to be a real one from a supervisor, although he knew from experience that wasn't always the case. He had seen damn near every imaginable situation in ten years at JFK. He had even delivered twins in an airport bathroom for a woman who claimed she didn't know she was eight months pregnant, and the paramedics took too long to get there after he called them. The mother and twins had done fine, and she had named one of them after him, but he hoped he never had to do that again.

"She said she wasn't," the secretary answered. There were three of them who took the calls as they came in and relayed the messages to the next available security officer on duty. And Dave was the next one up.

"What's she got?" He looked puzzled by the message.

"Something suspicious in the X-ray bin, but not a bomb."

"That's good news at least." He grabbed his jacket off the back of his chair and left his office. It was a short drive to the terminal where Bernice was working. He asked for her by name when he got there. They'd gotten busier again, the lines of departing passengers were long, and he asked one of the supervisors to point her out, which he did. A passenger was arguing with Bernice about what he claimed was a service dog, but he had no paperwork to prove it. The dog was huge and looked like a pit bull, and the passenger wanted the dog in the cabin with him unconfined.

Denise overheard Dave Lee question one of the male supervisors about Bernice, and asked him about it.

"What's that about? What's airport security doing here?"

"I don't know. Bernice must have called them," her colleague said, unconcerned. "Maybe about the dog. That dog looks like he could take someone's arm off." The other passengers standing near it were looking nervous, and the dog had started to growl and bare its fangs. Its owner wouldn't relent on wanting to take it with him, and not putting it in the cargo hold in a crate, and was using every argument to support his position. Bernice was happy to be removed from the situation, when Dave Lee approached her and introduced himself to her.

"Thank you for that," she said softly as they walked away from dog and owner and left it to one of the supervisors.

"Looks like you're having a fun day," he said easily, and she laughed.

"Yeah. I got bitten by a Chihuahua some woman asked me to hold last week. I didn't think they had teeth." He smiled and she followed him into an empty supervisor's office, and he got right to the point.

"So what do you have? What did you find in the bin?" She seemed alert and intelligent and looked hesitant for a minute, and felt stupid now that he was here. "Did you tell your supervisor about it?"

She nodded.

"And?"

"She thinks I'm crazy, and I might be. I've just got a weird feeling about this. It's been bugging me since I found it this morning." She pulled the postcard out of her pocket and handed it to him.

"That's it? A postcard?" He looked startled. She seemed smarter than that, and more sensible than to get worked up over a postcard, unless it had a threat written on the back. He flipped it over, and it didn't, just the message Bernice had read when she first saw it.

"I don't know," Bernice said apologetically. "The message seemed aggressive to me, especially with 'forever' underlined like that, and the picture of the bridge. If it had flowers on it or something, or hearts, but the bridge and that message looked weird to me." He thought about it for a long moment, staring at it as though something additional would appear if they looked at it long enough, but nothing did, and then he looked back at Bernice.

"I see what you mean. It would seem romantic or sexual to me, or something in that vein, but I can see how the image and the message could seem threatening to you. What does your gut tell you?" he asked her, narrowing his eyes as he looked at her, trying to evaluate her as much as the message. Being able to assess people and guess right was the most important part of his job, and he was good at it.

"I don't know why," she said honestly, "but it doesn't feel right to me. I kept wanting to throw it away, but I couldn't. Something kept stopping me." She knew she probably sounded like a nut job to him, but it was true.

"How long have you worked here?"

"Five years. I've caught a couple of drug dealers going through. But I've never felt like this before about something I found in a bin. We find all kinds of things, jewelry, money, cellphones, a handgun once. I know this is just a postcard, and I'm probably wrong, but it scared me. What if someone is targeting the bridge?" He nodded. The same thought had occurred to him, even though it sounded like a long shot to him too. But who would have believed that 9/11 could happen before it did? That had been a wake-up call to anyone in security. They couldn't take anything for granted ever since.

"When did you find it?"

"We had two San Francisco flights this morning at eight A.M. It was right around then, just before or after they took off. They canceled an A380, and I was told they accommodated all the passengers by breaking it into two flights, with equipment they had on the ground." He nodded. So they had at least two flights to check out, if he decided to pursue this, which would be twice the complications and twice the work, to figure out which flight the danger was on, if there was any at all. Or it could be a wild-goose chase, and just a postcard with a message that meant nothing. He sat staring at the card in his hand, as though he were psychic and expected to know if the potential danger was bogus or not. The postcard of the Golden Gate Bridge seemed to link the possibility to the two flights heading to San Francisco.

"If you want to know what I think," he said to Bernice, as though they were partners in this and had discovered it together, "I think it's probably nothing. Maybe a guy who proposed to some girl on the bridge, got turned down, and is saying she'll regret it. Or someone who's never even been to San Francisco, and was flying to St. Louis this morning. You can never tell about these things. Most of what we get like this is totally random, you have to be a mind reader to figure it out, and you never know what really happened, and nothing comes of it. There's a 99.999999 percent chance this is just a postcard, but there's that tiny fraction of a percent that says it could be something. That's what's talking to your gut, and what I work with. I think we're probably both off base, but it's my job not to ignore stuff like this. I don't want the responsibility of deciding it's nothing, and find out I'm wrong when the bridge blows sky high. Chances are, that won't happen. But if it does, you and I will know that we could have made a difference. I'm going to call the main office of Homeland Security and hand this baby off to them. If they decide it's nothing, then you and I are off the hook. I can't make this decision without them or, let's say, I don't want to." As he said it, and Bernice nodded seriously, listening to him, wondering if she had started a tempest in a teapot, Denise walked in and scowled at Bernice ferociously.

"What trouble are you causing?" she accused Bernice, as Dave Lee watched her, intrigued by the dynamic. She obviously didn't like the agent who had called him, and he wondered why. The senior TSA officer exuded disapproval and contempt for the younger, prettier woman. But Bernice seemed smart and efficient to him. Maybe that was the problem. And he didn't think she'd been wrong to call him. In his opinion, she had done absolutely the right thing, following her instincts.

"Are you Ms. Adams's supervisor?" he asked Denise, with a serious expression.

"I am," she said reluctantly. "What's going on here?"

"Dave Lee, senior officer, airport security," he introduced himself. "It's about the postcard she found. I think she told you about it."

Denise looked frightened for a minute, afraid that she was in trouble. This was beginning to sound official, although she thought Bernice was stupid to call them, and she was furious she hadn't asked her first. She wouldn't have let her, and Bernice knew it.

"I have the same concerns she did," Dave said. "I'm almost positive it's nothing, and so is she, but I'm not willing to stake my life on it, or anyone else's. I'm calling in the main office of Homeland Security. We can let them figure it out. If they don't want to pursue it, that's their business." He picked up the desk phone as he said it and dialed a number. He told whoever he spoke to where he was and what was happening, and then listened to them and hung up a minute later. He looked at both women.

"They'll be here in twenty minutes. I'm going to get a cup of coffee. I'll be back before they get here." And without saying another word, he left them then, as Denise looked at Bernice in a fury, and waited till he was out of earshot before she said anything.

"You realize, don't you, you're going to be in a world of trouble, if you stirred up all this shit for nothing?"

"I know," Bernice said meekly. She'd been thinking that herself, and had called security anyway.

"You'll be lucky if you don't lose your job over this," Denise said angrily. And she realized that she herself looked bad, because she had not acted on Bernice's concerns. If Bernice turned out to be right to be worried, it was Denise's ass that was going to be on the line, not hers.

"I understand that, but I couldn't ignore it, Denise. I don't know if there's anything to it or not. But I couldn't take the chance that it might be real."

"You better pray that it is, girl. Or you're going to be ten feet under a pile of shit."

All Bernice could think as Denise threatened her was that she only had two more months of law school to finish, and she could apply for a job as a paralegal, if nothing else. But there was no way she could ignore a possible risk of some kind of terrorist threat, assuming the worst case about the postcard, which seemed unlikely, but you just never knew, as Dave Lee had said himself.

Denise walked out of the office then, and Bernice followed her, torn between feeling worried about her job and about the postcard, and the possible danger it represented if it was a terrorist threat of some kind, however far-fetched that seemed. Homeland Security would have to make that decision. She didn't have the authority to do that at TSA. Even Dave Lee felt he couldn't, with all the experience he had. It validated Bernice's concerns somewhat, as Della came up to her and whispered.

"What's happening? Someone said that airport security was here to see you, and Denise said Homeland Security is showing up, and boy, is she pissed."

"I know she is. I found something in a bin this morning. It's probably nothing." She tried to tone it down for Della, until they knew more.

"Why didn't you tell me?" Della looked surprised that she hadn't. They told each other everything at work, or so she'd thought.

"I thought I was just being paranoid. I told Denise and she blew it off, which is probably why she's so pissed now. It kept bothering me so I called AS, without telling her, and the AS guy decided to call the main Homeland Security guys to check it out. They're probably going to decide I'm nuts and have me fired, or at least that's what Denise said."

"Screw her. It sounds like you did the right thing, if they called Homeland Security. Is it some kind of threat?"

"Could be," Bernice said vaguely. She didn't want to tell Della before Homeland Security made a decision about it.

"Keep me posted," Della said and went back to the spot where she was working, directing people into the body-scan machine. Bernice was on a break now, and Homeland Security was due any minute, so there was no point going back to work yet. She stood there waiting, while Denise ignored her, and prayed that it would all turn out to be nothing. She didn't want anyone to get hurt, even if she

lost her job. She could hardly wait to leave anyway when she graduated. She'd had enough of Denise's abuse. It was time to move on.
Her five years at TSA had served her well. They had given her the
time she needed to go to law school, and a salary she could live on
and support her son with while she was doing it. But she didn't
want to put up with Denise, or anyone like her anymore. Thinking
about it made her feel braver as she waited for Homeland Security
to arrive.

Ben Waterman sat at his desk, after his third cup of coffee, feeling
slightly jangled, but his nerves were on edge these days anyway. It
was his first day back at work after a month's leave. The highly pub-
licized hostage situation that had gone sour a month before, in an
airport warehouse, had left sixteen people dead when a SWAT team
rushed in to rescue the hostages after a twenty-four-hour siege, and
the hostage takers had killed them all, including a child in the final
shoot-out, and then killed themselves before they could be captured. The decision to go in had been made by the captain of the
SWAT team, in conjunction with the police and the head of Homeland Security, but Ben had been part of the decision, and urged
strongly for it. The hostage takers were starting to panic, Ben could
feel it, and he was sure innocent people would be killed, so he had
fought for the SWAT team to take action, and in the end they had all
died anyway. No one blamed him for it, and from everything they
knew now, it had been a no-win situation. The perpetrators were
seeking worldwide attention for an extremist cause, and his superiors had told him afterward that there probably had been no way to

spare the hostages right from the beginning, but it was no consolation with sixteen people dead.

In spite of a month of intense therapy and debriefing, Ben blamed himself for his part in the decision, and knew he always would. How did you forgive yourself for the blood of sixteen people on your hands? How could you ever know or believe that there had been no right decision? What if there was and he had missed it? He had been among the first on the scene after everyone had died, and it had been carnage. They had almost had to drag him away. He had done everything he could to save them and keep them alive.

They had given him permission to take up to three months off, or longer if he needed it, but he was back in a month. Staying home was worse. It was all he thought about, the terrible scene when they had gone in after the final shoot-out. Ben had sobbed when he saw them. And now he was back, feeling a little shaky but anxious to work.

He had been at his desk for exactly an hour and a half when Dave Lee called him and said they had a possible "situation" at Terminal 2. The last thing he needed right now was a "situation." He had come back to handle customs issues, people who didn't declare large amounts of money they were bringing into the country, jewelry some socialite hadn't declared for duty, even drugs being smuggled. The easy stuff. He didn't want to have to make any big decisions. And Dave Lee had said to him that they needed a decision about a possible situation. He wanted to hang up on him when he heard it. Dave had said it was time sensitive, and involved two flights that were in the air at that moment, heading to San Francisco. So there was no time to waste, but Ben felt rooted to the spot and didn't want to move, as he sat at his desk, wondering who he could reassign it to so he wouldn't have to go.

Ben was forty-five years old and had had an impeccable career until the recent incident, and his superiors were sure that he would recover from it. They were more certain of it than Ben was himself. He felt as though there would never come a time when he would wake up in the morning and not think of what he'd seen in the warehouse that day. He saw it in his mind's eye when he went to sleep at night and when he woke up in the morning. He had told the shrink about it, and the therapist had said it would get better, which seemed hard for Ben to believe. It was as sharply etched in his mind as it had been the day it happened. He was thinking about it again when Phil Carson, his boss, walked into his office.

"I just got a call from the chief supervisor of airport security," he said with a serious expression. "Apparently, they called you to assess a situation. Are you okay with that?" Ben wanted to tell him that he wasn't, not by any means, but he was back, and he didn't want to tell him he wasn't up to it. And then there were all the bullshit beliefs about getting back in the saddle. Homeland Security was not a job for the fainthearted, or agents who couldn't recover from seeing sixteen people dead on a warehouse floor after a shoot-out, especially if the decision to go in had been in great part their fault. It went with the territory, and he had to live with it if he wanted to keep his job. This was how it started, with a "situation" and a decision you would be responsible for, whether people died or not.

"Yeah, I'll do it," Ben said, standing up slowly. "Though if we've got someone else to send, I'd prefer it," he said honestly. "Who've we got?"

"I don't have anyone today. Harkness broke his ankle last week. Thompson and O'Dougherty are out with the flu. And Jimenez is on his honeymoon, again. He's got to give that up, he can't afford the alimony and we can't afford the vacation. So that leaves you," his commanding officer said, looking worried. He knew that Ben was still badly shaken by what had happened, and he had come back to work sooner than Phil expected. "It doesn't sound like a big deal. You can check the manifest if they're worried about a passenger, and make sure that no one on the no-fly list is on it. Call me if you have a problem," he said, looking sympathetic. Ben was one of his best men, and he didn't want to lose him, or kill him by putting too much on his shoulders on his first day back. And then he had a thought just as Ben was about to leave the office. "Take Amanda with you. If it's not too dicey, you can let her handle it. It'll make her feel good."

Ben groaned audibly. Amanda Allbright was the latest addition to their team. She was thirty-one years old and had a double master's in psychology and criminology, both of which were worthless, as far as Ben was concerned. She had a theory for everything, and none of it had any reality to it. She never stopped talking, and she was the new breed of Homeland Security agent, whose entire philosophy went against everything Ben believed. He could barely say good morning to her without getting seriously irritated.

"Now I know you hate me," Ben said, looking miserable. "Does she have to come with me?" He looked like a kid who didn't want to take his medicine, or his little brother to a ballgame.

"She'll be good for comic relief. Just try to bring her back in one piece. Don't kill her. I don't want to be visiting you in jail." Amanda liked to believe she was a dedicated feminist, but as far as Ben was concerned, she was a pain in the ass, whatever her gender, and her theories drove him up the wall.

"You might have to. I've been cleared to return to duty, not to work with her. I'd need another year of therapy for that."

"Just don't listen to her. Talk to her about baseball or sports or something."

"If I have to listen to her tell me about her Stanford and Columbia credentials again, I may have to strangle her."

"Be nice. Tell her about the Yankees."

Ben grinned ruefully, and went to find her. He didn't like anything about her, although as a rule he liked women. He had been married and divorced twice, and had no kids. Both his wives had said that his passion for his work and the amount of time he spent on it were not compatible with marriage, and he agreed.

He dated women his own age when he found any that interested him, which wasn't often. He didn't like frivolous women, or know-it-alls, which was Amanda's stock in trade. Just talking to her annoyed him. She was young and sexy, and wore skirts that barely covered her ass, but nothing about her appealed to him, least of all her endless theories about criminals and crime. She had no experience to back up what she said, just what she had learned in books, and Ben and most of the guys in the office thought she was full of shit and didn't like her. She didn't like them either. She thought they were a crusty bunch of older guys who told disgusting jokes, and she threatened to write them up for sexual harassment and discrimination regularly. Ben admitted that she was probably right, but it didn't make him like her any better, and none of the men were going to change. She was chasing a lost cause.

She was at her desk, filling out a report. She had handled a drug bust the day before. She was competent and overeducated. In the field, she was considered green by the men she worked with. Amanda looked up when Ben walked in, and didn't smile. She felt sorry about what had happened to him, but their overt hostility toward each other made it hard for her to express her sympathy. "How are you feeling?" she asked him. "Welcome back."

"Thanks. I have nightmares," he said, mostly to provoke her. "Phil wants you to go to Terminal 2 with me."

"And you don't," she challenged him.

"I didn't say that." He didn't have to. They both knew he didn't.

"What's up at Terminal 2?" she asked, as she stood up. She was going with him. She just needed to give him a hard time about it, as he saw it. She always wanted to know the details of everything, to an unnecessary degree, in his opinion. Most of what she wanted to know was irrelevant to anyone but her. But her question had been reasonable in the context. He just wouldn't have admitted it to her.

"I don't know. They said it's not a threat. They need a decision about something. We'll find out when we get there."

She followed him out in what Ben considered a shockingly short skirt. He was more than willing to admit she had great legs, but her personality ruined it for him. He didn't care what she looked like, he hated everything she stood for. But on the way over, he decided to take Phil's advice. "Do you like baseball?"

She looked at him like he had lost his mind. "No. Why?"

"The Yankees are on a winning streak," he said benignly, trying not to laugh. Maybe Phil was right. "I thought you might be interested."

"Are you asking me on a date?" She looked stunned. Maybe he'd had electroshock therapy as part of his recovery. She thought he'd have to, to ask her out.

"Shit, no. I just wondered if you liked sports."

"I just don't like baseball. It's boring. I played volleyball in college. We won the championship two years in a row. I play badminton and tennis. And I go to a gym to stay in shape. What about you?" It was a ridiculous conversation, but they were at Terminal 2 by then, and hadn't gotten into an argument yet, which was a first.

"I lift weights in my living room now that my wife moved out. I'm a black belt in karate, but I quit the last time I broke my shoulder. And I played beer pong in college," he said smugly.

"So did I," she said, always competitive with him and any of her male colleagues.

"You would," he said, as they got out of the car and walked into the terminal. Dave Lee was waiting for them, and Ben introduced Amanda. Something about the way he did it conveyed the impression that they weren't friends. And Dave walked them into the chief supervisor's office in the TSA area, where Bernice was standing. Neither Ben nor Amanda was wearing a uniform. The TSA agents did, but the senior Homeland Security agents wore street clothes, if they chose to. Dave showed them the postcard. Ben looked at it for a long moment, and then back at Dave. "And the question is?"

"The question is, what is it? A big nothing? Something between

lovers? It sounds faintly pissed off to me, and maybe a little menac-
ing. Or is it a threat on the Golden Gate Bridge?"

Ben whistled and looked at it again, narrowing his eyes. "That's
pretty unlikely, don't you think?"

"Could be. Nowadays, who the hell knows? We've all seen worse,
with less to go on." They all knew it was true, and sometimes they
got no warning. This wasn't much of a warning. But was it a clue?
That was the crux of the issue. Did the postcard mean anything or
not?

"What have you got in the air right now?" Ben asked him.

"Flights all over the country. And two to San Francisco that left
an hour and a half ago, about fifteen minutes apart. An A321 and a
757."

"And you've checked the manifest for both flights?" Ben asked
seriously.

"I assume someone ran them against the no-fly list before they
took off," Dave said calmly. "I only got called after they were in the
air." They were both aware that the no-fly list was compiled by
Homeland Security and the CIA, with highly sensitive information
provided by international government agencies listing people
known or suspected of terrorist activities, or who were undesirable
in the United States. Its purpose was to keep dangerous, subversive
people out of the country and off planes. There was a well-known
case of an Air France flight with two suspected terrorists on board
who had turned up on the sensitive lists. The plane had been kept
sealed on arrival. No passengers were allowed to disembark, and
the flight was refueled and sent back to Paris.

"Let's run the manifests again and see what comes up, who's on both those flights."

"We need a psychological profile of everyone, both passengers and crew," Amanda piped up, and Ben turned to look at her, trying to control himself.

"That would be a great idea if they were on a cruise ship in the Caribbean. We have four and a half hours to figure this out, at best. Maybe add another fifteen minutes, or have them circle for half an hour. We can get profiles on the crew and key passengers. There's no way we can get them on everyone on those two planes."

Ben turned back to Dave again then. "Let's get those profiles on the crew, and make sure we don't have some seriously disturbed employee up there that we don't know about. And I'll have them run the no-fly list again, and check for any passenger that stands out. I'll get my office to take care of it. We can get that pretty fast." Ben called his office then, and told them what he needed, and Ben, Dave, and Amanda sat down to wait. The answers started coming in quickly. Bernice listened closely to what was happening, but hadn't said a word. She had nothing to add. Amanda asked her a few questions about how long she'd worked here, and her seniority, and then Dave got the manifest by email on his phone, and shared it with Ben and Amanda. She spotted Susan Farrow's name and was impressed.

"Well, she's not our problem," Ben commented. They could see no one of interest on the manifest of the second flight. And then Ben saw the Arab last name on the manifest of the first flight, which attracted his attention but didn't concern him unduly. "I assume they were checked out on the no-fly list," he said to Dave.

"We check everyone," he confirmed. "There could have been a slipup, but I doubt it."

"I'm sure we checked too," Ben said quietly. "I'll run it again. Our office can tell us in a few minutes."

Dave nodded in response, looking serious.

"And I'm assuming we've got air marshals on both flights," Ben said, looking thoughtful, and called Phil to check it out. There was a pause at the other end of the line when he asked, which surprised him, and Phil sighed.

"We had a problem while you were gone. Apparently, someone ordered cutbacks without warning us. Some flights have been going out without marshals, and the pilots weren't notified. Everyone is pissed about it, but we have not had a hundred percent coverage in the air for the past month. I'll check on both these flights. But with the flight split into two aircrafts at the last minute, it's possible that we've only got one guy up there. I hope not, but it's possible. I'll call you back." He called back less than five minutes later and gave Ben the bad news. "We've got one on the second flight, but the A321 has no air marshal on board. The pilot has not been advised."

"For chrissake, are they serious?" Ben was furious at the idea, particularly in this case.

"That's the reality of it. There's no air marshal on that flight. And we checked the couple with the Arabic surnames. They're not on the no-fly list, but we don't know who they are. They could be perfectly innocent, or we could have a problem."

"Well, find out, for chrissake."

Phil was used to Ben's style, and he always brought home the results. He didn't object to Ben being cantankerous and even rough at times, particularly after what he'd been through. "Do you really think we have a problem?" Phil sounded worried, but Ben hadn't decided. He needed to know more.

"I don't know yet. We need the crew profiles on both flights. And I want everything we can get on the two Arabs, just in case." Ben was livid that there was no air marshal on the flight.

The only names that had caught their attention on the two manifests were the Arab man and woman, who could be anybody, and Susan Farrow, the famous actress, who was not a terrorist. Phil was going to call his source at the CIA to check on the two Arabs. Ben sat back with a sigh and looked at the others in the room.

"What we have here is basically a cover-your-ass mission," Ben said with a look of displeasure. "We don't have a goddamn thing. We have two aircraft full of random people, two Arabs who are not on the no-fly list and could be harmless or not. And no air marshal on one of the flights. If we put the whole thing to bed and forget about it, and some nut job dive-bombs the Golden Gate Bridge on a suicide mission, we've killed a hundred and eleven people on the flight and possibly more on the ground, *and* we get maximum publicity with a major movie star on the flight, just in case we needed that. In my head, I think it's nothing," he said to the others out loud. "In my gut, something is bothering me, and I don't know what it is. But just in case, I want to talk to the pilot of the A321 the two Arabs are on, so we're covered. I want to let her know she has a potential problem on board, and no air marshal on the plane. She'll be thrilled with that," Ben said unhappily, and then called Phil again. "Have we got satcom phones in the cockpit of the A321?" he asked him, and Phil said they did, which would allow them a private conversation with the pilot that no one else could hear. He said they'd get the number from the airline in five minutes and call him back.

As soon as Ben got the number, he called Helen on the flight and explained who he was. She sounded surprised to hear from him, and said that everything was fine on the flight.

"Almost fine," he corrected her. "Your air marshal wound up on the other aircraft. You don't have one on your flight." She paused for a moment as she listened to him, and decided not to tell the others. His decision to warn her on the satcom phone instead of the radio had been a good one. Only she could hear Ben on the phone, so no one needed to know they had no protection.

"Roger, I got that," she said quietly and didn't comment on it further.

"A TSA agent found a postcard we're not happy about. It could be nothing. It's not a direct threat, but slightly suspicious, relating to San Francisco. We're going to investigate it further. And you've got two Arabs on the flight the CIA is ID'ing for us now. They weren't on the no-fly list, and they're probably fine. I just want to check them out. And any passengers who stand out. I'll let you know if we have a problem after that, but I wanted to give you a heads-up about the air marshal. I think it happened when they split the flight," though it shouldn't have. They both knew that, and so did Phil and Dave. But it was too late to fix that now.

"Thanks for letting me know," Helen said in an even tone, and Ben promised to call her back. She turned to talk to Jason when she hung up. "We have two passengers in business who could be a problem. They're checking them out, and they'll tell us when they know more."

"What kind of problem?" Jason was suddenly alert. He wondered why they had called her on the satcom phone, and was suspicious it might be something about him. He'd had his share of clashes with the airline, and they had slowed down his progress toward promotion considerably, but she didn't mention that, and seemed unaware of it.

"Apparently, the two passengers in question have an Arab name, but they don't show up on the lists, so they may be fine. That's all I know for now. I'd like you to take a stroll back through the cabins, and quietly let the crew know, *discreetly,*" she emphasized. "Ask the business flight attendants to keep an eye on them, and let us know if they notice anything unusual about them or anyone."

"And if they do? Then what?" Jason asked her pointedly. That was going to be a serious issue, especially with no air marshal on board, but Jason didn't know that.

"We'll figure it out," she said, seeming unworried. Jason left the cockpit a few minutes later to carry out his mission, and Connor looked at her.

"Is there a bigger issue than that?" he asked, and she hesitated and shook her head. He wasn't part of the crew on this flight, and she didn't want to share the details with him. It might turn out to be nothing. "If there's anything you need me to do, let me know."

"I will," she said with a smile to reassure him. "Don't worry. Just enjoy the flight." As soon as Jason got back, the door locked behind him automatically. Ben had suggested she keep the cockpit sterile and let no one in except the flight crew until they knew more, and she agreed with him. "I think we'll skip lunch, gentlemen, until we know more about our passengers on this flight." She didn't want to take any chances. She looked remarkably calm and unconcerned as they rode on in silence after that. Ben hadn't said there was an actual threat to the flight. He had just superficially mentioned San Francisco. But Helen knew better than anyone that anything could happen in today's world, and it didn't have to be political. All it took was one dangerous person, determined to bring a plane down. And all they could do now was wait for Ben to call them with news from the CIA.

Chapter Five

They had the crew profiles in less than three minutes and passed them around. The airline personnel office had provided them immediately. Ben divided them into two stacks for the two flights as he read them. He was looking for danger signs, and Amanda scrutinized them minutely and read each one several times, before putting them back on each stack.

Ben kept going over the files of the three pilots on board the A321 again and again. Something wasn't working for him. They still didn't know if they had a problem, but if they did, it could have been one of the three pilots in the cockpit, a member of the cabin crew, or anyone on board. It sounded crazy even to him when he said it out loud. He remembered that Bernice was in the room then, and might have noticed something unusual about the people who went through security before the two flights. Everything seemed to be in order on the 757. He wasn't as sure about the A321. He questioned her, and she nodded slowly, thinking back to when she had come on duty and what she'd seen. But nothing had seemed unusual to her until she found the postcard in the bin.

"What did you notice about the crew?" Ben asked her intensely. "Any small odd detail?"

Bernice closed her eyes for a minute, trying to remember everything. "I noticed that the pilot was a woman, and she looked friendly and nice. She wasn't talking much, but she seemed pleasant. And the copilot was kind of a smart-ass. He made a nasty comment about most of the TSA agents being African American, and the pilot called him on it and threatened to write him up. He didn't say anything after that. The flight attendants didn't do or say anything special. They went through pretty quickly. They always do."

Ben nodded. It wasn't the flight attendants he was concerned about. It was the cockpit crew. "If we're looking for trouble," he said quietly, in the privacy of the room, after he asked Bernice to leave for a few minutes, "we have the potential for it with any of the flight crew on the A321. We have a pilot who had a TIA two days ago, which caused a decision to retire him immediately, after a distinguished forty-year career. He could be bitter about it, angry at the airline, or even suicidal. He has no psychiatric history, but his wife died last year. Now he's lost his job. He could be planning some kind of revenge on the airline, and if he is, this is his last chance. He's in the perfect place to do that. He's in the cockpit, and he sure as hell knows how to fly that plane.

"Helen Smith has gone through more than any human being ever should for the past two years. She left the Air Force, which is the only life she ever knew. She grew up with her father, an Air Force colonel. She came to work for the airline and expected her husband

74

to join her months later. Instead, he was shot down in Iraq, taken prisoner, and the whole world watched him get his head sliced off on TV. I'm not sure how you recover from that. She's living in an unfamiliar place, managing three kids. I don't know if she has money troubles or not, but she has every right to a psychotic break, or could even want to commit suicide. I can't imagine her doing it and taking a whole plane of people down with her, with her record, but if she snapped, no one would be surprised." He himself had been through so much less than that when the hostages were killed, and he had thought of suicide several times after it happened, out of remorse over the way it had turned out and the people who had died, but he didn't say that to Dave and Amanda, who were listening raptly to him. "She may feel guilty for leaving Iraq before he did, or have survivor guilt. There's no sign of it, but she would have a right to mental problems more than anyone I know.

"And Jason Andrews is a loose cannon. It's all here in his files. Every kind of insubordination and attitude problem. He's probably mad at the airline for slowing his progress down because of it. He's been passed over for several promotions, because of his attitude, not his skills. It says here that he's a more than capable pilot, but he can't keep his mouth shut, and he was referred to anger management classes two years ago. From what I'm reading here, I'm surprised that they haven't fired him. He sounds like a giant pain in the ass. And if they do fire him, he can look forward to life as a waiter. Flying is the only thing he knows, and no one is going to hire him as a pilot if the airline lets him go."

Ben summed it up. "So there you have it. We have three people in that cockpit, two of whom could want to commit suicide, especially Connor Gray, who has nothing to look forward to and no future ahead of him. And Jason Andrews is a wild card, with some kind of anger management problem we don't know enough about. How angry is he? How far will he go?"

"Does he have a girlfriend?" Dave asked Ben quietly, and Ben looked in the confidential file about him.

"I don't know. He lived with a woman he had listed as next of kin. But she's not listed anymore."

"Why don't you send someone to talk to her? She may know something we don't and shed some light on what he's capable of and just how angry he is. Maybe we have nothing to worry about. The girlfriends always know."

"Good point," Ben said, and was going to call Phil and ask him to arrange it, when Amanda finally spoke up. She had read the files thoroughly too, and had been unusually quiet. Now she had on her serious, professional face when she spoke.

"I completely disagree with you," she said to Ben. "I don't think you understand the psychology of these people, or two of them anyway. Connor knew he had to retire next year anyway. Shortening it by a year is not going to make a man of his caliber commit suicide. I'm sure he has plans for his retirement. He may be intending to start a business or spend time with his grandchildren. He's not going to take a plane down and murder innocent passengers on his way out. It's not in his character. His wife has been dead for a year—why would he commit suicide over it now? And it says in his file she'd been sick for several years. It doesn't sound like it came as a shock.

"And Jason Andrews may be a hothead, but he has a brilliant career ahead of him. Everything in his file says he's an outstanding pilot. So he has a big mouth, and he's been delayed for promotion a couple of times, so what? He's not going to destroy his life, take out a national landmark, and kill innocent people because it's taken him a year or two longer to become a captain. That would be insane. And even if he has an anger problem, he may put a fist through a wall or mouth off at a coworker, but he is *not* going to kill a hundred and eleven people, including himself. It's just not in his psychological profile. Trust me, he's not going to give up his future at his age.

"The one I'm worried about is Helen Smith. I don't think anyone can survive what she's been through without deep emotional scars and smoldering anger, none of which shows until the day she loses it and shoots twenty people in a supermarket, or takes down a plane. She has every reason to be furious at life. The truth is, she got screwed. What happened to her just isn't fair. I couldn't watch my husband get beheaded on video, and ever lead a normal life again. I think she's an accident waiting to happen, and I'm shocked that the airline didn't think so too, and that she is still flying. If we do have a problem, I think she's it. She has the potential to be a very dangerous person, to herself and passengers on the plane. She's our prime candidate for a suicidal psychotic break."

There was no arguing with the extent of Amanda's education, but Ben didn't agree with a word she said.

"I think you're dead wrong about her," Ben said firmly, "and about the others too. I think Connor Gray probably is suicidally depressed. And Jason Andrews sounds like such an unbridled asshole, he probably could kill a hundred and eleven people in a rage. More, if he were flying a bigger plane." Amanda looked seriously annoyed to be contradicted and kept arguing with Ben about it, when his cell-phone rang, and it was Phil. He had heard back from the CIA.

"Your Arab couple are okay," Phil said, sounding embarrassed. "They're both from prominent Saudi families. Ahmad, the husband, is a member of the Saudi royal family. They're here as students and starting classes at UC Berkeley in a few days. They're as far from terrorists as you can get. They're on student visas. He's enrolled at the business school, and she's getting a master's in art history. They're not going to take down your plane. So where does that leave us? Do we have a situation on our hands or not?" Phil asked, sounding worried, but relieved about the young couple at least.

"We're still trying to figure that out," Ben said quietly. "This narrows the field considerably. We're worried about the cockpit crew on the first plane. We have three potentially explosive scenarios and some complicated psychological issues. It's credible that any one of the three could try to take the plane down, though we don't agree on who. And I don't know if any of them would want to take out the Golden Gate Bridge in the process, but I think the copilot is capable of it. So do we pull out all the stops and try to stop something from happening that maybe was never going to happen in the first place? Do we make fools of ourselves trying to save a plane that's not at risk? Or do we let it go and end up regretting it when it turns out that we weren't paranoid in the first place? Intelligently, I don't think anything's going to happen here, it's all too unlikely, but my instincts are shrieking at me, and my gut tells me that a disaster is going to happen if we don't try to stop it." Dave was nodding as Ben said it. He agreed with him, and Amanda was pointing at Helen's personnel file with a look of determination.

"Personally, I agree with you on most points," Phil told him on the speakerphone. "I think we're all letting our imaginations run away with us. A random postcard does not a disaster make. And I don't see how any airline could be employing three pilots who would be capable of taking down a plane on a suicide mission, and those are three star pilots we're talking about, or two of them, at least. But having said that, I don't know why, I have a bad feeling about this too. This is the kind of situation we read about now too often, and no one saw coming. If we think there is *any* chance that what we fear here could in fact become a reality, then I think we have to do everything we can to stop it, even if we look like idiots later; if we turn out to be wrong, I'd rather look like a fool than have dead passengers."

"That's kind of the direction I'm leaning," Ben said, reassured to hear what Phil thought about it. "I just have a nasty feeling that as crazy as it sounds, all based on a flimsy postcard, I think it could happen."

"Then let's get serious about it," Phil said, relieving Ben of some of the responsibility of the decision. "Let's put up all the roadblocks we can, and hope to hell the problem isn't on the 757 and we missed it."

"That's not going to happen. I don't see any potential there. No passengers stand out and the crew are clean," Ben said firmly, with conviction. "I think we know where the problem is, if there is one, on which plane, and I think there is only one of the three pilots who would do it. Jason Andrews. The others are too responsible. It's not in their DNA to bring down a plane, for any reason."

"By the way, the airline gave us another detail on Helen Smith.

Her daughter is neurologically handicapped in some way. She has a mild form of disability. As her children's only parent, she's not going to abandon her, or any of her kids."

"That clinches it for me," Ben said firmly. "I think Andrews is our man. The question is what do we do to stop him." Ben thought about it for a minute and knew what he had to do, or to at least get started. "The plane is due to land at SFO at approximately eleven A.M. local time. I want the Golden Gate Bridge closed at ten, for 'construction.' They can tell people there's a serious gas leak, which will keep away the curious. And I want Coast Guard rescue boats in the water, in case he gets that far. Let's not take any chances."

Phil noticed that Ben sounded like his old self again, from before the hostage situation, and was pleased to hear it. He was not afraid to make decisions or trust his gut. "What about the captain? Are you going to tell her?" Phil wanted to know.

"I have to tell her something," Ben answered. "I'll clear the Arab couple, of course. But I need to warn her she could have a serious problem in the cockpit. She has to be prepared for it. Maybe it's a good thing that Connor Gray is there with her. I'll call her on the satcom in a few minutes, and then I'll come back to the office." He wanted to be at home base with all this happening, not in the TSA supervisor's office at Terminal 2. Ben suggested they take Bernice with them, and Dave had already said he would come along. Ben hung up with Phil, and saw Amanda staring at him in a fury.

"Do you realize what you're doing? You're backing the wrong horse here. What if I'm right and Helen is the most likely to bring that plane down? The death of more than a hundred people is going to be your responsibility if you make it possible for her to do that."

The force of what she said hit him like a wrecking ball, especially after what had recently happened with the hostages.

"It's a chance we have to take. I'm in charge here, and I take full responsibility for my decisions," Ben said in an icy tone, which didn't stop her.

"If you're wrong, I'll see to it that our superiors know about it, and that I advised you against it."

"Don't worry, Amanda," he said bitterly. "If I'm wrong, you won't have to get me fired. Next time, I'll quit." He almost had this time, and Phil had talked him out of it and insisted that no one could have foreseen that the hostages would be killed, and any of them in authority could have made the decision to go in when they did. They had agreed with Ben on it 100 percent.

"You have no psychological training or insights," Amanda insisted, adamant in her own position. "I listened to you, it's all a grab bag of guesswork with you. There's no science to it." She was frustrated and furious at him. She thought he was sloppy and unprofessional.

"It's called experience," he responded. "With you, it's all out of books you read. You don't know what you're talking about. I've been in the field here for twenty years. You can't learn this stuff in books. You have to know people."

"Like you knew the hostage takers?" It was a cheap shot and she knew it, and regretted it as soon as she said it. "I'm sorry. I shouldn't have said that. I just think you're wrong about Helen Smith. I think she's going to be the one to bring that plane down." Amanda was certain of it.

"Maybe none of them will," Ben said honestly. "We're starting from a postcard that may not mean a goddamn thing. It's *all* guess-work. All we can do is prepare for the worst and see what happens. And if nothing happens and we all look like fools, so much the better. I'd like to have egg on my face for a change. It might feel better than watching people die when we could have prevented it." He couldn't have stopped the hostages' death, but he still thought he might have.

"That's my point," Amanda said grimly. "Get Helen Smith out of the cockpit. Jason Andrews is the only one up there with a future. Trust him. He's not going to bring that plane down. He may save it for you."

Ben looked at her and shook his head. "I'm sorry, I can't," and with that he walked out of the terminal with Amanda and asked Bernice to join them. He wasn't going to explain it to Amanda again. She didn't get it.

Bernice looked overwhelmed by what she'd heard before she left the room, and the knowledge that she had started it. Denise watched her leave the building with them, and wondered what would happen next. Ben had made it clear to all that no one was to talk to the press. Dave was lagging behind, talking on his cellphone. When he caught up, he looked at Ben with an exasperated expression.

"Great. We've got a guy on the plane who kidnapped his infant son from his estranged wife. She's hysterical. He left a note telling her he's on this flight. He's on the A321 and the police are going to pick him up at the San Francisco airport. He's in arrears on child support payments, he's got the kid, who's ten months old, and he has a connecting flight to Japan. So we've got to nab him at the gate and put the kid in protective custody. Jesus, can anything else happen on that flight?"

"Let's hope not," Ben said as they drove back to his office, where Phil was waiting for them. Phil could easily sense the tension between Amanda and Ben when they sat down for a meeting. She shared her theories about Helen, and Phil listened to her intently and spoke to her apologetically when she finished. Her theories made sense only to her. No one else agreed. And neither did he.

"I've got to go with Ben on this," he told her kindly. He didn't want to offend her, but after reading the personnel files himself, he thought Ben was right. Helen had been through hell, but was solid as a rock. Connor was an honorable man, and must surely be depressed over losing his career, but not to the point of killing 111 people. If there was a plot, which no one knew for sure, Jason was their man. They all believed it after what they'd read about him.

The first thing Ben did when he got back to his office was to call Alan Wexler, the head of the San Francisco Homeland Security office, to have him send agents to talk to Jason's ex-girlfriend in San Francisco. She was a nurse at UCSF Medical Center, and he wanted to know more about Jason's anger problem, and just how far she thought he would go, if she would talk to them.

And then he called Helen on the satcom to bring her up to date. "We're not sure, but we think we have a problem on your flight," he said cautiously. "We don't know anything certain at this point, we're just guessing, based on what we do know and can piece together. But I don't think the concern is with the passenger list," he said quietly. "Your Arab couple are fine, by the way. They're Saudi royals on their way to grad school. I think the problem may be in the cock-pit." There was silence at her end for a long moment as she tried to absorb it and what that meant for her. "Do you understand me, Captain?"

"I think I do." She didn't suspect Connor Gray. Her copilot was a far more likely candidate to cause trouble. And she didn't argue with Ben about it. She thought he might be right, if there really was a problem.

"Are you having any issues now?" Ben asked her.

"We're fine," she said and sounded convincing. And it was true. Jason had been quiet for the last hour, and hadn't spoken to her or Connor. He had been lost in thought, as he sat in his seat with the plane on autopilot, but there was no way to know what he was thinking.

"We'll stay in touch with you," Ben told Helen. "We're gathering more information now. By the way, we've got a parental abduction situation in coach, but that's under control and it's not your problem."

She laughed ruefully as he said it. "Anything else?" And she had thought it would be an easy flight.

"We'll keep you posted," Ben promised.

"I'll look forward to it." She sounded cool and calm. The fighter pilot in her had taken over, her head clear even under fire in combat.

"And don't let him do the landing at SFO," he warned her.

"Definitely not," she said pointedly, and hung up a moment later. She glanced over at Jason after the call ended, and told him that the

Arab couple had checked out, were Saudi royals and weren't a problem. He listened to her and nodded and didn't say a word, and she
went back to watching the blue sky ahead of them. They were three
hours out of San Francisco. Halfway through the trip.

As Ben hung up after speaking with Helen, Phil Carson walked into
his office with the manifest of the first flight in his hands. The second flight was no longer an issue.

"I just saw an interesting name on here," Phil said as he sat down
and handed Ben the list, and pointed to a name close to the top. "It
rang a bell for me and I looked him up. Thomas Birney, he's the
American rep of the manufacturer of the plane. I read somewhere
that he had some corporate issue with the CEO of the company and
he was going to quit. He's ex–U.S. military, and he has top security
clearance. Maybe he can help us on the flight." With no air marshal,
they needed all the help they could get. "He's retired Air Force; if we
need someone to check out what's going on in the cockpit, he could
step in and see what's up. He has a plausible excuse for a courtesy
visit to the flight deck. Captain Smith may need a helping hand. See
if you can get his email address from the company. They've got WiFi
on the flight, we could send him an email." It sounded like a good
idea to Ben, and he called the New York company office immediately. He noticed that Amanda had gone back to her office. Bernice
was sitting in a chair in the waiting area. And several of the senior
agents had walked into Ben's office after Phil explained the problem
to them. They had a possible suicide flight, without absolute cer-

tainty about who the suicide pilot might be, and only a hunch to go on. All they knew, whatever the plot, if there was one, was that it had to be foiled. And they had exactly three hours to do it.

The head of the aircraft manufacturer's U.S. office in New York took Ben's call, was extremely cooperative, and gave him Tom Birney's email address, as soon as he established that Ben worked for Homeland Security, and that there was a security issue that they needed to contact Tom about. They asked if there was anything they could do to help, and Ben said there wasn't, but they were fully supportive and sympathetic.

As Bernice sat in the hallway, waiting for further news and developments, Della called her and asked what was going on.

"A lot right now, but maybe nothing. A lot of wild stuff is happening." And she had started the whole thing with the postcard she'd found, but she didn't say anything to Della. She called Toby's school then, and asked them to keep him in day care. She could see that there was no way she'd pick him up on time, because they wanted her to stick around. If it got too late, she'd have to ask her neighbor to pick him up. After she hung up, she sat thinking about everything she'd heard since she'd called airport security. She just hoped that Homeland Security would manage to save the plane and the people on it. She didn't even want to think about what might have happened if she'd listened to her supervisor and hadn't called.

Chapter Six

Robert Bond had been holding his baby for the past three hours and Scott hadn't stopped screaming, as though he knew that something was wrong. His father couldn't explain to him that everything was going to be okay. They were going on a nice trip together. They would stay in San Francisco for a day, and that night they were flying to Japan. Robert just needed time to think, and he wanted to be alone with Scott, without Ellen telling him how many hours he could have the baby for and what time he had to be back with him. It was always less time than he wanted and seemed fair to him. And in their provisional custody agreement, the female judge had agreed with Ellen that the baby was too young to spend the night with his father, and to make sure it stayed that way, Ellen was still nursing him full-time. She had added baby-food fruits and cereal to his diet, but she wanted the baby to be dependent on her. Robert had thought they had been ready for children, but clearly they were not. Everything had changed, and not for the better, the moment Scott arrived and even in the months before.

He had no ties to Japan, he just wanted to get as far away from her as he could. He was going to bring the baby back eventually, in a month or two, and maybe by then, she'd be more reasonable. He had left her a nice note, explaining everything to her, and how he felt about it. He had been so in love with her before they married and for the first year, but her pregnancy had changed her. She focused only on the baby, and when Scott had been born, it only got worse. Now she was obsessed with their child and no longer cared about him, or even wanted to be married to him. Everything had to be perfect and baby-proof. They lived with monitors and gates, and baby equipment everywhere. It all had to be done the way she wanted it. She refused to go back to work, and they couldn't even afford to go to a movie. Her parents paid for everything and ran the show.

Robert had been saving for months, without telling her, and now he was going to Tokyo and Kyoto with his son. He loved everything he'd seen about Japan on the Internet. The people were polite, the country was clean. He was going to rent a room in a mountain town somewhere, after they visited Tokyo, and he was going to discover fatherhood on his own. He was twenty-five years old, and he hadn't been ready for it, and didn't want the baby at first, but now he was going to embrace being a parent wholeheartedly. They had been separated for six months. Ellen said he was irresponsible, and she wanted a divorce. Her parents had invited her to live with them, and she had agreed, which was intolerable for him. His own parents had never approved of her and refused to let him stay with them now. They said he had wanted to be an adult, so he had to be one and figure things out for himself. So he had. He hadn't hidden what he was doing or where he was going, he just hadn't told anyone. He had gotten Scott a passport one afternoon when Ellen had to go somewhere and she let Robert take him to the park.

Since no one would help him, he had taken the baby without Ellen's permission, letting himself in through the garage. He knew what time she showered after her parents left for work. It had all been easy, until now. All Scott had done since they boarded the flight was scream and pull on his ear.

Robert was sitting next to a heavyset woman with bleached blond hair, wearing sickeningly sweet perfume. She was the leader of some kind of group of girls who were sitting all around them, and ignoring whatever she said to them. The woman had told him that she thought the baby had an earache, but Robert had no idea how to tell. He had never been with the baby for long on his own till then. He was planning to email Ellen from Japan in a couple of days and tell her they had arrived and the baby was safe. She'd have to live without him until they got back. She couldn't tell him what to do now, and neither could the court. He had taken matters into his own hands. In his mind, now he was what they all had kept telling him to be, an adult. It all made sense to him.

On Robert's other side was a couple who hadn't stopped arguing since they sat down. They were going to his sister's wedding in California, which she didn't want to do. She said his family was always nasty to her, and Robert knew just how she felt. She hated the sister who was getting married, and reminded her husband that he didn't get along with her either, and couldn't stand the man she was marrying, who he thought was a crook. So why were they going, and why did they have to stay with his parents, who criticized her the whole time they were there, whenever they went? But he said he didn't like her parents either, and they treated him like dirt. Her sisters wouldn't talk to him, her brother was stoned whenever they saw him, and her cousin was a drug dealer and belonged in jail.

It had gone on endlessly. Robert missed hearing some of it because of the baby's screaming, which drowned them out, but it was like watching reality TV. On top of it, she said she hated their apartment in Queens, and if he'd get a better job, they could move into a decent apartment and she could get pregnant. She was thirty-six years old, they'd been married for eight years, and her clock was ticking. But he said he wasn't ready for kids, and he liked the job he had. He just didn't like her family, any more than she liked his. It sounded like one of those "Can this marriage be saved?" programs. And in Robert's opinion, it couldn't. The two flight attendants were talking about them too.

"Oh, Jesus, have you been listening to the pair arguing?" Bobbie asked Annette. "I think they're going to kill each other before we land."

"Maybe we should make an announcement, asking if there's a marriage counselor on the plane," Annette said and rolled her eyes and laughed.

"They're a great reason to stay single. She's been crying for most of the flight, and he sounds like a jerk," Bobbie agreed with her.

"I had a relationship like that once. I stuck it out for four years. I have no idea why. I think I was just scared I wouldn't find anyone else. I felt like I'd gotten out of prison the day he left," Annette said with a sigh.

"My parents' marriage sounded like them," Bobbie commented. "They got it right the second time, with other people," she added with a smile.

"Do you think that baby will ever stop screaming?" Annette said with a look of despair.

"Yeah, he'll fall asleep in the last five minutes of the flight. Kids like that give babies a bad name," Bobbie said, and they both laughed.

"It's not the kids, it's the parents. The dad has no idea what he's doing with that child. I think it might be sick."

"That's what the woman sitting next to him told him."

"Watch out for the little choristers, by the way. They keep stealing our snacks. Don't you just love working in coach?"

"Yeah, love it. Not." There were two of them, and with seventy-two passengers in coach on a fully booked plane, a screaming baby, and fourteen young girls running around loose, it had been a tough flight. Someone had smoked weed in the only toilet that was working, and the flight attendants were convinced it was one or several of the older girls from the chorus, and the chaperone didn't give a damn. The girls had told them that they were going to San Francisco and Seattle to perform, and then flying back to New York. They were a rowdy group, and the chaperone paid no attention to what they were doing. As far as she was concerned they were safe on the plane and couldn't go anywhere, so she didn't have to watch them. She'd had her earphones on for most of the trip and was watching a movie, but at least she couldn't hear the baby crying, although for those sitting near her, the smell of her perfume was almost worse than the screaming infant.

Bobbie went up to business class to visit Nancy and Joel again and looked at them with envy. It had been a peaceful trip for them, except for the momentary alert about the Arab couple, which turned out to be a false alarm, and they were both asleep in their seats. He had mellowed out after the first two hours on the flight and watched a movie until he dozed off. And the word that had filtered down was that they were a Saudi prince and princess.

The report from coach was dizzying, and made the business class flight attendants happy they weren't in the main cabin. The two flight attendants in first class had reported that Susan Farrow was a dream, and had signed autographs for them. It had warmed them up considerably. And Nancy hadn't wanted to tell anyone, but finally couldn't resist and confided to Bobbie that she had just found out that morning before the flight that she was pregnant. She couldn't keep it to herself a minute longer. She beamed while she said it, and Bobbie congratulated her and hugged her.

"I'm old enough to have a kid in college," she said seriously, "but I don't care. We've waited so long for this. I don't want to do anything to screw it up. I'd probably never get pregnant again. This was a miracle." They talked about it for a few more minutes and then Bobbie left. Joel came back from delivering a drink to a passenger and started talking about his wedding again. They all had their lives to go home to, and couldn't wait. They would be landing in two and a half hours.

*   *   *

On the ground, Ben, Phil, Dave, Amanda, and half a dozen Homeland Security agents were actively debating if they should instruct the captain to bring the flight down at another airport before they reached San Francisco. But they didn't have enough conclusive evidence to go on, just a postcard that might mean nothing and their collective gut. And if they landed early, roughly halfway through the flight, it could cause panic and drama on board, possibly for nothing. Phil's conclusion, as senior officer, was that they didn't have anything concrete to justify landing the flight now. If something changed, they would, or could consider it seriously. But for now, they all agreed after half an hour, it was best to let the flight proceed to SFO. They still had time to change their minds. They all felt confident that Helen was competent enough to handle whatever happened in the air, which hopefully would not include a harrowing detour to the Golden Gate Bridge. And if they changed the flight plan now, they were afraid that Jason might try something dangerous or dramatic wherever they were. They had one advantage with the A321: If they did decide to land early, they wouldn't have to dump fuel, which could have been an additional problem on another plane. The plane they were using could land fully loaded, so full fuel tanks were not an issue. But their decision in any case was to keep the flight on course and in the air.

"Let's go for it," Ben said quietly. "We'll stay with the approved flight plan and land at SFO." Helen didn't know that they'd been thinking of changing the final destination, and they didn't tell her, since their conclusion was to stick with landing the plane at SFO, but it had been a serious debate. Ben and his team had to take it all under serious consideration, and they had no certain knowledge that the flight was in danger, only a postcard and a guess. And admitting to a threat of some kind would attract the attention of the media even before they landed, and could provoke an instant reaction from Jason. It seemed safer to identify and neutralize him, and bring the plane in according to plan.

Catherine James was still wide awake and sending emails, and had been for several hours. She had taken her suit jacket off and rolled up the sleeves of her silk blouse. She was having a town car pick her up at the airport to take her to Palo Alto for her meeting. She desperately wanted the job, and to make a good impression, so she didn't drink any more wine or champagne after takeoff, although she was still slightly nervous about the flight. But there had been no turbulence. It had been a smooth ride all the way from New York, and they only had two hours left. As much as she hated flying, she knew she could manage that. The man next to her had worked as long as she had, and when she asked him what he did, he said he was an aeronautical engineer, and she looked impressed.

"The company I work for built this plane," he said, and smiled at her. She had turned out to be neither drunk nor talkative, so he was friendlier than he had been at the beginning of the flight. He had asked her where she was going, and she said to a meeting in Palo Alto. She said she was hoping to move to California, if things went well. He didn't tell her that he had quit his job recently and had been interviewing in New York. He had another month to finish out his contract and was staying till the end. As one of the top people in management in the company, he felt he had a responsibility to them, especially when his leaving was reported in *The New York Times.* They were still trying to convince him to stay, but Tom thought their disagreements had been too severe. He didn't like the attitude of the CEO. There was a battle of wills between Tom and the head of the New York office, and he felt the CEO hadn't supported him, so on principle he was leaving. He'd been interviewing with similar firms in the East, but he hadn't found one he liked as much yet. He had loved working where he was and didn't want to change, but he felt he couldn't stay, with a personality clash with his superior. He had one more company in L.A. to meet with in two weeks, and then he planned to make a decision about his future. In his current job, he commuted between their New York office and one in San Francisco.

He asked Catherine then about her job, and she said she worked in finance, at a Wall Street firm for the moment, but it had been her dream for years to work in venture capital in Silicon Valley, and now it was happening. The job she was interviewing for had fallen into her lap.

"I broke up with my boyfriend recently," she said as they chatted, "so it seemed like a good time to make the move." Tom had wondered if she was single or divorced and whether she had kids, but hadn't wanted to ask. And he thought her comment about her recent breakup was an encouraging detail, having noticed again how attractive she was, and how shapely her legs were.

He was chatting with her when the email from Ben Waterman came in. It said only that they were having some security concerns about the flight, and would appreciate it if he would stop in the cockpit for a few minutes and then give them a temperature reading in New York about the atmosphere he encountered and any observations about the flight crew. Tom frowned as he read it, and Catherine noticed his change of expression immediately. The email also said that they had advised Captain Smith of a courtesy visit from him, once they knew he was on the flight.

"Something wrong?" Catherine asked. She hoped she didn't sound too neurotic, but was sure she did. But given what she knew of his job now, she figured he'd be one of the first to know if there was a problem with the plane.

"Of course not." He smiled at her. "Everything's fine," he said calmly. "In two hours, we'll be on the ground, and you'll be off to your meeting, and you'll knock 'em dead," he said pleasantly, and as he stood up, presumably to use the restroom, she pulled her legs close to her so he could get by her. She smiled as he walked past. She watched him go, thinking that he was good-looking. She noticed that he wasn't wearing a wedding ring. She was wondering if he just didn't wear one or wasn't married, when she saw him walk past the restroom, stop and say something to the purser in first class, and then knock on the cockpit door, and she stiffened.

The copilot opened it immediately when Tom identified himself, since the captain had been advised of a social visit and she had just notified the purser that Tom had clearance to enter and was expected.

Catherine saw the exchange, and Tom disappeared inside, which made her anxious again about what the email had said. Why would her seatmate go to the cockpit immediately after receiving an email?

He had looked serious as he read it, and had gotten up and gone forward almost immediately. She wondered if he had lied to her, knowing how nervous she was on the flight and had been in the beginning. Maybe something was wrong with the plane. She glanced out the window but saw no sign of smoke or fire in the engines.

Once inside, Tom greeted all three pilots, and Helen looked happy to see him when he introduced himself. They chatted easily for a few minutes, since she and Tom had both been in the Air Force. He commented that it had been a pleasant flight, and noticed that Jason was watching him intently. Tom turned to talk to him then, and thought the young copilot looked tense.

Tom asked about the plane's performance, to justify his visit and not arouse suspicion, and Helen said it was a pleasure to fly.

"No complaints then? Nothing you'd like to see changed? We like feedback from our pilots on an ongoing basis." It was true but also covered his appearance in the cockpit. He didn't know what problems they were having, but he sensed that the atmosphere was strained although Captain Smith seemed cool and professional.

He lingered with them to try to understand the tension he was feeling. He wasn't sure if the pilot and copilot didn't like each other, or if there was a problem or had been a disagreement of some kind. He could sense the newly retired captain watching him too. There was definitely an odd atmosphere among the three pilots, but he couldn't put his finger on it. Nothing in Helen's face betrayed it. He saw her make some notes in a log as they drew closer to San Francisco, and Jason seemed anxious for Tom to leave.

He finally ran out of excuses to stay, shook hands with all three of them, thanked Helen for a smooth flight, and was startled to feel a small slip of paper in the palm of his hand when Helen shook his. Fortunately, he had shaken her hand last. As he left with a final wave, he slipped the paper into his pocket, went into the restroom afterward, and read it. She had given him all the emergency access and override codes to the cockpit. Ben had been right. Something was amiss if she felt a need to give them to him. After that, he hurried back to his seat to contact Ben, waiting with the others at Homeland Security for his report.

"Everything okay?" Catherine asked him again, as he got back into his seat, after carefully stepping over her. "I saw you go into the cockpit," she said, worried.

"Courtesy visit." He smiled at her and picked up his computer again. The codes were in his pocket, and he wanted to fill Ben in immediately. He told him what had happened, and said there was a feeling of tension in the cockpit, but he couldn't explain it or see any reason for it. The captain had been congenial, Connor Gray was quiet, and the copilot seemed anxious and in a hurry for him to leave. Ben didn't like the sound of it. The whole day had been fraught with the same kind of feeling, of some major piece of the puzzle missing, and all his instincts shrieking. Why was Jason in a hurry for Tom to leave? And Helen must have sensed danger if she'd given Tom the access codes to the cockpit.

"I think there's trouble on the flight," Ben said to Phil, and told him about the paper Helen had given Tom, and Phil looked unhappy about it.

"That doesn't sound good to me." It confirmed their suspicions and fears about the flight and gave credence to their theories, even if they had no proof of a problem, or solid evidence of it, until the slip of paper with the codes.

"It doesn't to me either," Ben agreed, as Amanda walked into his office and sat down. She had gone back to her own office for a while, in order to get away from what she considered too much testosterone in one place, which in her mind accounted for their refusing to believe any of her theories about Helen Smith. She was a woman and knew how women's minds worked, and she was sure she'd gotten it right and the captain was about to snap, or already had, and they were going to see some terrifying sign of it. Ben and Phil were afraid of something even worse.

When Tom Birney left the cockpit, Jason looked at Helen suspiciously.

"What was that about? Was he checking up on me?"

"Of course not. Why would he?" she said, starting to put her things away, to get ready for their approach and landing. They were still two hundred miles away, which wouldn't take long to cover, and she was going to report to the tower in a minute. She had already done so earlier, but needed to check with them again when they were in closer range. "He doesn't work for the airline," she reminded Jason. "You heard what he said. They like getting feedback from the pilots, about how their planes perform. It's nice for them to have some input and for us to talk to them directly."

"Then why didn't he ask me?" he asked angrily, glaring at her, and she could see his temper starting to flare.

"He did, he asked all of us." She included Connor in her answer too, since he had been flying the same planes until only days before, and Tom didn't know he was recently retired. "You could have said something if you wanted to."

"I didn't want to," he snapped at her. "I don't care how they build their goddamn planes, the airline doesn't let me fly them anyway." He sat in the copilot's chair and sulked, waiting for her to let him do the landing at SFO. She hadn't told him yet that she wasn't going to. She was saving that piece of news for the last minute, so he'd have less time to react, in case he flew into a rage over it.

Ben responded to Tom's email immediately, and told him to be on the alert for anything unusual happening. And Catherine continued to scrutinize him as he answered Ben's email. She had a sixth sense that something was wrong and Tom wasn't telling her. But they were strangers, and he was too professional to say anything about Ben's warnings to him from the ground.

Nancy was making cookies in the galley, and Joel was plating them to offer passengers before they landed. They still had to pick up the earphones in business and first class and do minor housekeeping before the end of the flight.

Nancy used the opportunity to send her husband a quick email. She had never done that before but suddenly wanted to, and all she wrote to him was "I love you."

His response came back almost instantly, concerned about her. "Something wrong?" he asked.

"Of course not," she answered back, and his response was quick. "In that case, I love you too. See you tonight." He was just leaving Miami on a delayed flight. But she could wait to tell him the news until that night. It had taken twelve years to get here. A few more hours wouldn't hurt, and they had a lot to talk about, like the adoption of the little girl in China. What were they going to do about that now? And then, trying not to think about it, she took the trays of cookies around, while Joel collected the headphones.

The Saudi couple each accepted a cookie and smiled at her. They were excited to be approaching their new life in Berkeley. He looked far more relaxed than when he boarded, as he chatted with his wife. Nancy gave two cookies each to Mark and Nicole, who were looking forward to seeing their grandparents, and she noticed that Tom Birney and Catherine James were talking, and they were smiling. She wondered if a romance had started on the flight. They were both good-looking people in their early forties. Stranger things had happened, and they'd had plenty of time to talk.

When she finished offering the cookies, she went back to the galley and a few minutes later, Joel returned with the headphones. People hated to give them up before their movies were over, but the crew had to pick them up an hour before they landed, and warned people of it at the beginning of the flight, but no one ever remembered, and then got annoyed at the flight attendants when they followed the rules and reclaimed them.

In coach, the screaming baby had gotten worse, and Monique Lalou, the chorus chaperone, turned to Robert again with a look of concern.

"Your baby is bright red. I think he has a fever." As she said it, the baby projectile vomited all over her and she looked horrified. The smell was ghastly and Bobbie rushed to the bathroom to bring them wet towels, but there was very little they could do to repair the damage. Robert apologized profusely.

"I don't know what's wrong with him," Robert said, looking panicked.

"You should take him to a doctor," Monique said angrily. "He's been sick for the entire flight. You shouldn't be traveling with him." The smell of vomit was everywhere, and the couple on his other side covered their noses in revulsion, as the husband whispered to his wife.

"You want one of those? I sure don't."

"He was cute before he threw up," she said halfheartedly.

"No, he wasn't. He's been screaming since we took off."

The remainder of the flight in coach was going to be very unpleasant, and Robert was wondering what to do when he landed. He didn't know where to find a doctor, and he couldn't call Ellen to ask her. He didn't want to contact her again until he got to Tokyo. He had a plan, and he was going to stick to it. For once in his life, he was going to do what he wanted, and not what everyone told him to do. But he could feel how hot the baby was in his arms. The woman from the chorus was right, he had a fever. He'd have to take him to an emergency room for some medicine. Robert just hoped they didn't miss their flight to Japan. He had a nonrefundable ticket that couldn't be changed, and he didn't want to lose it. He was sure the baby would be all right once they got to Tokyo.

Bobbie took refuge in the business class galley again for a few minutes, but when she showed up she reeked of vomit, and they held their noses and told her she had to leave.

"I'm sorry, that baby threw up all over everyone. I got it all over me, while I tried to help them clean up."

"Don't you have a change of uniform?" Nancy asked her, as Bobbie shook her head and tried to keep her distance. But you could smell her from a block away, and she finally left them to return to coach.

"I'm not working coach again," she told them, and then ran back down the aisle, as people's heads turned, wondering where the awful smell came from. She wondered if the others would even let her take the airport shuttle with them. She'd have to take a cab in from the airport, and the cab driver wouldn't like it either. It was a hideous end to an already bad flight for her, and she heard the same couple arguing again as she rushed past them. They never stopped and she wondered if they enjoyed it, or why they didn't just get divorced instead of torturing each other.

In the cockpit, Helen had asked Jason to tidy up their paperwork, and to continue to keep the cockpit sterile after they descended to ten thousand feet until they landed. He did as she said, and then sat down and glared at her, wondering when she was going to give up the controls and let him land the plane, as she had said she would. She didn't say anything to him, as she continued to watch the skies for visible air traffic. Connor Gray's eyes were closed, and he looked as though he was praying. He was about to land in his captain's uniform for the last time. It was a day he had never thought would come, and he knew only too well how much he would miss flying. He hadn't been ready for this sudden end to his career, but now he had to face it, just as he'd had to come to terms with his wife's death. He had a sense of inevitability about his life, as though he no longer controlled any of it. Destiny made all the decisions. He didn't see Jason watching him, with a look of contempt. He thought Connor was a pathetic old man.

Helen appeared calm as the flight drew to a close. She looked completely unperturbed, and no one would have suspected that her heart was pounding in her chest. She could sense danger all around her. She'd had the same feeling of impending doom when the terrorists had released the video of Jack. It was as though her body knew that something terrible was about to happen before her mind did, and every fiber of her being was on the alert. She just didn't know for what. But like with the video that had changed their lives forever, she knew she'd find out soon enough. All she could do was brace herself and deal with it when it happened, whatever it was. She was ready, and anticipating the worst.

Chapter Seven

Two Homeland Security agents showed up in plain clothes at UCSF hospital, at the new campus downtown in the vicinity of the ballpark, and parked in the garage. It was a long walk to the surgical floor where Jason's ex-girlfriend worked. They'd been given a code by their boss that told them it was urgent and a top-secret investigation. They knew the identity of the subject they were to ask about, but didn't know exactly the reason for concern. They knew he was a pilot, he was currently on a plane, and it was time-sensitive, the plane was due to land in less than three hours, but they had no other details. They'd been told he had anger issues, and their boss wanted to know more about his potential for violence.

Alan Wexler, the head of the San Francisco office, had assigned a man and a woman to do the job. Paul Gilmore and Lucy Hobbs had worked together for two years, and Paul had agreed to let Lucy do the talking. The girl they were seeing was young, and more likely to open up to a woman about her ex-boyfriend. She was twenty-seven years old and a surgical nurse at the hospital. Lucy was only a few years older. In jeans with a long ponytail, running shoes, and a baseball cap, she looked like a kid. Paul Gilmore was fifty, nearing retirement, and had children older than she was, but he had learned from working with her that Lucy was a dedicated agent, and one of the smartest he'd ever worked with. He had done everything possible to avoid working with her when they were assigned to each other as partners, but had defended her hotly ever since. She had kept him from getting shot on their first operation together, and she had won his undying loyalty. He trusted her instincts about the girl they were about to see.

"How much do you want to bet that if she moved on to a new guy, her ex considers that cheating on him? Guys with anger issues do that," Lucy commented on their walk to orthopedic surgery, where the girl worked.

"Stop being such a cynic," he told her. "Not everybody cheats, only my ex-wife." She had left him for his former partner, which had caused him to be reassigned to Lucy. He had been a mess when they started working together, but with her easy, breezy, down-to-earth and sensible way of looking at things, she had gotten him through it. He had talked of nothing else for their first year as partners, and had had a crazed moment of wanting to go out with Lucy. She had told him reasonably that it was a dumb idea, he didn't mean it, and he'd regret it, and she'd been right. For the past six months, he'd been dating an undercover DEA agent, and was happier than he'd been in years.

Lucy had been dating the same guy for the past four years. He was a flying instructor and glider pilot and didn't give a damn about the kind of work she did. He was just happy to see her whenever she was free. They never talked about her work, and he had gotten her into skydiving, which Paul told her was insane. He said he'd rather be shot than jump out of an airplane with a parachute, but Lucy loved it. She said it relieved all her tension after work, which he said confirmed what he'd known about her all along, she was insane, which she admitted freely.

"I didn't say she's cheating. I said that if her ex has anger issues, he probably considers a new relationship infidelity to him."

Paul knew Lucy was probably right. She was smart about people and relationships. The direction they'd been given was about the subject's rages, if he was ever abusive with her, or ever hurt her physically, and if she considered him dangerous to other people. He didn't sound like a good guy to Paul, nor to Lucy, although they'd both heard worse about other people they investigated, and they knew time was of the essence.

They asked for Bianca Martinez when they got to the nursing desk of the orthopedic surgical floor and were told by the attendant on duty that she was in surgery and wouldn't be out for some time. Paul had done the talking and they hadn't shown their badges, but the answer they'd been given was not the one they wanted, or that Ben needed in New York. And the code assigned to their mission told them that "some time" was not going to do it for them.

"I'm sorry," he said quietly, with a voice of authority that didn't require a gun or a uniform. Most people reacted instantly when he put that voice on, and Lucy always laughed about it and made fun of him. She called it his Voice of God act, and it usually made people jump when he told them to. The woman at the desk was not impressed, and Paul discreetly took out his badge and showed it to her. "We need to see her on an urgent matter of national security," he said in his God voice, and the attendant looked up at him, evaluating him.

"Is she in trouble? Are you arresting her?" He could tell that the attendant was indulging her own curiosity for the sake of gossip later, but he decided to satisfy her, if it got them what he wanted. He was a good judge of people, and so was Lucy. They were an efficient team, and he wondered if they should have come in uniform, even if they didn't have to, but Lucy had thought it would be a bad idea. They had changed into street clothes intentionally, so as not to scare off the young woman they had come to see.

"No, she's not in trouble," Paul said quietly. "We need her help with an investigation. How long will she be in surgery?"

The woman consulted a list and looked at her watch before she looked back at him. "Another seven or eight hours. They just started, if they went in on schedule. It's a spinal surgery. She should be out by five or six." It was nine o'clock in the morning, and they had only gotten the assignment at eight-fifteen and had come as quickly as they could. The flight was due to land at eleven.

"We can't wait," Paul said bluntly, with his God voice getting stronger, and the look on his face told her that he meant it. "They need to get her out of surgery so we can talk to her." The importance of the matter came through his pores as he looked at her. The woman hesitated for a moment, and then nodded and got off the stool where she was sitting.

"I'll see what I can do. I don't know if they'll let her out to talk to you."

"I'd hate to have to go into the operating room to get her," he said, as Lucy smiled sweetly at the woman and looked innocent. No one would have guessed that she was a master marksman and deadly with almost any kind of weapon in her hands. Her father had been a cop, and she had wanted to be in law enforcement all her life, and was good at it. She had four brothers who were SFPD cops, and she had trumped them all by signing on with Homeland Security. She had been debating between that and the FBI as soon as she got out of college, and had worked undercover drug cases for several years before she and Paul teamed up. His specialty was more national security and international terrorism, which Lucy always told him was tame by comparison. They were both pros, and her brothers had always called her the Gladiator, because she would fight them to the death once they picked on her, and she never gave up, no matter how much pain they inflicted on her.

The woman from the nursing desk came back ten minutes later. "She'll be out as soon as they can replace her."

"How long will that be?" Lucy asked her, impatient with the woman's vague explanations. "If it's more than five minutes, we're going in to get her," Lucy said with steel in her eyes. The woman disappeared again without saying a word and came back five minutes later with her supervisor. Both agents reached for their badges and showed them to her, with stern faces that usually frightened people, especially once they saw the words "Homeland Security." The supervisor looked appropriately nervous when she saw them.

"I'm sorry, we can't just pull a surgical nurse out of a spinal surgery in two minutes. We have to get another nurse to take her place."

"I'm sure you do," Lucy said, without missing a beat, as Paul let her take the lead on it. "But we need to see her. *Now.* We're trying to be respectful, but we don't have time to waste here. There are lives at stake other than just your patient. We'll go into the operating room if we have to, to get her out." The supervisor was about to explain the situation to them again when a spectacularly beautiful young Hispanic woman appeared behind her, looking worried. She was wearing surgical scrubs and had taken her cap off. She had thick dark hair that fell past her shoulders, and she looked at Paul and Lucy with a puzzled expression.

"You want to talk to me? I'm Bianca Martinez." She spoke English without an accent, and was obviously American despite her exotic looks.

"Yes, we do," Lucy said, smiling at her, as they flipped open their badges again, relieved that she had come out to see them without further battle with the two women. "Is there somewhere private we can go to talk?"

Bianca nodded and led them to a small room set up as a rest area for surgical personnel. "I'm sorry, it took them a few minutes to replace me. I couldn't leave till they did." She sighed and glanced at them, and started talking before they could ask her any questions. She was sure she already knew what this was about. ICE, Immigration and Customs Enforcement, had come to see her before. "I know you've had problems with my uncle in Texas, but I honestly don't know anything about it. My father had a fight with him years ago, and I haven't seen my uncle since I was about four years old. Whatever he's doing on the border has nothing to do with me. I wouldn't even recognize him if I saw him. My parents are respectable people. We've never had anything to do with illegal immigrants." Lucy and Paul could see that she had said it all previously and was tired of the story, and the headaches it must have caused them.

"Wow," Lucy said, "that sounds unpleasant. It must be embarrassing for your parents. But that's not what we're here for." Lucy smiled at her, with her girl-to-girl look. "We're here to talk to you about your boyfriend, Jason Andrews." And this time Bianca looked shocked and genuinely surprised.

"Jason?" And then she corrected them quickly. "He's not my boyfriend. We dated for about a year. I've been seeing someone else for a year and a half now, a surgical resident here at the hospital. Jason and I were always on and off." Lucy shot an innocent look at Paul, and he nodded. She'd been right again. They were no longer dating, and she was seeing someone else.

"What can you tell us about Jason?" Lucy asked her almost casually, so she'd open up. "Is he a nice guy? How did it end between you?"

"Badly," she said immediately, and didn't seem reluctant to talk about him. Lucy got the feeling that she almost wanted to, to vindicate herself for leaving him. "We had a love-hate relationship right from the beginning. That's how he does everything. He loves you or he hates you. He had a lot of issues about my family being Mexican. He hates all kinds of social groups, blacks, gays, Hispanics, Asians, Republicans. When I finished nursing school at USF, it took me a while to get the job here, so I did some modeling, which I did in college too, for extra money. We met at a party, and he liked the fact that I was a model, and he loved showing off with me. I did a few jobs in New York and L.A. too, and he thought I should stick with it. He thought being a nurse was stupid. I was just modeling until I could get work in my field. I was on a waiting list for this job for two years. He thought I was an idiot to give up modeling. I think he felt it made him look good that I was a model, but I never cared about it. Half the time he was showing me off and bragging about me, the other half he was making nasty comments about my origins and accusing me of cheating on him, which I never did. He refused to meet my parents for the whole year he went out with me, and my family is very important to me," she said and then smiled, with a look of embarrassment, "except my uncle. I'm not proud of him. We think he takes money to smuggle people across the border, but we don't know for sure. I have two sisters I'm very close to, and my parents. My older sister is a lawyer, and my younger sister just finished medical school. She's an intern here. Jason never wanted to meet them either. He'd get really nasty about it whenever I said anything about my family to him. He has a terrible temper."

Lucy nodded sympathetically. She'd let her ramble on to get a better sense of her and how reliable her information might be. She sounded credible to both of them. "Tell us about that—his temper, I mean." Lucy looked at the beautiful ex-model with sincere interest.

"He used to fly into rages or get in really bad moods. He was always up and down, either he was crazy about me, or he acted like he hated me. We tried living together for a while, and I just couldn't do it. He'd get mad at me and not talk to me for weeks at a time. He was always accusing me of something. I wanted him to get counseling for it and I offered to do couples counseling with him, and he wouldn't.

"He was having trouble with the airline at the time. He got into arguments with his superiors, and once with a pilot. They sent him to anger management classes, and it didn't change anything. He just thought it was a joke and told them what they wanted to hear and made fun of them and how ignorant they were when he got home. I don't think he respects anybody. The airline put him on probation a couple of times, which he didn't care about either, but they stopped promoting him, and he got really upset about that.

"He's very charming. He always gets what he wants, and he knows how to work people. But they kept him stuck in the copilot seat and he was furious. He's really smart. His IQ tests show he's practically a genius, but his temper and mood swings blow it for him. He's lucky the airline didn't fire him, and gave him a chance to clean up his act. Maybe because he's smart, and because he's young. But he hadn't been promoted in a while when he started dating me, and he got angrier and angrier as time went on. He kept saying they'd be sorry for it one day.

"He used to threaten me a lot too, but it was mostly talk. I don't think he's an evil person, he's just very unhappy and very screwed up. He makes everyone around him miserable. If he ever got his temper under control, he'd get what he wants. Maybe they've made him a captain by now. I haven't talked to him since I left him, and I don't want to. It's been more than a year since he called me. He wanted to see me and he called me a lot of ugly names when I wouldn't." She looked momentarily panicked then and looked from Paul to Lucy. "Will he find out I talked to you about him?"

Lucy was quick to shake her head and reassure her. "Never. You're doing this to help us, not to hurt him. And we really appreciate it. He will never know anything about it. Did he ever hurt you physically?" That was a key question, and Lucy waited for the answer, listening intently.

Bianca hesitated before she answered. "Just once. He threatened to a lot, though, especially when he accused me of cheating on him."

"What about the 'once'?"

"He slapped me hard and gave me a black eye. It was about Raf, the man I'm dating now. He saw him and thought I was sleeping with him, but I wasn't then. I never cheated on Jason. He just thought I did."

Lucy believed her. She looked like an honest woman, and Jason sounded like a nightmare, the consummate terrible boyfriend that everyone hopes she never falls prey to, or thinks she can change "if only things were different." Bianca had been smart to get out of it.

"I left him after the black eye. I don't think his anger was really about me. It was more about the airline. They were always doing something to upset him, or calling him on his behavior. They were on to him every time. They gave him a lot of chances, but they would never promote him, as long as he behaved like that, and they told him they'd fire him eventually if he didn't get his temper under control. It's what keeps him from everything he wants, but he doesn't see it that way. He thinks it's everyone else's fault, and he thought they really screwed him over. He doesn't get that his reactions are unacceptable."

"Do you think he'd ever hurt anyone else? Do you think he's capable of harming people, or even killing someone?" Lucy knew that the girl's answer would be of little real value to their investigation, because she wasn't a psychiatrist or a professional trained to evaluate him, but as a nurse she might have some insight. Even as his ex-girlfriend, her response would be interesting. Bianca slowly shook her head as she thought about it.

"No, I don't. Killing someone, definitely not. He's not that kind of person. He's just a guy with an uncontrollable temper and a lot of prejudices. He's mad at the world, and a lousy boyfriend, but he's not a murderer. I don't think he's crazy, just an asshole." She smiled as she said it, and Lucy smiled back at her.

Bianca had given them plenty to work with, but Lucy didn't share her opinion that Jason was "just an asshole." He sounded like a deeply troubled guy to her, with a big beef against the airline and profound resentment for their not promoting him, although he had done it to himself, as Bianca suggested.

"He made a lot of nasty racial slurs about me after I broke up with him. He was really pissed, and he made a big issue about my being Mexican, called me a slut and a lot of bad names. He texted me for a long time. I stopped answering him. I never went to get my things out of his apartment. I was afraid he'd beat me up if I did. I still have my key in my locker. I meant to throw it away, but I found it the other day. He's probably gotten rid of my stuff by now.

"Threatening people and beating people up are all he knows. He had kind of a rough childhood. He says he used to get in bar fights all the time when he was growing up, just like his father. He told me his father beat him whenever he got drunk, which was all the time. He died in an accident when Jason was in high school, but he hated him anyway. And his mother had taken off when he was a kid, because his father beat her up too. He never saw her again. I think he has issues with women because of it. He's complicated. Therapy would have helped him. And that's why he never understood what my family means to me, because he really didn't have one."

He seemed to be a portrait of half the criminals in the world, as Lucy and Paul listened to her. Abusive, broken family. Bad, drunk father. Mother who abandoned him as a child. Deep-seated anger and rages he was unable to control. Issues with women whom he then abused and blamed them for it. No respect for family values. Inability to accept authority. Profound resentment for anyone he perceived to have wronged him, a desire to get even with them, and projection of that anger onto anyone available. The picture Bianca had painted for them was terrifying, far more than she realized.

"You were smart to get out of it, and lucky that he let you without hurting you."

Bianca smiled at what Lucy said, unaware of the danger she could have been in, both with him and afterward.

"Raf is a big guy. He wouldn't let anything happen to me. He's Venezuelan, and from a close family like mine. My parents and sisters love him." She smiled warmly as she said it. "We might get married next year. And I'm sure Jason has forgotten about me by now. He must have another girlfriend."

She wasn't fishing, just being generous about him. Lucy could see it in her eyes. Then she thought of something that could be vital to them, especially since New York had said it was urgent, and they needed all the information the San Francisco office could get on him.

"I have a favor to ask you." Lucy looked ingenuous as she said it, and she was hard to resist when she looked honest and sincere like that. Looking at her, it was hard to believe she could take down a sniper or a hostage taker without hesitating, and almost never missed her shot. She looked like any other nice girl her age. Paul loved that about her, how tough she was and how dedicated, but still capable of relating to people at a real level. He knew plenty of good agents who couldn't do that. "Bianca, would you lend me that key you found in your locker? I'll give it back to you, and no one will know you did. It could make a big difference to us, and maybe to a lot of innocent people. Would you do that for me?" Lucy nearly held her breath as she waited for her answer.

Bianca thought about it for a long moment, weighing risks and whether it was wrong for her to do, and then she nodded. What Lucy had said about protecting innocent people had made the difference to her. Lucy had chosen her words wisely, and they had resonated. "I'll get it for you," she said, left the room, and was back three minutes later. She handed the key to Lucy, who promised again to return it to her.

"No one will ever know about this. I promise." And she meant it. What they were thinking of doing next was in a gray area of the law.

"I don't know if he lives in the same place." She jotted the address down for them on a scrap of paper, with the door and elevator codes, and handed it to her.

"We'll check it out," Lucy said. But the address she'd given them was the same as the one in his personnel file. He hadn't moved.

And then Bianca looked at her with genuine concern in her big, dark eyes the color of bittersweet chocolate. It was easy to believe she'd been a model, she still looked like one. Jason had good taste in women, whether he liked them or not, or respected them, which clearly he didn't. "Has he done something really bad?" she asked, worried about him. She had thought she loved him once, even if only briefly, and he had proven himself unworthy of it.

"Not that I'm aware of," Lucy said honestly, not knowing all the details of the case. "We're trying to protect him too, and keep him from doing something that would hurt people. It sounds like he needs to be saved from himself when his temper gets the best of him."

Bianca nodded instant agreement, and felt better about talking to them after what Lucy said. "I hope everything turns out okay."

"You helped us a lot," Lucy said gratefully. "You really made a difference." It was important for Bianca to know that, and to feel she had done a good thing, not that she had betrayed someone she once cared about. Lucy knew how vital that was in an investigation like this one, and she was mindful of it. "Thank you," she said again, as the three of them shook hands, and Bianca slipped her surgical cap back on and they walked out of the room together. Paul and Lucy headed toward the exit then, and Bianca back to surgery, as the attendant at the desk stared at them and wondered what had happened. For a minute, she had thought the two Homeland Security agents were going to arrest her if she didn't get Bianca for them fast enough. But whatever it was, it must have been important.

Bianca looked thoughtful as she got in the elevator to go back to work. She just hoped that Jason wouldn't do anything stupid, and that she had helped to stop him. She didn't think he would do anything really terrible to hurt anyone, she hoped not, but he was dangerous when he got in a rage. It all depended on how angry he got, and how severely he thought he'd gotten screwed over. That was the trouble with Jason. You couldn't reason with him, and you never knew for sure what he would do. Hopefully nothing.

When Paul and Lucy got back in the car at the UCSF garage, Lucy pulled the key Bianca had given her out of her pocket and held it up to Paul.

"Bingo!" he said, grinning at her. "You were brilliant with her, Lucy." Paul had hardly said a word while they were with Bianca. He knew when to keep quiet, and Lucy appreciated that about him. She had worked with a number of partners who had two left feet and a big mouth, and managed to get both feet into it with regularity. She had hated working with them, but not with Paul. "What do we do now? Go back to the office and call them in New York, or take a quick look in the apartment?"

They knew he was on a plane, so they didn't have to worry about his being there. It was one of the few things the New York office had shared with San Francisco, other than the urgency of the matter, which led Paul and Lucy to believe that there was a plane currently in danger because of him. They had figured that much out. They weren't novices. And they also knew that searching his apartment could really give them a fast leg up. It was illegal to do so without a warrant, except in very unusual circumstances, but it was worth a shot, despite the impropriety of doing it on their own authority. But

119

they could justify it later, if they had to. Homeland Security had full autonomy and were able to use their own discretion, although they were supposed to get their orders from their superiors and a search warrant, but sometimes that wasn't possible, and a quick decision had to be made. They could have called their office, but decided not to.

"I vote for the apartment," Lucy said as Paul smiled at her.

"I knew you would. Me too. It could save us a lot of time and heartache later." They were both willing to cross the line to get the job done in this case.

"Let's hope he doesn't have a girlfriend in bed when we get there," Lucy commented.

"We can always tie her up and put her in the closet," Paul suggested.

She gave him the address off the piece of paper, and it wasn't far away. He had an apartment in the newly gentrified section South of Market, near the water. The building looked clean and modern when they got there. There was a code for the outer door, which Bianca had given them and they were relieved to find hadn't changed. And another one for the elevator, which still worked too.

"Smooth as silk," Paul commented, as they rode up to the seventh floor.

"Don't talk until we see if he had the locks changed." They had checked the mailboxes and knew he was still living there. If he had moved, they would have lost a major advantage. Bianca had given them the key to a gold mine, if it panned out.

They got into the apartment easily. He hadn't double-locked the door. There was no alarm, and there was no one in the apartment. It was a small one-bedroom box, but was probably expensive in that location, and it had a view of the bay, facing east, with the newly rebuilt Bay Bridge just beyond his windows, leading to Oakland and Berkeley and the suburbs in the East Bay. There were dishes in the sink, the bed was unmade, and there were clothes strewn around on the floor, but it looked no worse than any bachelor's apartment, and wasn't unusually disorderly. Everything looked normal for a guy living alone with a decent salary and a good job.

Paul checked the bedroom and bathroom and the closets, while Lucy went straight to the desk. They didn't want to stay long, in case someone else had a key, even a cleaning person, and showed up. Paul announced from the bedroom that there was no sign of women's clothing, so he must have thrown Bianca's away, and had no woman living with him to replace her.

Lucy looked in all the drawers first, and found nothing special there. There was a stack of books on the floor, which she paid no attention to at first, his computer was locked and they didn't have the password. It would have been too much to hope for to expect Bianca to give them that too. The key to his apartment was gift enough. And then Lucy sat down at the desk, and dug through some papers to see what was on the surface of the desk. She found an iPad under some magazines, and expected it to be locked too. It wasn't, and opened easily. She was startled at first by how easy it was, but he hadn't expected his apartment to be invaded. They had noticed that he lived in barren circumstances. There were no photographs, nothing on the walls, nothing personal, just basic furniture that almost looked like it might have come with the apartment as some kind of furnished rental.

There was nothing personal on the iPad either, no favorite songs, email, no family photographs or videos. And then she opened a section called "Notes" that looked like some kind of research. He had put it on there under the heading "weapons," and she started to go through it, and rapidly realized that all the weapons posted on it had one thing in common—none of them had component parts that were metal. All were made of plastic or materials that could not be seen by a metal detector. They were mostly handguns one could assemble oneself, and there were diagrams that showed how to make them. Some were surprisingly efficient-looking, and could be built by 3D printers. Others could be made of household items. He had posted an ad as well of a gun that looked like a ballpoint pen. There were many plastic guns listed, and he had gotten them all from the Internet, along with the instructions of how to build and assemble them. She was stunned as she went through the file.

"What'd you get?" Paul asked her as he walked by to search the kitchen, and she looked up at him with amazement.

"Shit, Paul. This is a whole arsenal of plastic guns and weapons you can get past any metal detector or X-ray machine, like the ones at the airport." Paul stopped and came to look, and whistled as she scrolled through them to show him. "Jesus, how can they put stuff like this on the net, so any kid can build them, or anyone who wants to take over a plane?" There were dozens of different models.

Lucy sped quickly to other sections then, and found every article that had been published on the German plane that had been taken down by a suicidal pilot no one had suspected in 2015, in the French Alps, and killed 150 innocent people. And there was another whole section on different forms of suicide, also from the Internet, with the pros and cons listed in each case, as to how effective, complicated, or painful they might be. But the section on plastic guns that could be easily built, with diagrams, told them the story they thought New York was looking for, and the articles about suicide completed it. Then she examined the books she had seen on the floor, and discovered they were all about weaponry and suicide. He had put time and effort into this. Whatever they were afraid he was going to do on a plane was no accident, and had been carefully planned, either for that day or another one. It was clear Jason Andrews had a plan. The big question was whether or not he had one of the homemade, easy-to-assemble plastic guns with him on the aircraft. There was no way to know that, but it was a distinct possibility. He certainly knew how to build them.

"We'd better get back to the office," Paul said quickly. Everything they needed, and New York had feared, was on the iPad. They were afraid they could have a rogue pilot on their hands, and there was no question of it now. "Take the iPad with you," he said to her, and she rolled her eyes at him.

"Obviously. I wasn't planning to leave it."

"Sorry." They took a last sweep of the apartment and left immediately, leaving the top lock undone, as it had been when they arrived, pressed the button for the elevator, and were in it a minute later. Paul put a flashing red light on top of the car so they could run red lights on the way back, but he didn't put the siren on. Lucy called the office as he dodged through traffic.

"I think we've got what you're looking for," Lucy told their boss, Alan Wexler, on her cellphone.

"Do I want to know how you got it?" he asked.

"Probably not. But it's an iPad full of information about plastic weaponry you can build yourself and get through any X-ray machine or metal detector. He's got a ton of stuff on suicide, and all the articles about the German plane that was brought down by the suicidal copilot in the Alps. We're bringing the iPad with us."

"I'll call New York. Did you get anything from the girlfriend? Does she know anything about a plan?"

"Ex-girlfriend. She hasn't heard from him in a year. He has an uncontrollable temper, and is pissed at the airline for keeping him deadlocked as a copilot until he deals with it. She gave us the key to his apartment."

"I figured something like that if you've got his iPad. At least you didn't break in."

"Walked in through the front door, and out with the iPad," she said simply.

"I'll set up a conference call with New York as soon as you get back. How fast can you get here?"

"Look out your office window. We just pulled up," Lucy said, as Paul screeched to a stop and they both jumped out. Lucy had the iPad in her purse, and they went straight to the chief's office. He stood up when he saw them. She flipped through what was posted and he nodded, as she handed him the iPad.

Now they had a problem. A big one. As big or bigger than Ben, Dave, and Alan Wexler had feared in their worst-case scenarios. They had a pilot who was angry at the airline, bent on suicide, and probably armed with weapons he had been able to get through the X-ray at JFK. And just in case that wasn't enough, he might be planning to take the Golden Gate Bridge with him, to make sure he garnered maximum attention.

Alan Wexler thanked Paul and Lucy for their extraordinary work in record time, and told his assistant to set up the conference call with Homeland Security in New York. One thing was for sure. He knew Ben Waterman wasn't going to be happy with what they got. Paul and Lucy had done a masterful job.

Chapter Eight

After Amanda had gone to her office to cool off following her disagreement with Ben about who their real risk might be, she thought about it for a while and then made a phone call. It was her only hope of getting through to them. She knew that she couldn't do it alone. She needed backup. The name that came to her readily was Mildred Stern, the psychiatrist they often used in hostage situations, either to help them assess the situation and the risk to the hostages, or to help them communicate better with the hostage takers. She was highly respected in her field, and had written several books about relationships and how they could sometimes be compared to hostage situations. She had a background in criminology like Amanda herself. And she also evaluated and treated Homeland Security officers who had been affected by traumatic situations and were suffering from post-traumatic stress disorder. She had an office right at the airport in one of the Homeland Security administrative buildings.

Amanda called her and was lucky to reach her. The eminent psychiatrist said she was between patients. Amanda described the situation to her. She said they were faced with a potentially high-risk situation, and the officer in charge was barking up the wrong tree in his assessment. He was focusing on the copilot, who she was convinced was not a threat, and refusing to correctly assess the pilot, who Amanda felt was a bomb waiting to go off and was capable of bringing the plane down.

"Sounds like a tough situation," Mildred said quietly. "I haven't seen any news bulletins on it, so you've kept it quiet so far. What kind of time are we talking about here?"

"Two hours at most," Amanda said succinctly, "maybe an hour and a half, worst case an hour, before the plane is due to land. We're not even sure it's a real threat, but it could be very real. It sounds like a suicide possibility, and we've got three pilots in the cockpit who all qualify. It started with a postcard found by a TSA agent, and nothing may come of it, but we can't take the chance," Amanda explained reasonably. What wasn't reasonable, as far as she was concerned, was Ben Waterman's assessment of it. And she needed the psychiatrist's help to change his mind.

"Landing here?" Mildred asked, as she stood up and grabbed her purse from under her desk. Her office had an institutional-looking desk, two chairs, and a narrow bed a patient could lie down on. There was nothing attractive about it. It was purely functional. But her passion for criminology had led her to give up a lucrative Park Avenue practice twenty years before. She'd been working with SWAT teams ever since. As the daughter of a famous criminal lawyer in Chicago, she had finally found her niche.

"Landing at SFO," Amanda answered her. "The flight left here at eight A.M."

"Why three pilots?"

"We have a senior captain flying deadhead on the flight. He had a TIA on the ground two days ago, and they retired him on the spot. He's flying home in the cockpit. His career is over, and he lost his wife to cancer last year. He's a suicide risk too. Can you possibly come over and help me get through to the man in charge on this? We've got less than two hours to do it, with a hundred and eleven passengers and flight crew on a sold-out flight."

"I'll meet you at your office in five minutes," she promised, and Amanda smiled, relieved that she had called her. She was sure Mildred could help her turn the tide. Amanda admired Mildred enormously and had read all her books, although she'd never worked with her before. But like Amanda, she was a woman functioning in a man's world, and she knew how to deal with it. Amanda was still learning the ropes of how to make her male colleagues and superiors respect her, and she knew they didn't and made fun of her behind her back. She was getting tired of it. She was always pushing the machine of bureaucracy uphill, while they pooh-poohed her theories and ignored her degrees in favor of their instincts and experience, which she knew were valuable but weren't everything. And they refused to acknowledge that what she contributed was important too. She assumed it was only because she was female, and they were sexist.

True to her word, Mildred was in Amanda's office five minutes later. Amanda introduced herself to the small, thin woman with well-cut white hair, and they walked into Ben's office together where he was conferring with Phil, the head man on the scene, and Dave from airport security. They looked up, startled to see another woman come in with Amanda. Dave didn't recognize her, but Phil did immediately. He had worked with her many times. Ben looked shocked to see her. Mildred greeted Ben in a cool, professional manner, and neither she nor Ben acknowledged the fact that she was the psychiatrist he had been seeing ever since the hostage situation had gone sour and he felt responsible for the deaths of sixteen people, which she'd assured him wasn't true.

"Hello, Mildred" was all Ben said to her, as she and Amanda pulled up chairs to join the others. Phil looked at her in surprise.

"What are you doing here?" Phil asked. To his knowledge, no one had called her, and in his opinion she wasn't needed, at least not yet, but Ben understood immediately and glanced at Amanda with a disgruntled look.

"Called in the cavalry, did you?" Ben said to Amanda.

"Yes, I did," she said in a stubborn tone. "None of you listen to me. I thought you might have more respect for Dr. Stern's theories than for mine." She didn't mean to, but she sounded petulant and immature.

"I'm sorry you feel that way," Phil interjected, "but just for the record, you need your superior's permission to bring in a psychiatrist, even one who works for us. That means Ben or me. Next time, ask before you drag Dr. Stern over here." He smiled at Mildred, and she smiled back. She knew the drill too, and had assumed Amanda had permission to bring her in. She was not happy with Amanda for putting her in an awkward position. "Mildred and I are old friends and have worked together a lot, but our staff psychiatrists are not to help agents convince other agents of their position, but to try and assess the risk in a situation and how to deal with it, or to deal with hostage takers with the benefit of their knowledge added to our own."

"I think you're all focusing on the wrong person," Amanda insisted. "I have a master's in psychology and another one in criminology, and Jason Andrews is not your problem. We're wasting time on him. He's a smart, ambitious, talented pilot, with a thirty-five-year career ahead of him. He's not going to blow that with a suicide mission."

"The guy in Germany who killed a hundred and fifty people in the Alps was twenty-seven or twenty-eight years old, and a talented pilot too. There's no accounting for what drives people over the edge, or what they'll do. Age has nothing to do with it," Ben countered.

"I think Helen Smith is the risk here. No one can come through what she did and stay sane or normal. She saw her husband beheaded on TV," Amanda said stridently, desperate to convince them and hoping Mildred Stern would help her do it.

"People *do* come through it and worse, and do lead sane, normal lives afterward," Mildred said in a strong voice. "Look at concentration camp survivors and what they lived through. Many of them went on to lead impressively productive lives. I know of Captain Smith's case and I've never heard anything to suggest she was suffering from mental disorders. Has something changed?" Mildred Stern asked everyone in the room, and they shook their heads.

"It all started with this," Ben explained to her, pushing the postcard across his desk toward her. "It may mean absolutely nothing, or it could mean a lot. We decided not to take the chance. And total shit luck, we have no air marshal on the flight. We had an equipment failure on an A380, and split the passengers onto two smaller planes. The air marshal who was scheduled is on the other one, so we have no protection in the air for the crew and passengers on this flight. And it's a crapshoot as to who the problem is, or if we even have one. We've been going crazy trying to assess it ourselves.

"I think Captain Smith is the best thing we've got going for us up there if there is a problem, and Phil agrees. She flew fighter planes and she was in the military for twenty years. She can take care of herself and the plane. And we have a copilot who has a disciplinary record a mile long, a terrible attitude, an anger management problem, and is pissed off at the airline because they haven't promoted him in two years. It's a fucking wonder they haven't fired him yet, and he's probably close to it and knows it, so he's angry at the world."

"Does he have a psychiatric history of suicidality?" Mildred asked him, and Ben shook his head.

"No, he doesn't. Neither does Helen Smith. The pilot who just got retired is probably a bigger suicide risk, but if so, I'd like to think he'd do that on his own time, not take a planeload of passengers with him. He's one of our best pilots, and it's rotten luck for him that he had a TIA."

"I'm sorry to hear it," the psychiatrist said sympathetically, and looked at all of them in the room. "To be honest, you've got a hell of a problem. It's damn hard to second-guess people, and problems like this can come out of left field. On the surface, I'm inclined to agree with Ben and Phil: Helen just doesn't have any of the warning signs of doing something like this, unless there's something I'm not hearing. But a young hothead like the copilot you describe could do something like it to garner attention and 'get even,' without thinking about his own bright future, as Ms. Allbright describes it. And I'm not so sure his future is all that bright. It sounds like he's been skating on thin ice with the company. And what's he going to do if he gets fired? That's it for him. No one is going to hire him if they let him go. And let's face it, most pilots don't want to do anything else. It's their passion, their whole life, and all they know. Getting fired might seem worse than suicide to him."

"He hasn't been fired yet," Ben corrected her, "but it sounds like he could be headed there."

Mildred nodded thoughtfully, and Amanda looked at her with disappointment.

"You agree with them?" she asked in a small voice.

"I think I do. The truth is that none of us will know anything for sure until something happens or it doesn't. The plane may land without a hitch, or you could have a tragedy on your hands. What are you doing about the bridge?" She was used to situations like this and thrived on them, and her suggestions were usually brilliant.

"We're closing the Golden Gate in a few minutes," Ben answered her. "At ten o'clock Pacific time." As he said it, an assistant walked into Ben's office and said that Alan Wexler, the San Francisco chief, and two agents were on the line for a conference call with them. Ben put the call on speakerphone immediately, so they could all hear it.

"We're all here," he spoke up clearly. "Did you get anything from the girlfriend? Would she talk to you?"

"We got everything you need," Alan Wexler responded in a grim tone. "I've got agents Paul Gilmore and Lucy Hobbs with me. They spoke to her and searched his apartment, although that's off the record." None of them liked advertising the fact that they took liberties at times. Homeland Security could get away with it, but it wasn't something they wanted the public to be made aware of unnecessarily, or at all. It was a breach of proper procedure, in an emergency, for a valid cause. Sometimes rules had to be broken to save lives.

"Hi," Lucy said by way of greeting, and told them everything Bianca had told her about Jason Andrews, none of which was reassuring, and confirmed their fears about him to a great degree. "We went to his apartment then. She's the ex-girlfriend and had had no contact with him for a year, so she couldn't speak to his state of mind now, but she said that the whole time they dated he was angry at the airline for holding him back and not promoting him. He thought they were ruining his career, and he took no responsibility for his part in it and his attitude problems with them. Anyway, she gave us the key to his apartment. We've got some interesting info. We've got his iPad, and there are pages and pages on it of guns you can build yourself out of plastic materials that won't show on an X-ray. The diagrams are very detailed, and the weapons look pretty lethal. We found no weapons in the apartment, only the information on the iPad. There's also a lot of research on suicide methods, and on the German pilot who took the plane down in the Alps. But the plastic weapons were the most disturbing. We're going to send you everything electronically now, so you can see it yourself."

Ben looked around his office at the others in dismay. He had been afraid of something like this. He had a computer screen on one wall, and within seconds, the plastic weapons and diagrams started to appear.

"Shit," Phil said and ran a hand over his eyes as Ben stared at one plastic gun after another, until he felt sick looking at them.

"I think we all agree, Andrews is the threat here," he said to both the people in his office and those in San Francisco, "and now I think we can assume he's armed. We'd better give Helen Smith a heads-up."

With that, the San Francisco chief said he had to jump off for a minute, and he was back two minutes later. "They just closed the bridge," he informed them. "Emergency vehicles are lined up, traffic is rerouted, they're calling it a gas leak, and we've got three Coast Guard cutters in the water," he told them. "We're ready. All of which won't do us a damn bit of good if Andrews kills the captain and takes the plane down."

Ben wanted to put his head down on his desk and cry. Knowing that Jason Andrews was armed with any one of the plastic guns changed the whole picture. It would be infinitely harder to stop him now and save the plane, especially with no air marshal on board.

"Do you think the retired captain would be any help?" Alan asked on the phone.

"I doubt it," Ben answered. "I'd put my money on Helen, but I'm not sure what she can do with a gun pointed at her."

"She's a tough woman," Phil said quietly. "I read her personnel file very closely. She's a black belt in martial arts, and an expert marksman."

"Yeah, and she's got a house full of passengers and a plane to fly."

"Where do you want us?" Alan asked them. "At the airport or the bridge?"

"In the cockpit with a gun to that bastard's head, and not a plastic one," Ben said angrily. "I don't know. Both locations, I guess. Maybe the three of you should be at the bridge. It sounds like that could happen, if he gets control of the plane, but let's have plenty of men at the airport, in case there's a problem when they land." Ben felt helpless sitting at a desk in New York, hearing about it from the distance, and what he wanted to do next was warn Helen Smith that her copilot could be armed. "Keep us informed, will you?" Ben said, as Mildred Stern watched him, and was satisfied that he was doing well. He looked stressed but he was handling the situation to the best of anyone's abilities. The trouble would come later, if everything went wrong, only a month after the last time.

Amanda had gotten very quiet. What they had discovered in Jason's apartment in San Francisco confirmed Ben and Phil's suspicions. This wasn't about psychological theories now. It was about weapons, and a man who had been researching methods of suicide and hated the airline he worked for. Even she couldn't deny it now, and had nothing more to add. The psychiatrist leaned toward her a few minutes later, and spoke in a low voice.

"None of us can be accurate a hundred percent of the time. We're bound to be wrong some of the time. We can only work with what we've got, and a lot of the time it's not enough to be absolutely sure, and we have to roll the dice and guess."

"It sounds like I guessed wrong on this one," Amanda said, looking mortified.

"If that's true, you'll be right on the next one," Mildred encouraged her.

"They don't listen to me. They think I'm stupid because I'm a woman." She had tears in her eyes as she said it.

"This is a boys' club," Mildred Stern said firmly. "If you want to work here, you have to earn it. Going behind their backs is not the way." It was good advice. As she said it, Ben put through the satcom connection to Helen Smith.

As she had before, Helen answered in a calm voice, as though she didn't have a care in the world and was in full control of the situation. Ben wanted that to be true but knew it wasn't, since they'd been warning her of potential problems for several hours, from terrorists to rogue copilots, with no air marshal on board for support.

"Ben Waterman here," he identified himself to her again, although she knew his voice by now, and no one else had reason to call on the satcom for a private conversation with her. "We want to let you know, Captain, that we have reason to believe your copilot's armed. Possibly with homemade plastic weapons, but they're just as effective and lethal. He's done a lot of research on the subject. We know that without a doubt. And on the subject of suicide, and the German pilot over the Alps. We think you've got a very serious problem on your hands. His target could be the Golden Gate Bridge. We closed it five minutes ago, and if he brings you down there, we've got rescue teams standing by, helicopters, and Coast Guard in the water. We've got you covered. Just be careful up there with him, and keep the controls out of his hands if you can."

"I'll see to it, without question, Ben," she said cryptically with a pleasant lilt to her voice as though he had just given her good news. "Everything is just fine up here. It's a beautiful day to land at SFO."

"I'm sorry we don't have any armed backup for you up there. I promise it won't happen again."

"Not a problem, Ben. Thanks for letting me know. We'll try to get everyone down to make their connections. See you next time in New York," she said confidently. "We'll be in touch with the tower after this," she said easily and hung up, as Ben's heart sank thinking about her, defenseless in the air, with an armed gunman next to her, more than likely.

"What was that about?" Jason questioned her. "Since when do they call on the satcom all the time?"

"I think they don't want to tie up the tower radios with chitchat. They just wanted us to know there may be a delay getting us a gate. They've had an overflow of planes at SFO today. We'll try to protect the passengers' connections. That's the best we can do."

"That's all they ever care about," Jason said angrily. "The fucking passengers. They don't give a damn about the pilots on this airline. Look what they did to him," he said, gesturing to Connor, who appeared to be asleep in his seat. "Canned him at a moment's notice, after a nearly forty-year career, because he had a headache."

"He had a TIA," she said calmly. "That's a serious thing. He could have another one while he's flying. I'm sure Captain Gray agrees."

Jason didn't answer her. He just looked straight ahead, while she thought about what Ben had told her. They considered Jason armed and dangerous, and although she hated to admit it, she was almost certain they were right. Nothing on her face betrayed it, and she was ready for whatever happened. She had one hundred and eleven lives to get down safely, and she didn't intend to lose a single one.

*   *   *

The scene at the Golden Gate Bridge was one of organized pande-
monium. There were trucks from the Office of Emergency Services
blocking entrance lanes to the bridge. Fire trucks, ambulances, and
paramedics were standing at the ready. They had brought a crane
in, in case they needed to lift some part of the plane after it crashed,
in order to rescue people. There were hundreds of emergency personnel lined up on either side of the bridge, waiting for something
to happen. Two helicopters were hovering. The three Coast Guard
cutters were stationed in the bay, and someone had thought to call
in the *Phoenix,* the fireboat often used to greet dignitaries and cruise
ships, which could shoot water onto the plane if it was on fire when
it came down or hit the bridge.

No one knew the whole story of why they were there. Most of
them had been told about a gas leak and potential explosion, but
experienced emergency workers knew from the equipment gathered
that they were dealing with something much bigger than that, like an
air strike of some kind, or a plane crash, or a terrorist threat of major
proportions on the bridge. The San Francisco chief of police showed
up, and was quietly talking to the director of emergency services.

"What does this look like to you?" the chief of police asked him.

"Honestly, it looks like they're expecting someone or something
to take down the bridge. Probably a plane." It didn't look like a
bomb threat to either of them, unless it was a nuclear missile of
some kind.

"Military?"

"Maybe. I doubt it. Between us and the Coast Guard, they have
us ready for a hundred and fifty survivors. That's not military. That

would be a commercial flight. Maybe they have a hostage situation they're not talking about, and some fanatic suicide bombers have taken control of a plane. We'll find out soon enough."

It felt like a long wait to all of them, as they tried to figure out what was really happening. No one believed that what they'd been told was the whole story. And twenty minutes after they were in their positions the news trucks started to arrive in droves with cameras and reporters everywhere, asking questions no one knew the answers to. The gas leak story was the one Homeland Security had ordered them to stick with, but the media wasn't buying it, nor was anyone they spoke to, least of all the rescue workers themselves.

"This must be the biggest gas leak in history," one of the reporters said cynically after grilling every fireman and rescue worker he could get to talk to him. Two news helicopters had joined the rescue copters above the bridge, which was eerily empty, free of traffic. It was an odd sight in the bright sunshine, and every time they saw or heard a plane, they looked to the sky, but nothing was happening. The news channels interrupted normal broadcasting to show what was going on. Civilians were being warned to stay away in case the bridge blew up. There were no gawkers on the scene, only professionals, as Ben switched on the TV in his office and they all watched. Mildred Stern had stayed with them.

"We're going to look like the biggest idiots in the history of aviation if that flight lands peacefully at SFO," Ben said as they watched the enormous preparations that had been made in case Jason flew the plane into the bridge.

"I'd rather look like an idiot than be notifying the victims' families," Phil said grimly. It couldn't be helped. They had to do what they had to do. Watching it reminded Ben of the TSA agent who had found the postcard and been sitting in the reception area for hours in case they needed to talk to her again.

"Why don't you bring her in here?" Ben said to Amanda, and she went to get Bernice, who entered the room shyly a minute later, in awe of all of them and what she'd started.

"Oh, my God," she said, when she saw all the emergency vehicles on the screen, and heard the announcer describing the dangers of the gas leak that was threatening the Golden Gate Bridge in San Francisco. "There's a gas leak too?" She looked shocked.

"That's for public consumption," Ben explained to her. "We can't tell them we may have a rogue pilot in the air who plans to take out the bridge. Besides, we don't know if it's true. But we think it might be," he said to reassure her. She looked frightened by what she was seeing. Denise and Della had been texting her all day: Della to ask what was going on, and Denise calling her irresponsible for starting trouble. Bernice wasn't thinking about that now. All she could think of were the people on the plane and what would happen to them if it went down. She remembered the disorganized man with the baby, the girls from the chorus in Queens, and the two little children traveling alone whose mother had cried when she left them. Bernice had told her they'd be safe. What if they weren't? And if they died? She wanted to be wrong now, just as the others did, but it didn't feel that way, looking at the rescue workers swarming around the bridge, in case the plane crashed into it. It suddenly seemed all too real, and entirely possible, as it did to all of them in the room.

*   *   *

A passenger rang the buzzer for a flight attendant to ask for a glass of water before they landed, and switched on the news on the screen at her seat, with her own headphones in. She was sitting mesmerized by the report on CNN, as Nancy stood there watching too.

"Wow, what happened?" Nancy asked her when she recognized the Golden Gate Bridge on the screen.

"I don't know. There must have been an accident or something. The bridge is closed and they just said there's a gas leak. I live in Marin and I won't be able to get home. I have to pick up my dog from the place where I board him before five o'clock." They could see the helicopters hovering, the Coast Guard boats, the fireboat, and hundreds of vehicles and ambulances, as they both watched it. Nancy couldn't hear the sound without headphones but the images were enough.

"That must be one hell of a gas leak," Nancy commented and then went back to the galley to talk to Joel. She told him about the gas leak and the emergency vehicles.

"That sounds like more than a gas leak," Joel said, concerned.

"It looks like a war zone," Nancy told him and described what she'd seen.

"I guess we'll hear about it when we land," Joel said, locking up the last of their supplies.

Several other passengers had seen the report by then too, and were talking about it across the aisles.

"Does this mean we can't get to Berkeley?" Ahmad asked Sadaf, looking worried.

"I think we get to Berkeley on a different bridge," she said to reassure him. She took off her abaya then, the long gray garment she wore to cover her clothes, and folded it neatly. She was wearing a sweater, jeans, and running shoes, like other young women her age. And for a moment, Ahmad looked shocked.

"What are you doing?"

"I don't need it here," she said quietly, and he was instantly upset. Many of his friends' and relatives' wives wore ordinary street clothes in foreign countries, but he didn't like the idea of Sadaf doing it. She still had her head scarf on, which was white and framed her face. She made no move to remove it.

"You're still with me. I don't want men seeing you in jeans."

"I'm not going to be a student in Berkeley wearing an abaya like my grandmother," she said firmly, and he turned away from her and closed his eyes. He was angry at her for breaking the tradition. He didn't want everything to be different here, or at least not so soon. They had left their familiar world and didn't know the new one yet. He was feeling lost.

In the cockpit, they hadn't heard about the gas leak yet. Connor had woken up. Jason looked anxious and finally asked Helen the question she'd been dreading, although her face was peaceful and showed nothing untoward.

"When are you turning over the controls? You said I could land," Jason reminded her in a voice that sounded impatient and harsh. There was nothing casual about the question, and Helen turned to him with an easy smile.

"I'm sorry, Jason. I don't know why, but they told me they want me to land. It's not a big deal. It's not a thrill on this plane, like the big one. It's all yours the next time we fly together."

"That's a load of crap," he said angrily. "They don't trust me, do they? I give a couple of pilots a hard time, and they punish me for years. I'm so goddamn tired of being in this seat. I can fly anything you can, and probably better. They have no reason to have you land today, except to humiliate me again."

"I'm sorry. I really am. We both have our orders. You know how it works."

"This isn't the military. They can't order us around like that. Why don't you tell them to get stuffed!" he shouted at her.

"Because I have three kids to feed and I like my job," she said quietly. "I've been following orders all my life. It's not personal. Sometimes they have reasons we don't know about. I'm sorry you're upset," she said kindly, trying not to inflame him further, and hoping he'd calm down.

"You're damn right I'm upset. I'm fucking furious and fed up," he said, shouting at her, as he grabbed his flight bag, unlocked the cockpit door, and stormed out, presumably to use the bathroom before they landed. "You don't need me around if they're not going to let me land it," he said over his shoulder and then slammed the door. It locked behind him, as Connor looked at her and sighed. Helen didn't like the fact that Jason had taken his flight bag with him, but didn't say anything to Connor. And he wasn't supposed to go to the restroom right before they landed, but she decided not to make an issue of it and make things worse.

"You're a lot more patient than I am. I'd have had him fired on my watch," Connor said with a look of irritation, as she realized that she had to say something to warn him, and with Jason gone, now was the time.

"I had a lot of young guys like him under my command in the

military. Some of them shape up eventually, others don't." And then she spoke to the senior pilot in a soft voice. "Connor, we think we have a problem."

"Mechanically?" He looked surprised. He hadn't noticed anything on the flight, but had dozed off several times.

"No, with him. Homeland's been calling me on the satcom. There could be a plan of some kind to take over the plane before we land. No one's sure. If something happens, I'll do whatever I can, but I may need your help. I'm sorry to worry you." She didn't want him having another TIA or a full-on stroke, but he had to know. "It could be nothing, but that's why I didn't let him land. I can handle the plane and maybe him, but I wanted to warn you something may be up." He nodded thoughtfully and looked at her seriously.

"I'm not surprised. I know your flying record, Captain. You can bring us down safely. I'm sure you can do it, whatever happens. You've been in worse situations." She nodded, grateful for the re-minder and his confidence in her.

"Yes, I have. I hate to scare the passengers, but I may have to. Homeland thinks he may be armed, possibly with a homemade plastic gun. Be careful. Don't do anything foolish. Just keep an eye on him. We'll get the plane down. And you're right, I've been through worse."

"Just remember that." He smiled at her, and saluted her. He was an old Navy pilot. She had read it somewhere.

They both fell into an uneasy silence then, waiting for Jason to return. He took a long time, and Helen wondered what he was doing, and if he had a gun on him, if Homeland Security was right, or if it was all a fuss over nothing.

Jason was gone for fifteen minutes, using the first-class restroom, much to the flight attendants' annoyance, and came back as Helen was circling the bay and getting ready to make her approach. She had no reason not to allow him back in. He had done nothing threatening yet. It was all guesswork for now, and maybe wrong.

The tower wanted her to stand by for five more minutes, so she didn't have to wait on the ground for a gate, and she was ready to take the plane in as soon as they told her to do so. She glanced at Jason, and he was smiling. All signs of his anger were gone. He looked happy and relaxed, and she wondered what he had done in the bathroom to calm down and what he had in his flight bag, guns and maybe drugs. She concentrated on what she was doing, as Jason continued to smile at her as though he didn't have a care in the world.

"It's been nice flying with you," she said to him, and he nodded. She saw him pat something in his pocket, and prayed it wasn't a gun. They were almost home. Just a few more minutes and they'd be down.

"Nice flying with you too, Captain," he responded. "This might just be the best flight of my life," he said and then he laughed.

Chapter Nine

Tom was acutely aware of the motions of the plane as he chatted with Catherine. She was infinitely more relaxed, knowing that the flight was almost over. And she was excited about her meeting. He could tell that she had no sense that anything was wrong, while Tom wondered why they were circling and hadn't been brought in yet. He didn't want to go back to the cockpit and ask. It could have been normal maneuvers dictated by the tower due to traffic into SFO, or maybe there was some other reason to keep them circling, while emergency vehicles on the ground got ready. He knew that Homeland Security wanted to keep it quiet, in order not to start a mass panic and in case it all turned out to be nothing. But he thought their approach to the airport was taking forever.

He had seen Jason leave the cockpit, looking annoyed, a while earlier, and saw that he was gone for quite some time. He used the first-class restroom, but he seemed happy when he came out. There was no sign of anything odd happening, or Tom would have gone forward. In the meantime, Catherine was easy to talk to, and he actually liked her. She had told him something about her job on Wall Street, and how hopeful she was about the interview in venture capital. And he decided to ask her the question on his mind before the end of the flight. If he didn't he might not see her again.

He apologized before he even began. "I hope you don't think me rude for asking." He smiled at her, and she liked the way his eyes lit up when he did. "I assume you're not married since you talked about breaking up with a boyfriend recently."

"No, I'm not." She smiled at him. "And now that you mention it, are you?"

"Not lately." He was relieved when he heard the landing gear grinding, and they came down in altitude slightly. He thought it was a little early for the landing gear but not alarmingly so. He was finely attuned to the plane, and for once she wasn't. "Actually, I haven't been married in a long time. I'm divorced," he confirmed. She was happy to hear it, so the absence of a wedding ring had been an honest statement of his status, not merely an oversight or a hoax. "Do you have kids?" he asked her, sincerely interested in knowing more about her. They had both worked on their computers for so many hours that they hadn't had more time for conversation.

"No, I don't. I kind of missed that opportunity. I've never been married, not that that seems to matter these days. I have a lot of friends who aren't and have children, their own or adopted. Being single is no longer a reason for not having children. I've just been too busy with my career for the last twenty years, and dating people I didn't want to marry, or who didn't want to marry me. I turned forty this year and I suddenly realized that I was kind of over it. So

I decided to do the things I've wanted to do but never got around to, like this job in California. I have no reason to stay in New York. I have no family there, no kids in school, no husband or boyfriend. I'm a free woman," she said, and she looked like she enjoyed her life.

"I was thinking that I'd like to see you again before you go back to New York. Would you have time for lunch or dinner, or a drink?"

She looked pleased by the invitation but qualified it. "I'd like that, but I'm going to be staying down in Palo Alto."

"I think I can manage to get down there," he said, undaunted. "It's about forty minutes out of the city. Or we could spend the day in San Francisco on Saturday, and I'll drive you back. Whatever you can manage."

"I'll be free after tomorrow. I left time for a second interview if they like me. I'm free on Friday and Saturday. I'm flying back on Sunday."

"That works well for me. Why don't I come down to Palo Alto for dinner on Friday night, and if all goes well, we can spend the day together on Saturday? I'll pick you up if you like," he offered.

"'Goes well' as in if I don't slurp my soup or start a food fight in the restaurant?" She was in good spirits, having survived the flight without incident. She always expected the worst to happen whenever she got on a plane, but it never had, and her fears were always unfounded.

"Something like that. I was thinking more along the lines of if you don't think I'm a jerk by the end of dinner. You never know how first dates will go."

"I've had a lot of them," she said, "I'm a pro." He laughed at her

149

and noticed that they were coming down slowly from their cruising altitude. Helen was handling the plane smoothly, which was to be expected, although some military pilots had rougher styles than others. Tom was fervently hoping that their concerns would turn out to be needless. It was beginning to look that way. The flight was almost over and nothing had happened.

Catherine jotted down the name of her hotel then, and handed him her business card so he would have her cellphone and email, and he gave her his. Nancy saw the exchange as she walked past them and smiled to herself. She was right. Something was starting between them. They had both been easy passengers, despite Catherine's nervousness in the beginning.

"I'll call you tomorrow to see how the interview went," Tom promised, and he looked out the window to see how they were doing.

Nancy was checking that all the passengers' seats were in the upright position and they had their seatbelts on, and she stopped to see that the two children, Nicole and Mark, were strapped in and doing fine.

"We're going to see our grandma soon," Nicole said to her with a big smile, minus her two front teeth. They had been angels on the flight, unlike the screaming baby in coach. "She's meeting us at the airport, and then we're going to call our mom." Her brother was looking out the window, as Nancy moved on to the seat in front of them, where the Saudi couple was seated. He appeared not to be

speaking to his wife, while she tried to reason with him about something. Nancy saw that she had taken her long gray coat off, and was
wearing jeans and Nikes. She was talking to him, but he was not
responding. He seemed to have other things on his mind as he
looked out the window with a pensive expression, and Nancy went
back to the galley. She could hardly wait for the flight to end, and
for her husband's flight to land from Miami. They had a lot to talk
about that night, plans to make, and a decision to face about the
two-year-old girl in China. Nancy didn't know what she wanted to
do about it. And Joel was reading a Martha Stewart wedding planner he had taken out of his flight bag as they got ready to land.
Their workday was almost over, and their private lives were waiting
for them at home.

And when she glanced into first class, Nancy could see that Susan
Farrow had put on a big straw hat and dark glasses. She had told
the flight attendants she'd chatted with that she hated to be recognized when she traveled, because she liked to wear comfortable old
clothes and didn't want to have to wear makeup and look glamorous. Nowadays anyone could snap your picture with a cellphone,
and it would turn up on the Internet, and she'd look awful. She had
already put her little dog in his carrier, ready to deplane and make
a quick exit. A representative of the airline was meeting her at the
gate, to accompany her to her car. The flight attendants had gotten
a confirmation on it, and she would be first off the plane, as a VIP
traveling with them.

And in the cockpit, Helen got clearance to make her final approach to SFO. She dropped their altitude for a smooth descent and

noticed Jason staring at her. He indicated the controls on his side-stick next to his seat. They each had one to fly the plane.

"That'll be it, Captain. Thanks for a nice flight. You can turn the controls over to me now, and switch off yours." For a minute she thought he was kidding the way he said it, or hoped he was. She almost thought they had escaped the problems that Ben had feared.

"I'm landing the plane, Jason," she reminded him quietly in a neutral tone.

"Actually, you're not. I am," he said, and switched the controls over to his seat. As he did, she flipped a small switch on her side-stick he didn't notice, which would allow air traffic control to hear everything that was happening in the cockpit on an ongoing basis. He didn't see her do it, he was so intent on taking over the plane, and she didn't fight him for the controls, so as not to destabilize the plane, as he made a sharp turn and headed north, in the opposite direction from the airport.

The tower came on instantly and asked her what she was doing, but they had already been alerted that any change in flight plan was to be reported immediately to Homeland Security. It was the only warning they'd been given, and controllers on duty noticed the change as soon as Jason took control.

"What do you want me to tell them?" Helen asked Jason, and he thought about it for a minute, and she knew that the tower could hear her ask the question, which would alert them to the fact that she was not flying the plane and someone else was.

"Tell them you're doing another loop around, and you aren't ready for landing."

She did as she was told, as she saw Connor get up from his seat out of the corner of her eye, and wondered if she'd been wrong to warn him about Jason. But Jason saw him too, as he set a straight course for the Golden Gate Bridge, and then turned toward the senior pilot and took a gun out of his pocket, where he'd concealed it. It had taken longer to assemble than it had when he'd practiced before, but it was functional now and had a silencer on it. He pointed it at Connor and spoke to him in a harsh voice.

"Get back in your seat, and don't do anything stupid."

"You're a lunatic. You know that, don't you? You'll never get away with it."

"Really?" Jason said in an icy voice. "Watch me." And with that, he shot Connor in the chest and stomach. Air traffic control could hear a pop, but not loud enough to be heard outside the cockpit. Jason lowered their altitude considerably. Connor Gray dropped to the floor instantly after he'd been shot, his uniform quickly soaked in blood.

"Stay calm," Helen said to Jason. "I'm going to go and help him. You don't need the gun. You have control of the plane now." She got up carefully from her seat, and Jason didn't try to stop her. He was intent on where he was headed. Helen got to Connor as quickly as she could, took off her own jacket and tried to slow the flow of blood, but he was badly injured and having trouble speaking. His eyes looked deep into hers, and she tried to reassure him.

"You're going to be okay. We'll be on the ground soon." She made him as comfortable as she could and went back to her seat next to Jason. The tower was demanding to know again what they were doing and where they were going. Neither Helen nor Jason answered, and the tower was insisting they come in, and warned them of air traffic just below them if they intended to drop altitude again. Helen looked out the window and could see a large plane just beneath them.

"Watch out for that plane," she warned him. "You're not going to be able to pull this off. You know that, don't you? If you give me back the controls now, I'll get us down safely. You can keep me as a hostage if you need to when we're on the ground."

"What are they going to do? Shoot me down? Fire a missile at us? They can't. We have a hundred and two passengers and nine crew on board. They're not going to endanger them, and you don't need to be a hero, Captain. Who gives a damn about these people?" he said confidently. He was on a joy ride he had waited years for, and nothing was going to stop him.

"You don't want to hurt anyone, Jason," she said firmly, but he already had. Connor Gray was dying on the floor behind him. And it was obvious where they were going. They were headed for the Golden Gate Bridge, just as Ben had feared would happen. Nothing was going to stop Jason now.

The tower had alerted Homeland Security immediately, who called their local chief, who in turn called Ben in New York. He was still watching the rescue teams at the Golden Gate Bridge. Ben put him on speaker the moment he got the call.

"He's got the plane," Alan Wexler told Ben from San Francisco. "She flipped the switch on the radio. Air traffic can hear everything.

He shot someone. It must be Captain Gray, because Captain Smith is still talking. They're headed for the bridge now."

"Shit," Ben said, listening to him. And he turned to Phil. "Where's Tom Birney? Email him and tell him to get in there. If Smith tries to get the controls away from Jason Andrews, he'll shoot her."

"He's going to shoot one of them, whatever happens," Phil predicted grimly. He emailed Tom Birney then, but got no response. Tom was already aware that something had happened when they dropped altitude sharply and nearly hit another airliner. He looked at Catherine for an instant, and spoke to her quickly.

"Everything's going to be fine, but it may get a little scary for a while. Trust me. You'll be okay. I promise." And with that, he took off for the cockpit at a dead run, sped down the aisle, and took the access codes out of his pocket. People were leaning into the aisle to try and figure out what was going on, and both groups he ran past in the galleys looked panicked. He stopped for only a second to talk to the purser, told her the captain had given him the access codes, and he had the security clearance to go in. And she'd seen him go into the cockpit earlier so she knew it was true.

Seconds later, as people looked down the aisle to watch him, Tom unlocked the cockpit door easily with the codes Helen had given him, and he crouched down as he crawled on all fours, let the door close behind him, and saw Connor Gray immediately. He was ashen and bleeding profusely, and Tom could hear Helen speaking to Jason in a calm, even voice, trying to get him to allow her to take the controls over again. They couldn't compete back and forth with the controls. They were flying over the bay by then, over container ships and tankers, and Tom could see the bridge in the distance, with the Coast Guard ships near it. He stood up then, trying to distract Jason from Helen. Jason turned to face Tom, standing behind him, and pointed the gun at him.

"You don't need to shoot me, Andrews," Tom said calmly. "You don't need to do any of this. Let's go home."

"Fuck you," Jason shouted at him. "How did you get in here?"

"My security clearance gives me the access codes on any plane I want." He didn't want Jason to suspect Helen, or he might shoot her for that. "Let's take the plane back to the airport." They were losing altitude but not at a rapid rate. They still had room to maneuver, and he knew Helen could do it. "Put the gun away. You don't need it."

"Yes, I do. Fuck the bastards I work for. They'd have had me in the number-two seat forever. They don't like my attitude," he said in a mocking tone. "I hate them."

"That's no reason to kill a bunch of innocent people for it."

"What difference does it make? At least they'll have had a thrill before they die. No one gives a damn about them."

Helen did, and Tom, and the airline, and Ben and his whole office in New York, and Alan's in San Francisco. They had been working frantically for hours to protect them.

The tower radioed to all planes in the area that they had a rogue plane in the air believed to be headed toward the Golden Gate Bridge, and suggested they gain altitude and to watch for visible air traffic. The tower warned them all to use great caution, and to stay away from the bridge. At the same time, the San Francisco office of Homeland Security was warning all emergency vehicles to be on the alert. The plane was heading toward them, and probably the bridge. And the FAA had just been informed that the captain was no longer in control of the plane and a rogue pilot was flying it.

Jason was still using the controls on his sidestick, while Helen sat watchfully beside him, waiting for an opportune moment to switch them to hers, before they got to the bridge. And Tom knelt to tend to Connor, who was gasping for air, as Tom loosened his collar and tie, which was all he could do for him.

Tim Shepherd, Helen's father, had just left the hardware store with a new power drill and some shelves he wanted to put in his younger grandson's room. He heard the news as soon as he turned the key in the ignition. He had left the radio on the news channel, and all the announcer said was that a plane, a commercial airliner, was flying in the San Francisco area out of normal flight plan, and the possibility that it was being piloted by terrorists had not been ruled out. Tim stopped, frozen in his seat, and glanced at his watch. It was ten forty-seven, and he knew Helen's flight was due to land any minute. His blood ran cold as he listened, and some terrifying instinct told him it was the plane Helen had flown in from New York. She had called him from New York the day before and asked if he wanted to have lunch with her. She said she'd be home by one. And as he often did, he told her he'd do some repairs around her house, while he waited for her to get home. Since retiring from the Air Force, he spent all his spare time with his daughter and grandchildren. His son-in-law's shocking death had convinced him that Helen needed his help. She couldn't do it all alone.

He had been one of the most dedicated pilots in the Air Force in his day, and had given Helen her love of planes. He was immeasur-ably proud of her. She was his only child, and as he sat listening to the news in the car, the announcer said that the plane had been sighted heading for the Golden Gate Bridge. They didn't identify what flight it was, but as soon as they said the airline, he knew.

"Come on, Helen," he said out loud without even realizing it. "Whatever's going on up there, you can do this. Get your plane back from those bastards and take control." He was clenching his jaw as he said it and fighting back tears. He put the car in gear then and sped toward his grandchildren's school. Whatever happened next, they were going to need him more than ever, and he wanted to be there when they heard the news.

"God damn!" Ben said, stomping around his office, as everyone made calls to try and get information. "Couldn't I be wrong for once? Here we go again. What the hell are we going to do to help her get that lunatic away from the controls? And where the fuck is Tom Birney?"

"He's in the cockpit with them. The tower can hear him. Tom gave Andrews some song and dance about having the access codes as part of his clearance. But at least Jason hasn't shot him or Helen yet. That's something," Alan said miserably on the speakerphone.

"The passengers must be panicking," Ben said, thinking aloud.

"We have a good crew up there. They know what to do."

* * *

Jennifer, the purser, made an announcement for all passengers to stay in their seats when the plane had started to drop. She told everyone to put their life vests on and where to find them, and reminded them not to inflate them while they were inside the aircraft. Susan Farrow had put her dog inside her sweater, with his leash in her hand, and had put the life vest over both of them. And Nancy and Joel were on their jump seats holding hands.

"I'm not letting whoever is flying this plane ruin my wedding. I can't do that to Kevin," he whispered to her, and they both knew that if the plane went down and they hit the water, they'd have to move fast. They had no idea what was happening, but it wasn't good.

Jennifer kept making announcements for everyone to keep calm, and to be ready for a possible water landing. She reminded them again to pull down on the red tab on their life vests only after they left the aircraft. When Nancy leaned into the aisle, she could see people holding hands, and some were crying. No one was screaming yet. She felt bad for the two kids traveling unaccompanied but didn't dare move out of her seat, and Catherine James was looking panicked. By then, everyone knew that something terrible had happened, and something even worse might come next.

Jason was grinning, with the bridge in plain sight by then, and Helen knew she had almost no time left to save them. Tom was sitting in Connor's seat, who was lying at his feet, and making no sound. Helen turned to look at Tom and nodded imperceptibly, and he understood. This was going to be their last chance. In a few minutes, they would be there. Tom got up quietly from his seat, and on silent feet, took two big steps to Jason, who was looking straight ahead at the bridge, and Tom hit him as hard as he could on the side of the head. It stunned Jason for just long enough to loosen his grip on the sidestick with the controls next to his seat. Helen flipped the switch on him and took control of the plane again, as Jason leapt out of his seat and pointed his gun at Tom.

"You sonofabitch," he shouted at him, "you're just like all the rest, the lying bastards at the airline, my cheating girlfriend, you're all liars and cheats trying to screw me over." He yelled at Tom, but he didn't pull the trigger. Helen tried to regain altitude as she pulled a sharp maneuver and alternately dipped the wings. She was trying to throw Jason off balance and get the gun out of his hands, so Tom could get it away from him.

"Sorry, Tom," she said, as she dipped the wings as sharply and extremely as she dared. It was a tactic she had learned as a fighter pilot, and it had always worked, but she needed more altitude to do it right. She knew she was terrifying the passengers, who had no idea what was happening. But it worked well enough, both men were knocked off their feet, and the gun fell out of Jason's hands as he tried to steady himself, and Tom got him in a grip and held him down, while Helen tried desperately to regain altitude, but he had taken them down too far. She could hear screaming in the back from the passengers, but there was nothing she could do about it, except steady the plane, and try and pull it up. It looked like she was going to make it, and the zigzag course of the aircraft was on CNN by then, and they saw her breathtaking maneuver alternately dropping the wings that had gotten the gun out of Jason's hands, while she continued to wrestle with the plane.

"I can't get us up any higher," she said through clenched teeth. "The goddamn plane is too heavy, and he's got us down too low," she said to Tom, and she flipped the radio switch again, so she could talk to the tower, while Tom held Jason down with his full weight so he couldn't move. "This is Captain Helen Smith," she said calmly, "we have a problem."

"We can see that you do. Who's flying the plane now?"

"I am. But I'm having trouble getting back upstairs."

"Can you land in the Presidio? There's some flat land there. It's to your left."

"I'll see what I can do," she said, but didn't sound convinced. The air traffic controller told Homeland Security what he had suggested to her. Amanda and Bernice were holding hands in a death grip as they watched the progress of the plane on CNN, and Ben stared at it in horror. They were still heading toward the bridge, and he knew Helen must be fighting the plane with everything she had to change their course before too late.

And as Ben watched the television screen in New York, Jason succeeded in throwing Tom off him with a burst of superhuman strength and fought Helen for the controls again. Tom had hit his head and was dazed. Jason was able to get control of the plane away from Helen and headed it straight for the bridge. Everyone watching from the ground could guess that Jason was back in the driver's seat again. It looked like the inevitable was about to happen, and as Jason shrieked with laughter, Tom picked up the fallen gun and aimed it at him.

Chapter Ten

There was silence in Ben's office as they watched the progression of the plane, low over the water, and heading for the bridge. No one was telling them anything from the cockpit. Helen was too busy trying to figure out how to get the plane away from Jason and save the passengers. But Tom had the gun and Jason didn't know it. Jason was in a state of euphoria watching them head straight for the bridge. This was what he had planned and it was happening. It was the most exciting thing he'd ever done. And he'd done it right. He knew Helen couldn't save the plane, or get them out of the nose-dive they were in. And he had timed it perfectly. They would hit the bridge, the plane would explode, and what was left of it would fall into the water and sink and the bridge with it. Everyone on the plane would be dead, and the airline would be embarrassed and have to pay millions of dollars in lawsuits, maybe billions. He didn't care who died, just so they all did. And he had nothing to live for now anyway. They were never going to let him fly as a captain now.

They weren't going to anyway. And he was going out with a bang. He was taking a national landmark with him. They would never forget the pilot who had destroyed the Golden Gate Bridge. They would remember him forever, just like the postcard said. He had left it in the bin on purpose, even though no one would know what it meant until afterward. He was savoring every minute, and suddenly felt the gun pressed against his head.

"Get out of that seat," Tom said in a murderous voice. "I mean it. Get up."

"Why should I?" Jason said smiling at him. "We're all going to die together."

"No, we're not," Helen said clearly. She reached down and switched the controls back to herself, as Tom dragged Jason out of the chair, and Jason didn't try to stop him. He knew it was too late for her to save them. His mission had been accomplished.

"Captain Smith here," Helen said to the tower. They had been listening too and watching the plane's erratic movements, as they helplessly stood by. "It's too late to get us out of this. We're going down," she said in a matter-of-fact tone. And as she said it, Jason grabbed the gun from Tom with an enormous smile on his face, put it in his own mouth, and pulled the trigger. Blood splattered everywhere, and Jason fell to the floor dead. He had wanted to commit suicide and he had done it. Helen looked through the blood-splattered windshield, trying to figure out what to do, and where to land. She couldn't make it into the Presidio, but she was determined not to hit the bridge, and she knew that if she pulled up now, she would.

"My copilot is dead, he shot himself," she said and then turned to

Tom. "Get back there, and have the crew get everyone out as fast as they can, once we're on the water. I'll do what I can, but we won't float for long." Tom nodded, and she stopped him for a second. "How's Connor?" They hadn't heard a sound from him in several minutes while they dealt with Jason. Tom looked down before he left the cockpit and answered her.

"He's dead." She nodded. She couldn't stop to think about it. She had a plane to land on the water, for as long as it would float.

"Go," she said to Tom, with urgency in her voice. "We have very little time to get them out. If I can keep it up for long enough, the slides will be operative," which would turn into life rafts. There was a slim chance that they could save the passengers, but she was going to try, and she was determined not to hit the bridge. She knew that if she tried to gain altitude from the course Jason had set them on, they would hit the bridge for sure, and there would be less chance of survivors.

"Captain, the Coast Guard is ready for you," the tower told her.

"I don't know if I'm ready for them. I can't get up, so I'm going down, I'm going to try to slide under the bridge. We may lose a few repeat customers on this maneuver. They may pick another airline after this," she said to the controller, concentrating on what she was doing, and trying to bring the aircraft in on a dime. It would put them in the choppy waters at the mouth of the bay, but she had no other choice now. She was in the cockpit alone with two dead men, and she was damned if she was going to lose a single passenger, whatever it took.

* * *

165

Tim had made it to his grandchildren's school by then, and without hesitating, he strode to the principal's office. She was just coming back after a meeting and he told her what was happening. The news had said it was a flight from New York, but admitted that there were two flights due in from New York within half an hour of each other and they didn't have a confirmed flight number for this one.

"Are you sure it's Helen's flight?" the principal asked, looking shocked. She had seen him at the school before, picking the kids up from sports games and after-school activities. He had an active role in their lives, and he shook his head in answer to her question.

"No, I'm not sure. But I'll be stunned if it isn't. She was due in now, on a flight from New York. I'd like to get the kids out of their classes. I don't want them seeing or hearing about this from some-one else." She nodded agreement.

"I'll have them brought to my office right now." And within min-utes, he had his arms around them in the principal's office. There was a TV in the room and he had turned it on and was watching his daughter's last desperate maneuvers to save the plane and fly under the bridge. He knew what she was doing, and it was a daring move.

"Is Mom going to be okay?" his younger grandson asked as all three children stood watching with them. The principal left the room out of respect for them and what the children were seeing. Possibly their mother's death in the next few minutes, and that of many other people when the plane went down.

"She'd better be," Tim said in a hoarse voice. "Your mom is a hell of a fine pilot," he said as tears rolled down his cheeks and the chil-dren clung to him like barnacles. "If anyone can pull this off, she will," he said, willing her to succeed, at least at saving the passengers and herself. He didn't give a damn about the bridge or the plane. All he wanted was for his daughter to come out of it alive. Her children needed her, and so did he.

Ben and everyone in the New York office had a perfect view of what Helen was doing from the camera in the news helicopter that was shooting live footage for TV. It was the same scene Helen's children and her father were watching in Petaluma, at their school.

"Oh, my God, what's she doing?" Ben could see that she couldn't bring the plane up. It was too late, and the only thing she could do was a water landing, but the plane would sink fast when she did.

Phil was pacing, Amanda was speechless, Bernice was crying. All she could think of was Toby, and how she would feel if they were on that plane and about to die. It looked like a long shot for Helen not to hit the bridge, keep the plane floating long enough, and get everybody out. Possibly only a few would be saved, those closest to the exits, or maybe none at all. Dave hadn't said a word since Jason got control of the plane, overshot the airport, and headed for the bridge. He'd never seen anything like this, and didn't want to again. It had been the most stressful day of his life.

Ben understood what Helen was trying to do by then, and he didn't think she could pull it off. It was a stunt kids had done in small private planes, daredevils, show-offs. Trying to fly under the bridge in an aircraft that size was insanity. But what other choice did she have? If she didn't go under it, she would hit the bridge.

* * *

Nancy had made the announcement as soon as Tom came out of the cockpit covered in blood, and told her Helen's instructions. She told the passengers they were going to make a water landing, reminded them again how the life vests worked, and said they were going to have to move fast as soon as the plane touched down. The crew would help them, but the plane couldn't float for long. She wondered for an instant what this would do to her baby, but she couldn't think about that now.

Tom got to his seat and grabbed Catherine's arm.

"I want you out as soon as we hit the water. Do you understand?" She nodded and looked at him, too frightened even to panic.

"What happened?" He was covered in Jason's blood, but unharmed himself. It was a gory sight.

"I'll tell you later."

The crew members were shouting to everyone to remove their shoes and take crash positions, which they all did, too terrified not to. As Tom glanced out the window, he saw them heading straight for the bridge. And by some miracle, Helen pulled the plane down just enough, leveled it barely above the water, and flew it under the bridge, close enough to touch it. Skimming the choppy waves beyond it, they glided on top of the water, and came to a stop. Tom knew that was their cue and so did the crew. They opened all the doors and shouted to everyone to head for the exits, leave their belongings, and not to wear their shoes. And before Nancy could get to the two children sitting behind them, the Saudi couple had taken off their seatbelts and pulled the children out of their seats. Ahmad put on their life vests as they stared at him.

"Don't be afraid. We will take care of you," he said, holding

Nicole in a firm grip. She was crying and Mark was close to it. Ahmad and Sadaf got them to the nearest exit, pushed them down the slide toward the part that became a raft and would detach from the slide later, and followed them immediately. They each held one of them on their lap in the boat bouncing on the choppy water. And all down the length of the plane, the slides were operating, the rafts were inflated, and passengers were sliding out as fast as they could. Catherine wound up in the raft with Ahmad and Sadaf and the two children, and she told them they would be all right. She was more worried about them than she was herself.

"Go!" Joel said to Nancy, as they shepherded their passengers out.

"I'm not leaving till we get them all out," she said fiercely.

"Bobbie says you're pregnant, get down the slide."

"I'm not leaving little kids and our passengers on this plane. If we make it out of here, you'd better invite me to your wedding."

"Promise. How long do you think we'll float?" he whispered to her.

"Not long," she said honestly. The plane was bouncing on the waves, and water had started to seep into the cabin. They saw Susan Farrow and her dog come down the aisle then, going the wrong way, heading toward coach.

"You've got to get to the slide," Joel said, trying to turn her in the right direction, with the dog sticking his head out of her life vest, which she hadn't inflated yet, since she hadn't left the plane.

"I'm seventy-six years old. No one's going to miss me if I'm gone. And if they do, they can watch my movies. I'm not leaving these people on a sinking plane. I'm heading back to coach to help," she said and marched past them before they could stop her. When she got there, she saw Robert with his baby in a front pack, helping the girls from the chorus down the slide. Their chaperone had been one of the first out, and the girls were crying and panicking, left to their own devices as Bobbie and the other crew members and Robert got them all out. There were other passengers with young children, and he helped a dozen of them off, after the girls, before he went down the slide himself. They were all sprayed with the salt water as soon as they got out, and the Coast Guard tenders were all around them, a flotilla of them, lifting people out of the rafts, onto the deck of the Coast Guard rescue boats. The helicopters were hovering to fish anyone out of the water, but so far, miraculously, no one had fallen in.

Ahmad had carefully lifted both children into the hands of the Coast Guard rescuers, and then lifted Sadaf up, and let the other women pass before him. He was the last one out of his raft, as it danced crazily on the water, but he kept his balance and managed not to fall out. Sadaf burst into tears the moment he reached the deck of the Coast Guard boat and stood sobbing, clinging to him.

"Captain Smith?" Air traffic control checked every few minutes to see if she was still there. She hadn't left the plane yet, and didn't intend to until the last passenger was out. It pained her to see Connor Gray's body in the rising water in the cockpit, but there was nothing they could do for him now. He had lost his life for a noble cause, trying to save her, the passengers, and the plane. He had died a hero's death. What remained of Jason was on the floor near his seat, where he had fallen. "You need to get out, Captain," air traffic control told her, sounding anxious. She was watching the evacuation from the windows, and they still had people coming down the slides and getting into rafts.

"I'm not leaving till everybody's out," she said firmly. "I think we're almost there. The water is up to my knees now."

"Get out!" the controller shouted at her.

"Not yet! I think we're going down nose first." It was what she had expected, with the weight of the plane. "I'm going to check the cabins now." She left her seat and headed back then. First class was empty, and business class. The crew had moved to the tail section and were all still there, helping the last people down the slides. A woman with two teenage children, a handful of men. Everyone was in shock but focused on getting out before the plane went down, and helping each other. The water level was rising at the back of the plane too. The last passenger was off, as they stood up to their thighs in the water, and Helen ordered the crew down the last slide and into the life raft. More Coast Guard rescue boats were waiting for them.

"You too, Captain," Joel said, as he turned to look at her. She had Jason's blood all over her shirt, on her face, and in her hair. Nancy was already out of the plane, and Bobbie was in a raft with Annette, waiting to be picked up, along with Jennifer the purser, who had stayed till the end. The crew had been remarkable. Joel went down the slide next and was the last person off the plane, except for Helen. She took a final look to make certain everyone was gone, and the plane suddenly sank lower in the water, and the opening to exit from shrank dramatically, and the slide detached. She slipped through the opening into the water, and knew that one of the boats would pick her up, and was surprised to find herself under the water for what seemed like a long time. She was a strong swimmer, and made it through the water, underneath the waves, and then felt a powerful pull trying to take her down deeper with it, and she realized that the plane was sinking. She fought to swim free of it, and had to fight hard. Her lungs felt like they were exploding as she bobbed to the surface. The current had taken her far from the lifeboats and she tried to float for a few minutes to catch her breath, and then another wave took her down with it, as she wondered if she would come up again. For her children's sake, she hoped she would, but she was sure that Jack had felt that way too before he died.

Chapter Eleven

"Where is she? What do you mean the Coast Guard didn't pick her up, and she's not in the life rafts?"

"She was the last one to leave the plane, after the crew," the head of emergency services in San Francisco told Ben, who was pacing in his office screaming at him. "They never saw her come down the slide. The last one detached just before she got out, and the plane went down. They didn't see her get out before it did."

"Well, for chrissake, are they looking for her? What are they doing? She's got to be in the water somewhere."

"She may have been pulled under by the plane if she got out too late. It went down pretty fast, and created a powerful undertow. She may not have been able to swim free of it. We're looking for her. We've got rescue boats in the water, and helicopters in the air. If she's out there, they'll find her."

"She's out there! *Find* her!" Ben shouted, and hung up for the third time since the rescue had started. They had all been watching it on CNN. The recovery operation had been brilliantly efficient so far. The crew had gotten the passengers out in record time and had been the last to leave. They didn't have a totally reliable head count yet, since there were passengers on an assortment of boats, as they were being transferred to the Coast Guard ships in the bay, particularly those needing medical attention. Ben wondered if Helen could be one of them. If the numbers they'd been given so far were accurate, they had lost no passengers or crew other than the three pilots, and they knew that two of them were dead. Ben was praying that the third one had survived.

It was another hour before Tom Birney called him from one of the Coast Guard boats and told him what had happened in the cockpit in the end. Jason shooting Connor, Helen getting the controls back and then losing them again, and then getting control of the plane in the final minutes, and Jason's dramatic suicide with the plastic gun. Tom said that both Jason's and Connor's bodies had gone down with the plane. For his family's sake, he hoped they would recover Connor Gray's. And Ben was sure they would find Jason's too when they pulled up the remains of the plane. It would be a costly operation, but the plane would have to be raised from the ocean floor at the mouth of the bay. The airline and the city would want it removed, before it was dragged out to sea by the currents or became a hazard to incoming boats.

The group in Ben's office began to move around. They had been sitting there for hours. It had been a day of agonizing tension that had left all of them drained. But if the passengers had been saved from disaster, it was a major victory, in great part thanks to Helen Smith's and Tom Birney's courageous acts in the cockpit.

The CEO of the airline had conferred with Phil several times, and they were preparing a statement to explain the situation to the public. In essence, the flight had been taken over by a mentally disturbed copilot, and the passengers had ultimately been saved by the heroic captain, a decorated pilot with long years of military experience as a fighter pilot. But they had some heavy explaining to do as to why someone like Jason was still working for the airline after countless warnings and behavioral problems that they knew about.

Ben spoke to Bernice quietly, after ranting at emergency services in San Francisco. She was still sitting there, waiting to see if they would rescue the captain. She hoped they would, but it didn't sound likely. Helicopters and rescue boats were combing the area, with no luck so far. The water was rough and the currents strong under the bridge, and she could have been pulled out to sea, or gone down with the plane.

"I'd like to credit you with finding the postcard and reporting it to us, if that's all right with you," Ben said cautiously. "It was brave of you to follow up on it, especially after your supervisor discouraged you from reporting it." Dave Lee had explained the whole sequence of events to him, and he was duly impressed with Bernice's intelligence and determination.

"Could you leave out the part about the supervisor?" she said hesitantly. "She hates me, and she'd probably kill me when I go back to work." She smiled at him, and he chuckled.

"We can leave out the part about the supervisor," Ben assured her. "You should get a medal for this, or some kind of citation, and a promotion." He looked warmly at her.

"I'm planning to quit soon," she said quietly. "I've been going to law school online. I'm graduating in June. I'm going to take the bar exam, and I want to get a job in a law firm. That's what I promised my son I'd do."

"You have a child?" He was surprised. She looked like a kid herself, barely out of her teens.

"I have a six-year-old son," she said proudly. She had been touched by how seriously Ben took everything, and how hard he had worked to make the right things happen. And he had believed her. After Denise, he had restored her faith in her fellow man. He wrote down the correct spelling of her name, and she went back to watching the big TV screen with the others, as the rescue continued. It was four o'clock in San Francisco by then, and seven in New York. Her neighbor had picked Toby up at day care, and he was spending the night with them. She didn't know what time she'd get home. The drama wasn't over yet, although the worst was behind them. Ben was upset about Helen and wishing that a miracle would occur and they'd find her, and so was everyone else. She was one of the main heroes of the day. It wouldn't be right if she didn't survive it, and she would leave three orphaned kids behind, since their father had died a hero's death too.

Amanda was watching too, sobered by everything that had happened. She had a lot to think about and some decisions to make. Mildred had left by then, and Dave Lee and Phil were among the diehards who didn't want to leave Ben's office until they had the final count of survivors and knew what had happened to Helen. They all were aware that if Helen wasn't picked up soon, she wouldn't be among the survivors.

*   *   *

"Where's Mommy?" Helen's seven-year-old daughter, Lally, asked her grandfather as they continued to watch the news in the principal's office. She had brought him coffee and milk and cookies for the children.

They had watched all of the passengers lifted from the inflatable rafts onto the Coast Guard boats.

"Is she on one of the big boats?" Lally asked him, sitting on his lap.

"Not yet," Tim said with an intense look in his eyes. This couldn't happen to them again. Life couldn't be that cruel to leave all three of them orphans at such a young age. Oliver was thirteen, Jimmy was eleven, and Lally seven. One of Lally's feet dragged slightly, and her right arm was weaker than her left, but other than that she was a busy, active, happy child and never let her slight disability slow her down. She looked somber now, though, as they waited to hear of Helen's rescue, but nothing came.

"Are there sharks in the bay?" Oliver asked his grandfather in a whisper, not wanting the others to hear.

"I'm sure they aren't that close to land," he said in a reassuring tone, but he had always heard there were. He hadn't even thought of that till then.

"If she's on one of the big boats," Lally insisted, "why don't they show her on TV?" She wanted to believe that her mother had made it to one of the Coast Guard boats.

"Because everyone there is very busy right now," Tim said reasonably, keeping an eye on his middle grandchild. Jimmy hadn't said a word for hours. He just kept staring at the TV. Tim wanted to get them home but he didn't want to miss anything while they were in the car. The news reports kept playing over and over the video footage of when the plane went down and disappeared under the water with a terrible sucking sound. He could easily imagine his daughter being pulled under with it, with a force that she couldn't fight.

The children's faces were pale when the principal looked in on them again, but Tim had a kind of dogged determination as he comforted the children and refused to believe his daughter had died.

Tom Birney and Catherine had become separated while he helped others out of the plane and down the slides. But he knew she had made it into the first raft, and was on one of the Coast Guard boats. No one had been taken to shore yet. They were being treated for minor injuries by the Coast Guard teams that had picked them up, and Tom knew he'd catch up with Catherine sooner or later.

Ahmad and Sadaf were on a Coast Guard cutter with the two children they helped rescue, Mark and Nicole. They had been allowed to call their mother to tell her they were on the boat and were fine. Their mother sobbed when one of the officers talked to her. She said it had been the worst day of her life. And her parents were waiting for news of them at their home in Orinda. She gave the officer their number, and he promised to have someone call them when they docked, which wouldn't be for several hours. He assured her again that they were in good hands, and hadn't been injured during the rescue. He said that Mark had just eaten a hamburger, and Nicole wanted pizza, and would be eating shortly. The crew members were taking good care of them, and so had Ahmad and Sadaf during the rescue, who hadn't let them out of their sight.

Nancy and Joel were picked up by the same boat somewhat later, and they were all happy to see each other, and Nancy was relieved to see that the children had done well and the Saudi couple had taken responsibility for them during the rescue. No one had expected the flight to end as it had when it left New York that morning. Bobbie and Jennifer and most of the flight attendants had wound up in a life raft together when it detached from the slide and from there they had been transferred to a Coast Guard boat.

"So, are you going to invite me to your wedding?" Nancy teased Joel again. He had called Kevin from the rescue boat, and his future husband had sobbed piteously when he heard Joel's voice.

"I thought you were dead when I saw that plane go down. Thank God you're all right."

"I'm fine," Joel told him gently. "It was scary as hell, but we were busy reassuring the passengers and getting them out."

"You can be my matron of honor if you want," Joel said to Nancy when she mentioned the wedding.

"I'd like that," she said, looking across the bay at the city she thought she'd never see again. She hadn't talked to her husband yet. His flight from Miami was due to land shortly. She wondered if she'd lose the baby after everything she'd just been through, but it couldn't be helped. She was alive, and she had Peter and the little girl they were going to adopt in China. Maybe that was all she needed. She suddenly felt extraordinarily lucky. She had stared death in the face and survived it. She and Joel stood on the deck of the Coast Guard boat, and he had his arm around her. She suspected they would be friends forever after this. They had been to hell and back together.

They brought out an obstetrician by helicopter to examine her, and she said that everything appeared to be in good order. She had no cramps or bleeding, although the doctor told her to take it easy for the next several days. But all was well so far.

Susan Farrow had wound up in the life raft with Robert and his baby, the girls from the chorus, and Monique Lalou, who was disgraced after abandoning her charges on the plane. She made a number of weak excuses, but the truth was that she had been terrified and wanted to save herself and forgot about the girls. The girls, Monique, and Annette, the flight attendant, wound up on one of the Coast Guard cutters together. Robert had called Ellen from the Coast Guard boat and apologized to her for taking the baby from her that morning. He was sorry about it now, and he sounded remorseful. He had almost gotten them both killed. He knew he wouldn't take the flight to Japan that night. Ellen still sounded frantic, and said she'd never recover from the shock of finding the baby gone.

"That was a terrible thing to do to your wife," Susan said seriously when he told her about it. "You have to give the baby back now." He was sleeping peacefully in his father's arms then and no longer seemed feverish, even after being exposed to wind and water.

"It was all so much harder than I thought it would be when we had him. She changed after she was pregnant. She was always telling me what to do, like I was a kid or something."

"Maybe you acted like one," the actress said honestly. "Maybe she grew up and you didn't."

"I'm not sure I want to," he said, thinking about it. "She'll probably never speak to me again."

"I'm not sure I would either. Stealing him from her was a pretty nasty thing to do." He nodded and didn't answer. The authorities had already contacted the airline and emergency rescue services, and when they got to shore, child protective services were taking the baby into custody. The baby's mother would be there in the morning to get him. She was flying out from New York.

The girls from the chorus were badly shaken by what had happened, and their chaperone said she intended to give notice. She knew the parents would fire her anyway when the girls told them how she had behaved, leaving them on the plane during the rescue. One of the mothers was coming out to continue the tour with the girls. Ms. Lalou insisted that she wanted to be admitted to a hospital when they landed, and said she wasn't up to continuing the trip, nor the job as the girls' chaperone. They were too much for her to handle.

The couple that had argued for the entire flight were on a different boat. They had been separated in the life rafts, and each thought the other hadn't survived. When they found each other on the same Coast Guard boat they realized how far they'd fallen and how badly they'd let each other down. And whatever happened in the future, they agreed that they weren't ready to give up on their marriage yet.

"I thought you were dead," she sobbed in his arms as she clung to him. Tears rolled down his cheeks, and he admitted that he had thought she was dead too. They hadn't solved their problems, and didn't know if they would, but being together was enough for now. They felt like they'd been given another chance and didn't want to waste it. And maybe they could work it out. They promised each other they'd try.

The bridge was still closed at eight o'clock that night, but they were planning to open it at midnight. Most of the emergency vehicles had left, except for a few ambulances and police cars. The fire trucks were gone and hadn't been needed, and the *Phoenix* had returned to port earlier.

Arrangements had been made to take those who needed it to local hospitals for minor injuries, and the airline had made hotel reservations for everyone else. Representatives from the airline were waiting onshore with buses, and clothing had been provided for all of them, at the airline's expense. And local passengers would be going home if they didn't need to be admitted to hospitals for injuries sustained during the rescue. There had been some cuts and bruises, a broken ankle, and some sprains. Two passengers with serious heart problems were being treated by Coast Guard doctors, and an elderly person had been taken to UCSF by helicopter.

But on the whole, they had fared surprisingly well in spite of the trauma and near-death experience. There would be months of trauma-related disorders and post-traumatic stress to deal with, and counseling for the crew. The survivors' recovery would be a huge undertaking. Legal issues would have to be decided and dealt with, including whatever restitution by the airline was deemed appropriate. There were bound to be lawsuits, no matter how well it had been handled, and questions asked forever about why Jason hadn't been dismissed earlier, at the first sign of his behavioral problems, which had ultimately led to this horror and the cold-blooded murder of a respected senior captain. Connor's family would undoubtedly sue the airline too. They were expecting it, and all the other lawsuits passengers and their families would file against them. It would be a long, arduous process and take years.

Ben, Phil, Bernice, and Amanda were still watching the continuing reports on TV in Ben's office, hoping to hear of Helen's rescue. But there had been no further news of it by eight-thirty after a press conference.

The final survivor count was in by then. No lives had been lost except Connor Gray, Jason Andrews, and possibly Helen Smith, the three pilots. The rest of the crew and all the passengers had survived. The rescue had been extraordinarily successful, and Helen's artful landing had saved the passengers and the bridge. She was already being declared a hero.

The CEO of the airline and head of PR had held a press conference at eight o'clock, explaining what had happened as best they could and apologizing to the passengers and their families for the trauma they had endured. They concluded by praising the captain and crew for their heroic acts during the rescue that had resulted in all the passengers surviving, and they expressed the hope that Captain Helen Smith would be found. Every effort was being made by the Coast Guard in a continuing search-and-rescue mission to find her at sea and in the bay.

Tom Birney had declined to be interviewed, but the press were camped outside his apartment once they heard about him. It was too soon for anyone to talk. The anchormen on all the news stations were starting to repeat the same things over and over, focusing on the most dramatic elements. Helen's water landing under the bridge had been shown again and again.

Helicopters were still sweeping over the area, looking for Helen, and a final report said that after nine o'clock that night, search efforts would be suspended until morning, when they would extend the area further, in case her body had been swept out to sea. The fog had begun to roll in slowly, as it did almost daily in San Francisco, which would complicate matters further for a rescue mission that night.

Helen's father had taken the kids home from school finally at six o'clock. They couldn't stay there all night. He drove them home and cooked them dinner, but no one ate it. They turned the TV on as soon as they got home. But there had been no further news about Helen. Tim told them that people had been rescued after surviving for days in the water, and he reminded them how tough and strong their mother was. She was a fighter, and if there was any way for her to come home to them, she would. He hoped he was telling them the truth, and wanted to believe it himself. He hadn't prayed in years, not since his wife's death fifteen years before, but he had been praying all day that they'd find his daughter. They had to, and she had to hang on, wherever she was, for the sake of her children.

* * *

Ben was just about to turn the TV off at ten o'clock in New York when a reporter on the scene announced that there was breaking news. They showed footage of two helicopters hovering over the water, with searchlights shining brightly below them. The reporter explained that they had extended the search for another hour, the tide was coming in, and one of the helicopters was dropping a harness by wire into the water, along with a second wire with a man in a harness also dropping to the surface of the water. All you could see was a head bobbing on the surface, and an arm come up to grab the harness as the man secured the person in it.

No one had confirmed who it was yet, but there was visible excitement among the rescuers. It took a moment to get the rescue gear adjusted, and then slowly, a slim form was lifted up as the wire shortened. The rescuer kept a grip on the person being rescued, and the arms of several rescuers pulled someone into the helicopter, and then the helicopter took off at full speed. The reporter said they didn't know who the rescued person was yet, but there was only one missing. All of them standing in Ben's office stood rooted to the spot as they waited. It was a full five minutes before the reporter announced that the plane's captain, Helen Smith, had just been dramatically rescued from San Francisco Bay, moments before the fog came in. She had been swept out to sea by the currents when the plane went down. She had held on to a seat cushion that had floated loose from the plane when it went down, and she had been treading water and floating for the past eight hours, and was brought back in by the tide. They said she was in stable condition but suffering from exposure, and was being airlifted to a local hospital.

Phil, Ben, Amanda, and Bernice let out a scream simultaneously, and had tears running down their cheeks as they hugged one another. She had made it! She was alive! Helen Smith had saved the passengers and the bridge with her remarkable landing, and now she had been rescued. The nightmare was over. All Ben could do was think that he hadn't botched it this time. His legs were shaking as he sat down at his desk and thanked the God he'd thought had forsaken him when the hostages died. This didn't change that. But somehow it made life worth living again. And whatever condition Helen was in, she would be all right, and so would her children. She was alive!

Tim was about to tell the kids to get into their pajamas when the bulletin flashed across the screen, "Heroic pilot Helen Smith alive," and they saw Helen's dramatic rescue as she was lifted into the helicopter from the water. At first they just stared, and then they hugged and screamed and clung to their grandfather.

Ten minutes later, she had someone put a cellphone in her hand, gave them the number, and called them. She could hardly speak, she was so exhausted. Her voice was barely more than a hoarse whisper but she talked briefly to each of her children, told them how much she loved them, and then spoke to her father.

"I'll be home tomorrow," she promised. They were admitting her to a hospital but Tim was right about her, she was a strong woman and a fighter.

"Didn't anyone ever tell you not to fly under bridges? That was quite a landing," he said, his voice shaking and filled with emotion.

All she could think of as she'd floated in the water was that she had to get home to them somehow, and survive until they found her.

"I love you," she said, as her voice faded to almost nothing, as the last drop of strength drained from her.

"I love you too. Get some sleep, we'll talk tomorrow."

It was a long time before he got the kids settled down and into bed. Lally fell asleep next to him on the couch. He carried her up to her bed after he tucked the boys in. Oliver still looked shaken but Jimmy was asleep before his head hit the pillow, and Tim sat in the living room for hours, thinking about what his daughter had been through and grateful that she'd survived it. He had never seen a more beautiful sight in his life than when they'd lifted her from the water. His prayers had been answered. There was a God after all.

The last four diehards in Ben's office hugged each other again. Ben finally turned the TV off, and he offered to send Bernice home in a Homeland Security car with an agent to drive her. It was the least they could do for her, and she thanked him for it. It was too late for her to want to take the train, and she couldn't afford a cab. She could hardly move, she was so tired.

She couldn't even speak in the car. When the agent dropped her off at her address, she felt as though she could barely crawl as she walked inside, went upstairs, and rang her neighbor's doorbell. Toby was standing next to her when she opened it, and Bernice picked him up in her arms, held him tight, and started to sob.

"What's wrong, Mama?" He had never seen her like that before.

"Nothing, baby. I'm tired, and I love you so much." All she could think of were the children who had been on the flight, and Helen's children who hadn't lost their mother.

"Everything okay?" Her neighbor knew what had happened, and Bernice nodded as she clutched her son to her. He was the perfect antidote to a terrible day. But it had turned out to be a good day after all. A very good day. She had started an avalanche that morning when she found the postcard and averted a disaster. But everything had turned out right. She took Toby home, left her uniform in a heap on the bedroom floor, pulled on her nightgown, climbed into bed with him, and just lay there holding him, thinking of everything that had happened, and incredibly grateful that Helen Smith and the others were alive. She couldn't ask for more.

Chapter Twelve

When the Coast Guard boats came to the dock they were using in San Francisco that night, an area had been set aside for family and friends to wait for the survivors. There was an auditorium for them to stand indoors, where food and drinks were laid out, and an enormous TV screen where they had watched the rescue. As the boats approached, everyone rushed outside. No one knew what kind of condition the survivors would be in, mentally and physically, as they were assisted to land and their loved ones ran toward them, unable to contain themselves anymore.

Ahmad and Sadaf were holding firmly to Nicole's and Mark's hands. They didn't let them go for an instant, and had become their self-appointed guardians. A gray-haired couple hurried over as soon as they saw them and swept them into their arms. There were tears and hugging, as the children told them everything that had happened, and introduced their new friends to their grandmother and grandfather. Representatives from the airline were on hand to check off names on the manifest and make sure that everyone was accounted for, and provide whatever assistance they needed. They had been waiting for the children, and a woman in the airline uniform stood by with tears in her eyes and watched the scene, and ticked Ahmad's and Sadaf's names off the list as well. She said she had children the same age, and could only imagine the agony their family had been through.

It took several minutes before Grant and Barbara Hollander could talk to the young Saudi couple calmly, ask them how they were as well, and thank them for staying with their grandchildren when they left the plane. Nicole and Mark were telling them all about it in vivid terms, and their grandmother couldn't stop crying as she hugged the couple again and again. Ahmad seemed very paternal as he stood by, looking embarrassed by the emotional scene, and Sadaf cried with them, out of relief for all of them.

Nicole explained to her grandparents that her new friends were going to school in Berkeley, and had come all the way from a place called Riyadh in Saudi Arabia. The four adults smiled at the exchange as others swirled around them and similar scenes were played out, and uniformed airline staff attempted to help people get oriented and find the people they were looking for, and shepherded others to the buses that were waiting to take them to hotels where rooms had been reserved for them. All possible amenities had been provided for them, including clothes from local stores, provided by the airline until they could get organized on their own. The Hollanders offered to drive Ahmad and Sadaf to wherever they were going, which the young couple shyly declined. They had signed up on the boat for one of the rooms at the Hyatt Union Square.

"You can stay with us if you like," Barbara Hollander suggested, and Sadaf insisted that they didn't want to impose, would be fine at the hotel, and had to sign up for student housing at Berkeley the next day. Grant asked them what they would be studying, and Sadaf said she would be studying art history, and Ahmad was going to business school. Both Hollanders were impressed by how polite and kind they were, and mature for young people their age. After talking for a few more minutes, the Hollanders gave them their phone number, the children hugged Ahmad and Sadaf, and they left for Orinda, where they lived in the East Bay. They wanted Ahmad and Sadaf to come to dinner once they were settled in Berkeley.

They had said that their daughter and son-in-law were flying out the next day to see the children themselves, and visit in Orinda for a few days. The vacation had gotten off to a terrifying start for Nicole and Mark, but they seemed to have weathered it, and they waved as they left to locate their grandparents' car in the parking area. Sadaf and Ahmad talked about what nice people they were as they got on the bus with others from the plane to be taken to the hotel.

When Joel came off the Coast Guard ship with Nancy and other members of the crew, he saw Kevin immediately, and made his way through the crowd to him. Kevin flew into his arms, and the two men stood hugging silently. Kevin couldn't stop crying as he held him.

"I thought I'd never see you again," he whispered as Joel smiled through his own tears.

"You didn't think I'd miss our wedding, did you?" He introduced Nancy to him then, and said she was their newly appointed matron of honor. Kevin's parents had come with him and were standing off to the side discreetly, and joined the two men when they saw Nancy.

"We were afraid we were going to lose you," Kevin's mother said to Joel in an emotional voice. Her son looked just like her, and she hugged Joel with deep feeling.

As Joel walked away with them, he spoke quietly to Kevin. It was nearly eleven o'clock at night by then. They had kept the crew on the Coast Guard boats to feed them and examine them, while airline representatives came on board to talk to them. Homeland Security agents had come out to the boats too to find out what they knew of the final traumatic hour of the flight. They knew little or nothing of what had gone on in the cockpit.

"I'm going to call my parents tomorrow," Joel said quietly. "I want to tell them we're getting married." He knew they would be shocked and wouldn't approve, but he felt he owed them that. He could have died that day, and he wanted them to know the truth about his life, even if they didn't like it. They were his family, and he didn't want to lie to them. He had made the decision in the life raft waiting to be rescued and vowed to himself to be honest with them, out of respect for Kevin and himself. And if they couldn't handle it and rejected them, that would be okay too. He didn't want to be like his brother, living a lie forever in order to be accepted by a community who would have ostracized him if they knew the truth. It seemed like a sad life, and Joel was grateful he had moved to a city where the way he lived was commonplace and he was respected by his peers.

"See you Friday!" he called out to Nancy as they left. He had told her the wedding was at four P.M. on Friday at city hall in San Francisco, and she had promised to be there.

She was still waiting for Peter when Joel and Kevin left with Joel's future in-laws. Peter arrived a few minutes later, still in his pilot's uniform, fresh from his delayed flight from Miami. He had come by cab straight from the airport. He had gotten the message that she'd been rescued over the radio from air traffic control, and he had left the plane in the command of the copilot for a few minutes so he could go to the restroom and compose himself.

He held her in his arms and felt her warmth against him as he closed his eyes, grateful that it wasn't a very different scenario.

"I'm pregnant," she whispered to him, as he held her. She wasn't sure what effect the stress and rigors of the rescue from the sinking plane would have on the pregnancy, but the doctor on the Coast Guard ship had said she was all right. Peter looked at her in amazement. It had been a day of miracles. "We have a lot to talk about," she said, smiling at him. She looked tired but uninjured in what was left of her uniform and the paper slippers they'd been given on the Coast Guard ship. They walked to one of the shuttles waiting to take them home. They lived in the house they'd bought in the Marina and didn't have far to go. All she wanted to do was be together, and try to forget everything that had happened that day.

There had been a sad scene being played out near them, as people pretended not to notice. The police had been waiting for Robert Bond when he came off the Coast Guard ship holding Scott. The girls from the chorus said goodbye to him. A chaperone from the San Francisco Girls Chorus was waiting for them and had volunteered to escort them. Monique Lalou had been taken to the hospital by ambulance. One of the mothers was arriving to continue the trip with them, and another member of the San Francisco Chorus had volunteered to help until she got there. The girls were shaken by the experience but excited to go to the hotel. They were going to be staying at the Hilton downtown.

The police tried to be as discreet as possible, under the circumstances, but it was obvious what was happening. A member of child protective services took the baby from Robert, and explained that Scott would be taken to San Francisco General Hospital that night to be checked out and would remain there until his mother arrived from New York the next day.

"I think he had a fever on the plane," Robert said, looking remorseful. He felt guilty now for what he'd done. At the time, it had all made sense to him, but now it no longer did. Nothing about the past year made sense to him, or even the year before when he and Ellen got married, despite everything their parents said, and her parents' vehement objections that they weren't ready and that Robert was too immature. And then she'd gotten pregnant and it all got worse. "He may have had an earache too," he said to the woman who was holding him, and she nodded. She felt sorry for Robert, but the baby seemed happy and didn't look sick. "He threw up a lot," he added.

"Your wife said he was sick when you took him," she said gently, having read the report. "She said he has the flu."

Robert nodded. He hadn't noticed anything until Scott started crying on the plane, and eventually projectile vomited.

"He looks fine now, though," the social worker from CPS said gently.

He was chortling happily and holding his arms out to his father, but Robert knew the police were standing by, waiting to take him to jail.

"When do you think I'll be able to see him again?"

"I don't know," the social worker said honestly. "That will be up to family court in New York. There will be a hearing. Your wife is taking him back to New York tomorrow."

"I guess her parents are bringing her."

"I don't know." She got into a car with the city's emblem on it then, after strapping Scott into a car seat in the back. Scott still held his arms out to his father, and had cried when the social worker took him away. Robert was waving at him, making funny faces, with tears rolling down his cheeks.

The police stepped in as soon as the social worker left. They read Robert his rights and arrested him for parental abduction, which was a felony in California, at the family court judge's discretion, and also a felony in New York.

"What happens now?" Robert asked nervously, as they walked him to a police car in handcuffs.

"That's up to the judge. You'll be arraigned. Someone can post bail for you. The rest will be decided later in court. Your lawyer can move to transfer the case to New York." The two policemen tried to go easy on him. They didn't agree with what he'd done, but he'd already been through a lot that day, and who knew what his wife was like and what he'd been running away from. The older of the two policemen commented on it after they'd dropped him off at the jail.

"He's just a kid." He felt sorry for him. Robert had looked like a deer in headlights when he saw the jail.

"He's a year younger than I am." The younger policeman was less sympathetic. "I've been married for four years and I have two kids. And my wife would kill me if I pulled a stunt like that. Imagine if the baby had died during the crash or when the plane went down. He had no business stealing him from his mom." His older partner thought about it and knew he was right, but he also knew that people grew up at different ages, and some never did.

"My younger boy could have handled being a dad at twenty. He's twenty-nine now and he and his wife just had their third kid. My older boy is thirty-four, and he couldn't manage it today. I wouldn't leave a hamster with him. He acts like he's fourteen. He's completely irresponsible—can't keep a job or a girlfriend. I'm not sure he'll ever grow up, or if I'll live to be old enough to see it. My wife makes excuses for him and gives him money all the time. He gets thrown out of apartments for making noise and smoking weed, and then he moves in with us and drives me crazy. Some people just grow up slower than others. This kid looks like one of those to me. Maybe what happened on the plane will wake him up and teach him that he's on real time, especially with a kid. Some people never get that. I have friends my age who still don't," he said, feeling sorry for Robert, especially with a baby, who would inevitably pay the price for his father's immaturity.

"I have friends like that too," the younger policeman said thoughtfully. "I just don't feel compassionate toward guys who screw up their kids or put them in dangerous situations."

"The boy will love him anyway," he said, and they both knew it was true. They had picked children up for protective services, or referred them to them, and the kids always seemed to forgive their parents and wanted to go back to them.

"I hope this teaches him a lesson," the young father said. And at that exact moment, Scott had just been admitted to SF General, and Robert was crying in his jail cell, wondering if Ellen would ever let him see Scott again. He felt like a total fool and realized now how wrong he had been. Too late.

By midnight, all evidence of the survivors' checkpoint on the dock had been cleared away. Those who lived in San Francisco had gone home. The others had gone to hotels, except for one passenger who had insisted on catching a one A.M. plane to attend an important meeting in Seoul. An airline rep had helped him buy clothes and a suitcase at the airport, and they had held the flight for him, given the circumstances and the fact that he had VIP status with the airline.

The crew had gone home to mull over what had happened, and how they could have handled it differently or more smoothly. They knew they would have counseling available to them if they needed it. Most of them felt they didn't. Things like that could happen. Planes crashed from mechanical failure and unusual weather conditions, and even terrorists. It was something they had to face every day. And a pilot with his own agenda to turn a flight into a suicide mission, taking innocent people with him, was not unheard of anymore either, and couldn't be predicted. These were the rigors of the job as much as drunk or nasty passengers, bad crew members to work with, crying children, or unexpected turbulence. It was all part of it. It wasn't just about serving hot rolls with dinner, or handing out earphones, and they accepted the risks with the benefits when they took it. None of the crew members had complained about what had happened. It had been handled flawlessly by the airline once it happened, and equally so by all the emergency service providers.

Catherine was lying on her bed at the Four Seasons Hotel in Palo Alto, trying to assimilate everything that had happened. She'd had to call the venture capital firm she'd planned to interview with to tell them what had happened and to reschedule the appointment, hopefully for Friday. And she wanted to buy some decent clothes to meet them in. The concierge at her hotel had told her about the Stanford Shopping Center, where she would find everything she needed. And he had extended his sympathy for what she'd been through. The hotel was comping her for the first night of her stay, which she thought was a compassionate gesture, and the airline had offered to pay too. And she would need to replace all her ID and credit cards and get a new cellphone.

She was surprised to hear Tom's voice when she answered the phone in her room. They had been on different rescue boats, and she hadn't seen him since he told her to get out of the plane as fast as she could before it went down, and pushed her toward the first slide in the business cabin.

"I just called to see how you are. I couldn't find you on the Coast Guard dock but I got there pretty late," he said, sounding exhausted. He'd been in a long meeting with Homeland Security about what had transpired in the cockpit. The FAA wanted to see him, and the CEO of his company had called him as well. It had been a busy night for him. And he'd called his son in Chicago to tell him what had happened and that he was okay.

"I'm all right," she said, sounding as wiped out as she felt. "The whole thing has had such an unreal quality to it," she added in a small voice. And it would have seemed even more so if she'd seen Connor Gray dying from gunshot wounds, and Jason Andrews blow his brains out at close range after grappling with Helen for the controls. "Are you okay?" she asked him.

"Just tired." He was at the apartment he had in San Francisco, which the company provided him, and had had to fight his way through the press outside his building when he got there. Someone had told them that he'd been in the cockpit before the plane went down, and they wanted the inside scoop from him. He told them that he had no comment, and there would be another press conference the next day, to answer all their questions. The airline had promised there would be one, with members of Homeland Security, and the director of the Office of Emergency Services present, to address all the issues. "I really enjoyed talking to you, Catherine, in spite of the circumstances."

"Yeah, me too," she said, yawning, and he laughed. "I knew something was wrong from the look on your face when you started getting emails."

"Homeland Security in New York wanted me to go into the cockpit and suss out what was happening. They told me there was a glitch, and there was no air marshal on the flight. It was brave of you not to start drinking champagne when things started to get dicey."

"I didn't want to be drunk at my meeting," she said honestly, "otherwise I would have. Although I'm not sure how much good it would have done me up to my ass in water in the life raft."

"You can order some now," he suggested.

"This may come as a shock to you, but I'm not an alcoholic, just a nervous flier."

"So you said." And then he laughed. "When you knocked down those three glasses before the flight, I figured I'd be sitting next to a chatty drunk all the way to California."

She laughed at the impression she had given him. "It just puts me to sleep."

"I noticed," he teased her. "But then you were great company for the rest of the flight. And knowing how you feel about flying, you were terrific during the evacuation, and before that."

"The crew did a great job. And I'm so glad they found the captain. She's lucky she didn't get eaten by a shark, or drown." The reporter on the news had pointed out that there were sharks in the ocean just outside the bay, and shark attacks occasionally.

"She did an amazing job keeping control of the plane when the copilot tried to bring it down. She's a remarkable woman and a hell of a pilot."

"That's too bad about the retired captain," she said, and they were both quiet for a moment, thinking about him. No one felt sorry for Jason, given what he'd tried to do, and nearly succeeded.

"The airline is going to have a lot of explaining to do."

"Will you be at the press conference tomorrow?" she asked him and suspected he would.

"Yes, I will. They asked me to be there. As window dressing, I guess."

"You were a lot more than that, Tom," she said seriously. She was fully aware of it, even though she didn't know all the details, and knew she probably never would.

"Are we still on for dinner on Friday night, or will I just be part of a bad memory for you now?" he asked wistfully, hoping that wouldn't be the case. But given how she felt about flying, it wouldn't surprise him.

"Of course we are. You're the hero in the piece, not the villain. Thank you for telling me to get out fast. That Arab couple were really nice to the two little kids flying alone. He grabbed them and got them out as quickly as he could. I think they were the first off the plane, and I was right behind them, thanks to you."

"I'll pick you up at seven on Friday, and try to think of someplace fun for dinner," he said sleepily. He was too tired to talk to her any longer, although he was enjoying it. He liked her looks too. She was tall and sexy and in great shape. She looked athletic and he guessed correctly that she went to a gym every day. "Good luck with the meeting."

"Thank you. I have to go shopping tomorrow. It sounds stupid, given everything else that happened, but I hate to lose those shoes. They were new Manolo Blahniks and my current favorites. I just got them."

"That's a new language for me. You'll have to teach me about it over dinner." They both laughed. "My wife wasn't interested in fashion, and I only know about airplanes. Get some rest," he told her gently.

"You too. I'll watch you at the press conference tomorrow."

"See you Friday," she said, looking forward to it. A moment later they hung up, as she lay on her bed and thought about him. And before she could reach up to turn off the light, she was asleep.

Chapter Thirteen

Bernice didn't get up to go to work the next day, and she kept Toby home from school. She wanted to spend the day with him, to savor every moment, after the stress of the day before.

She tried to explain to him in simple terms what had happened, without frightening him unduly, in case they ever flew somewhere, which hadn't happened yet. She couldn't afford it, but one day she hoped she could take him to Disney World in Florida or on a nice vacation, when she was a lawyer. She had big dreams for them.

She explained to him over breakfast that she had found a postcard at her job that had a picture of a bridge on it, and a bad man had left it there.

"For you?" Toby was fascinated.

"No, he just left it there. I think he forgot it. He wrote something on it that I thought was weird, like a message. It was a picture of a famous bridge in San Francisco. So I called the airport police and showed it to them, and after a while they figured out what plane he was on, but it took a while. He wanted to hurt the bridge, but they wouldn't let him. And everybody was safe." It was a severely shortened version, but told him what he needed to know. At his age, he didn't need to know about murder and suicide, water rescue, and a plane going down in the water.

"What happened to the bad man? Did he go to jail?" She hesitated for a minute before she answered, and took the easy way out. There was no way she could tell him the truth, although she might one day when he was older. Nothing like it was ever going to happen to her again.

"Yes, he went to jail," she lied to him. "Forever," she said echoing the word he had underlined on the postcard.

"Good." Toby was satisfied with her version of the story. "Did you help take him to jail?"

"No, I just gave the police the postcard I found, because I thought it seemed suspicious." He nodded, and looked a little disappointed. "And I was with them all day while they tried to find out who he was. And then they found him."

"And sent him to jail." Toby smiled and finished the story for her. "Bad guys always go to jail." Like Toby's uncle, her brother, she thought to herself, but Toby didn't know about him. She had just told him that her brother lived far away and they didn't see each other anymore. "Could we go to see the bridge one day?" he asked her, curious about it, and she liked the idea.

"I'd love to do that with you. It's called the Golden Gate Bridge. I'll show you a picture of it." She went to her computer, typed the words in, and a photograph of it appeared, similar to the one on the postcard, but from a slightly different angle. Toby studied it for a minute and nodded.

"It looks nice. Let's go there sometime. Maybe this summer," he said, planning for them. She liked the idea too, but knew she wouldn't have the money until she got a new job. And she had to pass the bar exam. She had already written to several law firms, and was hoping for interviews.

"Probably not this summer. But sometime." She never wanted to disappoint him by promising things she couldn't deliver.

"I want to go to Washington and meet the president one day," he said, grinning at her, and she laughed at him.

"Yeah, well, me too. But that's not going to happen."

"Why not?" He was full of bright ideas, and the future was full of possibilities for him. She had brought him up that way. She never wanted him to feel limited by their circumstances or who they were.

"The president doesn't just call you and say, 'Hey, come on over for pizza,' or something. You have to be really important to see the president. Like be a senator or a congressman. Maybe you'll be a senator one day."

"What do they do?"

"They speak up for people, and tell the president what they want."

"I'd rather be a policeman or a fireman, and send bad guys to jail, like you did yesterday. Or I could be president, and have you over for pizza." He laughed at the idea, and they went to get dressed. She took him to the zoo, and it was a beautiful day.

She got a text message from Denise while they were out. She

thought it was from Della at first till she read it again. She had never expected to get a message like it from her supervisor. "We're all proud of you. You're a hero here. Way to go, girl! See you back at work. Denise." She read it three times and smiled to herself. She heard from Della too, who wanted all the gory details. And so did everyone else. She thanked Denise for her text, and didn't answer any of the others. It was Toby's day, and hers, and she didn't want anything to distract her from him. More than ever, after the day before, she realized how precious their time together was.

Ben came to work with a small carry-on bag the day after the dramatic rescue from the plane. And he had a suit in a garment bag. He and Phil were flying to San Francisco for the press conference on the noon flight. They didn't have to check in until eleven, and he was at his desk at nine o'clock sharp.

He'd had nightmares the night before about the hostage takers. This time they had captured a plane full of hostages and killed them all. But he reminded himself when he woke up that this time what amounted to hostages had all been saved, except for the retired senior captain. They had only lost one man, not sixteen, or the hundred and eleven they could have. And no children had been lost. They had saved them all. Or Helen had with her historic landing under the bridge and the crew that got everyone off the plane in time. This time the story had a happy ending. He had to remind himself of that again and again to counter the painful memories of the past.

Mildred Stern had reminded him that it would take time. It had been strange seeing her the day before in his office, and he'd been shocked when she walked in. It had brought the traumatic hostage situation vividly back to life in an instant, although in some ways it was comforting to see her. He had Amanda to thank for that. And as though he had conjured her up by thinking of her, when he looked up from his paperwork, he saw Amanda standing in front of him. He hadn't heard her walk in.

"What are you doing here?" he asked, looking surprised, and was mildly embarrassed over how curt he'd been with her the day before, when they went to Terminal 2 together to see the postcard.

"I came to see you," she said awkwardly.

"I owe you an apology," Ben said. "I think I was hard on you when we went to see the postcard. I'm not used to working with girls . . . sorry, women, like you. And sometimes your theories are a little over my head."

"And full of shit, is what you mean," she corrected him, and he laughed.

"Yeah, sometimes. We're a bunch of grumpy old guys here, and I'm the biggest one of all. Once in a while, your theories make sense. Forget I said that. I won't admit it to you, if I can get away with it." He was smiling at her, as she handed him a sheet of paper, and he looked at her before he read it. "What's that? A love letter?"

"No. My resignation. I owe you that after yesterday. I screwed up big-time. Or I would have, if you'd listened to me. Thank God you didn't, and you thought it was Jason all along. And I'm not resigning hastily. I thought about it last night. My theories really are too abstract. This job isn't about what you learn in books. It's about knowing what you're doing at all times. People's lives are on the line. You can't make mistakes. I made a huge one yesterday."

"We all make mistakes, Amanda," he said seriously. "I made a bigger one a month ago. Sixteen people died because of it, including a child. I'm no smarter than you are. I've just been here longer. And you'll make more mistakes. So will I. We just have to hope that we figure it out and come up with the right answers before people die. That's a big responsibility, but it comes with the job."

"I don't think I'm cut out for this kind of work," she said quietly.

"No, with a double master's in criminology and psychology? What are you planning to do instead? Counsel jaywalkers?" She smiled at what he said. She liked him more than she realized after seeing him in action the day before. She just didn't like working for him and feeling stupid all the time, or being treated as though she were. But he wasn't doing that now. He was speaking to her like a real person. And she knew that she had a lot to learn by listening to others with more experience.

"You came to this by a different route than the rest of us. That takes time for people to get used to, and that includes me. Most of the guys here are old customs officers, were in military intelligence or with the police. Basically, we're all cops, in one uniform or another. We're not psychologists like you are. We're not catching spies stealing secret designs for nuclear missiles. We're all trying to protect the public from a criminal element. Yesterday was a perfect example of that. This office needs what you have *and* what I have, and together we can figure out who the bad guys are. Sometimes that's harder than others. I was never sure yesterday, until close to the end, that Jason Andrews was our guy. The only thing I felt sure of, from everything I knew about her, was that Helen Smith wasn't. Sometimes that's how you go about it. And I didn't think that Connor Gray had the personality for something like this. We got lucky with Andrews's iPad. After that it was a shoo-in, but before that, I was flying blind too."

"You didn't look like it," Amanda said respectfully, impressed by everything he had said.

"I fake it pretty good." He smiled at her. "You have to have balls for this job, Amanda. Grow a pair. Don't run away because you made a mistake. It will happen again. We need you here. We need smart people in this job, not just a lot of old hardened cops. I think you'll do a great job, if you stay. You've got to learn something about baseball, though, or the guys here will kill you. Go to a Yankees game. Consider it homework." And as he said it, he tore her letter of resignation into a million pieces. "That's what I think of your resignation. Any questions?" He sat with the confetti of her resignation on his desk, and she looked at him seriously.

"Do you really want me to stay?"

"Yes!" he barked at her. "Even if you don't know squat about baseball. Volleyball, for chrissake. Now get your ass out of my office before I start yelling at you. I have work to do. And if you really want to quit, talk to me about it in six months, and we'll discuss it. For now, get to work, and go catch a terrorist or something."

"Yes, sir." She smiled at him and hurried out of his office, as he admired her miniskirt and long legs and shook his head. That wasn't why he wanted her there. The bottom line was that she was smart, however she looked or how great her ass was. Even he could see beyond that. She had a brain, a heart, and a great education, and what he had said to her was true. They needed her, even though she had made a serious mistake the day before. He respected her for offering to quit, but he wasn't going to let her. He thought she was worth saving, if she had learned something from it and it had humbled her a little.

He looked at his watch after she left. It was nine forty-five. He had an hour before he and Phil had to leave the office to catch their flight to San Francisco. The top brass wanted them at the press conference there, with Alan Wexler, the head of the San Francisco office of Homeland Security. Tom Birney, Helen Smith, and the CEO of the airline planned to be there. They had some explaining to do to the public. Big-time.

When Ahmad and Sadaf woke up at the hotel the next morning, they decided to order room service. Sadaf was tired after the emotions of the day before, and they had a long day ahead of them registering for student housing and getting their assigned student apartment. They had been told the process could take all day. And they had to sign up for classes the next day.

They were both starting in the fall, and wanted to get unpaid internships for the summer, which they could do with their visas. They had a lot to do and organize when they got to Berkeley. Ahmad was studying the syllabus for business school, when Sadaf came to breakfast without her head scarf. She did that when they were alone, but whenever other males were present, other than her father or brothers, she had to wear it, and had since she was a young girl. Her family was more liberal than most, since the women didn't cover their faces, and wore ordinary street clothes when they were abroad. The women in her family all wore the abaya in Saudi Arabia, the gray coat she had folded and left on the plane the day before. But in the end, even though he had been angry about it, it had proved to be a blessing not to be wearing it when they left the plane and had to get into life rafts. The wet garment would have encumbered her and weighed her down, and might even have been dangerous.

But when the waiter served their breakfast, she didn't cover her head, and Ahmad, shocked, looked at her the moment he left.

"What are you doing?" he asked her angrily. "What was that about? Are you trying to prove how liberated and American you are? Don't forget you're a Muslim. And you're my wife."

"I never forget I'm your wife," she said quietly. "I love you. And I believe in our religion. Many of your female relatives don't cover their heads in London or Paris when they travel, or wear the abaya. Even my grandmother didn't. She wore clothes she bought in Paris."

"What difference does that make?" he asked, still angry at her. He was more traditional than some of their relatives and peers. By law in their country, and their religion, she was not supposed to show her hair to any man except her husband, and she knew it.

"It's only now with the new, more extreme positions in our country that we're supposed to follow the old ways. But we believe in modern ways too. That's why we're here to study. We can combine the old and the new ways, at least while we're here. I want to be a modern woman, while still respecting you and our families. We want to build a new life here. But that new life isn't just for you, because you're a man. It's my new life too. We are equals. I love you and respect you as my husband, whether I cover my head or not. I'll cover my head at home in Riyadh when we're there, but I don't want to cover my head here, or wear an abaya, or be different from everyone else. This has to be *our* new life, for *both* of us. Not just for you." She was twenty-three years old and he was twenty-four, and she wanted just a little taste of freedom, while they were in Berkeley.

She had spoken eloquently and with deep emotion, and he knew that what she said was true. He couldn't embrace modern beliefs for himself but deny them to her. But he hated to give up their traditions, whether old or new. His mother hadn't covered her head when she was abroad either, and his father had been fine with it. Sadaf was right. They had both come to America for a new life, and Sadaf had a right to claim it as much as he did, while she was here.

"I'll think about it," he grumbled and ate his breakfast in silence. Sadaf was far more ready to embrace new ideas and let go of the old ones, without giving up her religious beliefs. She loved her religion and her country, and in her mind, their God didn't love her any less because she didn't cover her head or wear an abaya in California. Ahmad knew she would respect their laws and do what was expected of her when they went home. She wasn't a revolutionary, just a modern young woman in a new place, in a new world, while he was clinging to the old ways. Some of what he expected of her was simply out of habit, on subjects that even his own parents didn't follow.

The airline had left simple clothes and basic supplies for them at the hotel, since their luggage had gotten lost. She was planning to go shopping, but for now she wore her own jeans, with a sweater they had given her, and they were both wearing flip-flops and had to buy shoes in Berkeley after they dealt with their housing. Now they needed all new clothes, since what they had brought with them had gone down on the plane, with her abaya.

She was ready to leave the room with him, and for the first time since she was a child, she wasn't wearing a hijab to cover her hair. It was second nature to her to put it on, and she felt naked without it. But it was a good kind of nakedness. She felt as though she had shed something she no longer believed in. Ahmad stared at her in displeasure as he picked up the small bag they'd been given for their belongings. "All right," he said under his breath, not looking at her, and she barely heard him.

"What?" She wasn't sure what he was talking about.

"I said all right. I love you because you're a modern woman and that's why I married you. I can't punish you now for being everything I love about you. I think I forgot how brave you are as a person. You were brave yesterday too."

"You're just as brave as I am," she said and kissed him. "And when we go home, we'll respect the traditions there," she said softly. "Thank you," she kissed him again. She knew that her not wearing a scarf on her head had been a shock to him. But he had taken it well. And they were both smiling when they left the hotel room hand in hand. They were going to their new life and everything they would discover. And whatever happened, they would face it together, just as they had on the plane.

*   *   *

Helen was kept at the hospital overnight after her rescue from her long siege in the water. She thought she had been delirious for part of it. The water had been freezing cold. When she had finally bobbed up to the surface after, with all of her strength, she swam free of the plane underwater, the cushion had been next to her, and she had clung to it until they found her. For part of the time, she had been sure she was going to die. And then she had been pushed back into the bay by the tide, and she had heard the sound of the helicopters at twilight, and saw the harness drop down next to her in the water. It had taken everything she had in her to hang on for eight hours and not give up. And then suddenly they saw her and lifted her into the helicopter. Strong arms had caught her and laid her on the floor. She couldn't even talk at first, until she warmed up. She had been shaking violently from the cold water and exposure. They had taken her to San Francisco General and at times before that, she was delirious, and thought she was back in Iraq in the Air Force, and asked for Jack. She hadn't remembered at first that he was gone.

A kind nurse stayed with her and told her what had happened.

"Did anybody die?" Helen was finally able to say in a hoarse croak.

"The copilot and a retired pilot, who was shot. But the rest of the crew and all the passengers got out before the plane sank. And of course they were looking for you for hours. I only know what I saw on the news, like everyone else. They said the crew was terrific, and got everyone out," she said, and Helen lay back against her pillows. She had an IV in her arm, and her lips were cracked from the salt water, and every inch of her body ached.

She managed to call her children in spite of it, and her father before the kids left for school that morning. They were ecstatic to hear her, and told her to hurry up and come home. She was planning to right after the press conference. Just thinking about going to it exhausted her.

When she talked to her father again, he commented seriously on what she had been through. "That must have been an ugly scene in the cockpit," he said, sure that there was a lot more than he'd heard on the news, and he was correct. The airline wanted to clean it up as much as possible, but there was no way to cover up the fact that a copilot had committed suicide in flight, a senior officer had been shot and killed, and an airliner had gone down in the bay, despite Helen's heroic flying.

"You're a good woman," her father said to her proudly, "and a hell of a pilot, even if you don't know how to land. Didn't your instructors teach you better than that?"

"Guess not." It was comforting to hear his voice. She had thought of him and her children the whole time she was in the water, and prayed that she would see them again. The mental strain alone had taken a toll on her, trying to control the plane in the final hour, and not get shot, and eight hours in the water. "I have to be at the press conference today at four o'clock. I'll be home right after that. They're bringing me home. I don't think they trust my driving," she said wryly. She wanted to see her father, but he wanted her to rest.

"We'll be waiting for you," he said, and she could hardly wait to see them. They sounded shaken up but okay. As kids in the military, they had a lot of friends whose parents had died, mothers as well as fathers, which was why she had mustered out, and Jack had wanted to as well. They didn't want that happening to their kids. But it had anyway, to him. And almost did to her, even as a civilian.

"You're a hero, Mom," Jimmy said to her proudly when she talked to him.

"No, I'm not, I'm just a pilot," she corrected him. "Dad was a hero. I was just flying the plane."

"Yeah, but somebody got shot, and you landed under the bridge. That looked really cool!" They had seen it all on TV.

"No, it was not cool. It was very scary."

"Were you swimming that whole time?" He wanted to know so he could tell his friends. Now that she was back, it seemed like an adventure. The day before it had seemed like a tragedy and almost had been for all of them.

"I was hanging on to a seat cushion you can use as a life preserver." But when she talked to Oliver, he was much more shaken than his younger brother, and she could hear him choke up at the sound of her voice. He was more sensitive and more aware than his brother.

"Are you really okay, Mom?"

"I'm fine." She tried to sound even more so for him.

"Thank God the crazy guy didn't shoot you."

"That's true. And I was lucky I could land the plane on the water, which gave everyone enough time to get out." They had evacuated the plane in under four minutes, someone had estimated, which was miraculous. And landing it under the bridge without hitting it hadn't been luck, but extraordinary skill.

Lally wanted her to come immediately, and pick her up from

school that afternoon. Her grandfather had said he would do it, and Helen hoped to be home shortly after. Hearing them reminded her how much she had at stake here. If something happened to her, there was no one to take care of them except her father, who was too old to raise kids again, although she knew he would do it if he had to. But being a pilot was all she knew.

She got up and walked around her room and down the hall after she talked to them, and was stunned by how stiff and weak she was. She felt like she'd been beaten. But she knew she had to be coherent and in good shape for the press conference, no matter how she felt. The airline had promised to bring her a new uniform in time to dress.

The doctors said they would have preferred to keep her for another day or two, until she was stronger and less battered by the trauma, but she insisted that she wanted to go home after the press conference. She needed to be with her children. She went back to bed then and slept for several hours.

They delivered the uniform to her as promised, and a nurse helped Helen dress for the press conference, and by the time she was in full uniform, she felt like she had been hit by a bus and had to sit down in a chair.

"Are you okay?" the nurse asked her. Helen had been discharged, but she was deathly pale. She pulled herself together then and stood up. The airline had a driver waiting for her, and all she could think about was going home to see her kids. The press conference was just a challenge she had to get through before she could go home and rest. The airline had told her that day that management wanted her to take a month off, with full pay, as compensation for what she'd been through. In the Air Force she got combat pay. In a way, this was no different.

When Helen walked into the hotel reception room the airline had rented for the press conference, her uniform was impeccable, her back was straight, her head was held high. She felt shy for a minute, recognized the CEO of the airline, and went to greet him. He knew instantly who she was and thanked her for coming, and for her courage and quick reactions the day before. He attributed the survival of the passengers and crew to her. He talked about her incredible landing, since he had been a pilot himself. And as she talked to him, she heard a familiar voice behind her but couldn't place it. She turned to see a man she didn't recognize. He was wearing a dark suit, and was in his mid-forties. He looked trim and had a handsome, craggy face. He looked a little bit like Dick Tracy, and then she realized who it was when he spoke again, and she smiled broadly.

"Hello, Ben." She knew that voice from their calls the day before. "Thanks for all your help yesterday."

"Thanks for not knocking the Golden Gate Bridge down. We would have looked like shit if you did," he said so no one else could hear him, and she laughed. "I'm sorry you had to go through that."

"I feel so bad about Connor Gray. He was trying to help me."

"The odds were that somebody was going to get hurt, or a lot of people. I'm glad it wasn't you," he said sincerely. Connor Gray was in his sixties and didn't have young children. His death was sad, but hers would have been a tragedy.

"It shouldn't have happened," she said with a serious expression. She was planning to go to his memorial service, whenever they held it.

Ben introduced her to Phil then, and Alan, the head of the San Francisco office of Homeland Security, whose agents had spoken to Jason's ex-girlfriend and found the iPad in his apartment. They had each played an important role in figuring out who wanted to bring the plane down in a suicide mission.

"You had us all worried yesterday when you disappeared," Ben said to her quietly.

"I got pulled out by the current, after the plane went down. First I was dragged under when it sank and then it just pulled me out. By the time I surfaced and realized what had happened, I was too far out to swim back or for anyone to see me. I was lucky the tide brought me back in."

"I don't think I've had a happier moment in my career than when I saw you reach for that harness and they pulled you up." He almost cried thinking about it again.

"Thank you. I was pretty happy too." She smiled at him, and he liked her eyes. They were big and blue and honest. She looked like someone who didn't hide from the truth. And then she saw Tom Birney walk in, and went to talk to him and thank him. He looked a little rocky too, the way she'd been feeling all day. They had all been through a lot.

"Are you supposed to be out of the hospital?" he asked her as though they were old friends and not two people who had met the day before. But wartime bred fast friendships, and this had been no different. They had been fighting a common enemy, and were the two soldiers left standing. She'd been told that he had worked tire-lessly to get the passengers out, and been one of the last to leave with the crew. She owed him a great deal.

"No," she said in answer to his question about leaving the hospi-tal, and then laughed about it. She was feeling better now that she was up and dressed, and the queasiness was gone. "My kids need me. I'm going home after this." He nodded and went to speak to the head of the airline, and a few minutes later, the press conference started. The CEO made a statement about how shocked and cha-grined they were that something like this had happened, that human nature was unpredictable, and it had taught them to be even more stringent in the future. They had been giving a talented young pilot a chance to develop, and they had learned the hard way that it had been a mistake. There was no way they could deny it now, and they didn't try to. He introduced Helen and Tom Birney as the heroes of the hour, acknowledged the bravery and efficiency of the entire crew, and said that Captain Smith had managed to pull off an im-possible feat, flying under the Golden Gate without destroying it, landing a plane that size on top of the water, and giving everyone enough time to get out before it sank. There was a round of ap-plause, and Helen made a brief statement afterward that heroes were accidents of circumstances. You couldn't train or learn to be one, or plan it. You did what you had to when the opportunity pre-sented itself and hoped you got it right.

Within minutes, all the members of the press who had attended were on their feet and giving her a standing ovation, and Helen blushed and looked embarrassed. Despite the medals she'd earned during her career, which attested to her skill and courage, she wasn't used to public acclaim. Ben, Phil, and Alan all spoke briefly for Homeland Security, and took questions from the press. It took almost an hour and at the end of it, half the people in the room came to shake Helen's hand and congratulate her. Ben smiled as he watched her. She was without a doubt the shyest person in the room, and probably the most modest.

"Cheer up, Captain," Ben said to her in an undervoice as she squirmed from the attention. "The next time you shake up their Bloody Marys with a little turbulence, they'll be writing the CEO nasty letters about you." She laughed out loud at what he said.

"I'm not used to this. They don't give standing ovations in the Air Force."

"They don't often in civilian life either. And I hope you never have to pull off another stunt like this one."

"Me too." She wasn't even sure now how she had done it. She was just compensating for the havoc Jason had wrought and the angle he had put the plane in at low altitude, and by some miracle, it had worked.

"Could we have dinner sometime when you're in New York, to celebrate the fact that we got through this?" It didn't sound like a date, just combat buddies grateful for their return from a tough mission in one piece.

"That would be nice," she said easily. "They just gave me a month off, so it won't be for a while," she added, relieved that the press conference was over.

Reporters had directed their toughest questions at management for not realizing how mentally unstable Jason was and firing him before this. But he was smart and charming, when he wanted to be, and Helen could see how he had slipped through the cracks. Even she had just thought he was a smart-ass and a harmless, badly behaved boy, and he was a great deal worse than that. He was a murderer who wanted to take 110 people with him, and had no remorse about it whatsoever before his death. He thought the airline deserved it for depriving him of what he considered his rightful place, so killing innocent people made sense to him, and didn't matter. But it was hard to justify to the press, and ultimately the public, that they hadn't fired him before it got to that point. The airline had a major challenge ahead of them and they knew it. The CEO had been deeply apologetic. And they all knew there would be major lawsuits as a result.

Helen got ready to leave then, and shook hands with Ben and Tom again, and the others, and with the CEO, who thanked her profusely. And then she left the room to meet up with the driver. Ben took off right after she did and saw her drive away in the town car. She had her uniform hat off and had removed her tie. Her shoulder-length hair was blowing in the evening breeze, and she was smiling at the prospect of seeing her children and spending a month at home with them. She owed them that after the fright they'd had the day before because of her.

Ben waited for Phil, and they had dinner that night at a great steak house. They drank a lot of wine, and Ben was drunk when he got back to his hotel room, and he didn't care at all. He knew he had earned it.

*   *   *

When Helen turned into the driveway in the unfamiliar car, all her children looked out the window, let out a shout when they saw it was her, and ran down the front steps to throw their arms around her as she got out. They almost knocked her down, and she followed them into the house where Lisa, the babysitter, had baked a cake for her, and she had helped Lally make cupcakes for her. Lally insisted Helen eat one immediately. They were her favorites, Lally pointed out, red velvet and dark chocolate. And Oliver and Jimmy were standing by at attention, waiting to hug her again. They couldn't get enough of her, nor she of them.

"I thought you drowned, or a big fish ate you," Lally said, looking worried.

"I'm a good swimmer and I'm not going to let a fish eat me, Lally. And I have a month's vacation." She had been thinking about it on the drive home, and thought of taking them to Disneyland. She wanted to do something fun with them, to celebrate the fact that she was alive. Suddenly, that was all that mattered. She wanted their time together to be about life, not death. They'd had too much of that in recent years.

Her father was at the house too, waiting patiently to see her, and all five of them sat at the kitchen table and had dinner together. Tim went out and got pizzas and two roast chickens, and it felt like a feast to Helen. Life seemed suddenly normal again although two men had died in her cockpit the day before. Her father couldn't bear the thought that it might have been her, or that the copilot could have flown them into the bridge and killed them all, as he intended.

Nothing seemed safe in the world today. But destiny had protected her this time. It was all they could ask for. He hadn't worried about her this much since she was in the military, although he tried not to show it.

Lally slept in her mother's bed that night. And they finished the cupcakes for breakfast the next morning. She had gotten them organized for school, and Helen smiled as she looked at her children at the kitchen table. Life was sweet. And however frightening the scene had been two days before, miraculously she had survived. It made every moment with them even sweeter.

Chapter Fourteen

Like the rest of the crew that had been on Helen's flight, Nancy had been given two weeks off, and Peter traded his trips for the next week to give them time together. They spent the next day in bed, sleeping and relaxing and watching movies, and that night, she dug through her closet to find something to wear, and found a dusty-rose-colored silk suit that seemed like the right attire for a matron of honor. Joel hadn't given her any details about the wedding, except that the ceremony was at four o'clock at city hall, and Kevin's parents were giving them a reception afterward at the Ritz-Carlton. But she had no idea how many people would be there or how dressy it would be when she teased him into inviting her.

Peter wasn't sure what to wear either, since it was their first gay wedding, and they agreed that a dark suit would be a safe choice. They arrived at city hall a few minutes before the appointed hour, and Nancy was startled when Joel introduced her to his mother. He had said that his very conservative family had never accepted the fact that he was gay, and Nancy was impressed to find herself face-to-face with a tall, attractive, youthful-looking woman, who looked just like Joel, in a chic navy blue dinner suit, and she smiled warmly at Nancy and Peter. After Joel had gone to greet several men who had just arrived, in suits similar to Peter's, Joel's mother spoke to Nancy in a quiet voice.

"I just found out about the wedding yesterday. Joel has always been very private about his life," she said carefully. "And his father has never accepted the fact that he's gay. It's been very difficult for Joel. I'm glad he's happy now. It meant a lot to me that he called to tell me, and invited me to the wedding. I wouldn't miss it. And Kevin is a wonderful man. I flew in from Salt Lake this morning. I asked my husband to come, but he just can't do it. But here I am," she said proudly, and Nancy was pleased for Joel. He whispered to Nancy about it a few minutes later, as he pinned a small white rose to her lapel, so people would know she was the matron of honor, and he had a white orchid for his mother to wear that he'd ordered at the last minute after he called her.

"Do you believe it? My mother came. She loves Kevin." It was a difficult breakthrough for him. "I decided to call her when we were getting out of the plane. I thought if I lived through it, I'd give it one more try with them. You never know, do you?" He was beaming, and Kevin's mother kissed him several times, and stood next to Jo-el's mother during the ceremony.

They had two best men, their closest friends who were also part-ners who had gotten married, and Nancy standing near them as witnesses, about a dozen friends, and their parents. The ceremony was serious and respectful, performed by a judge, which was the only disappointment for Joel's mother, she admitted later. She would have preferred a minister. Joel and Kevin exchanged narrow gold wedding bands, and had written their vows, which moved Nancy to tears, even more so when she remembered how close she and Joel had come to being killed two days before, and realized their friends and families could have been attending a funeral, not a wedding, which was a grim thought, and she shuddered when it crossed her mind.

Both mothers cried when Joel and Kevin were officially pronounced married, and everyone embraced the couple after the ceremony. Kevin had arranged for a white-coated waiter to be outside the room in the hallway and pour champagne into plastic cups. And the atmosphere was instantly festive. Everyone was happy for them. An hour later, they drove to the Ritz-Carlton, where Kevin's parents had rented a beautiful reception room with a garden, and a small band was playing their favorite songs. And there was a buffet for about eighty people. Nancy couldn't remember a wedding she had enjoyed as much, or which had been as tastefully done.

She danced with Peter before and after dinner, and he stayed close to her all night. Having nearly lost her, he didn't want to let her out of his sight, and Nancy could see that Kevin was feeling the same way. It had been a wake-up call for all of them that the worst could happen and life could change in the blink of an eye.

At ten o'clock Joel threw a bouquet to the single men and women in the group, and Kevin's niece caught it and was thrilled.

The wedding cake had been made by one of the best bakeries in San Francisco and was spectacular, with two grooms on it. Everything had been done with style and beauty and impeccable taste.

Not a single detail had been overlooked. The flowers throughout the room were exquisite.

Joel's mother left shortly after ten to catch her flight back to Salt Lake City, and she had a quiet, healing moment with her son, and looked genuinely sorry to leave. She promised to come back and visit soon. And at midnight, Kevin and Joel got ready to leave their guests. Their flight to Tahiti was leaving at the crack of dawn. The wedding had been absolutely perfect.

"If you ever decide to give up flying, you have a new career all lined up," Nancy said to Joel when she kissed him goodbye and wished him a wonderful trip. "You'd be a fabulous wedding planner," she complimented him.

"Kevin did everything. All I did was say yes or no, and cut a few pictures out of magazines." He looked lovingly across the room at his husband, and then looked at Nancy seriously. "I keep thinking how lucky we were this week."

She nodded, understanding what he meant. She felt the same way, and to be pregnant on top of it was the icing on the cake. She had seen her doctor the day before and confirmed that everything was fine, which was a huge relief.

"I'm glad I called my mom," Joel continued. "I think it meant a lot to her, and it did to me too to have her here. I always feel like an orphan with no family," although Kevin's family had embraced him like their own son. "My mom gave me back a piece of myself by being here and putting her stamp of approval on my life," Joel said with emotion. "It's too bad my father can't get there too. It's hard on my brother, who leads a secret life to keep them happy. I just couldn't do that anymore. At least my mom came." He kissed Nancy goodbye again. Most of the guests left at the same time, as the orchestra played "Happy Trails to You" and the party ended.

"I had a really good time," Peter said to Nancy. "It was the nicest wedding I've ever been to, except ours." He smiled and kissed her as the valet brought them their car, and they got in. And he looked serious for a moment on the way home.

"We need to talk about what we're going to do about Beijing now." She nodded. It had been on her mind too. "If we're going to back out, we should do it soon."

"Do you think we should?" she asked him sadly.

"I don't know. How do you feel about having two kids?"

"That doesn't worry me. I like the idea. I just wonder if we'd feel differently about having an adopted child and one of our own. I don't want to be unfair to her."

"I'm sure that we'd come to love her as much as our own. Our biological child could turn out to be a brat," he said, teasing her, as they drove home.

"Let's think about it," Nancy said, wanting to do the right thing, still coasting on the warm feelings of the evening. It had been a beautiful night.

Ellen had Scott in her arms when she visited Robert in jail, the day after she arrived, two days after Robert had kidnapped him from her parents' house. Robert had been arraigned the day after he was arrested. He was charged with parental abduction, and the judge had set bail, but Robert hadn't paid it and had nothing to post as bond. He looked depressed when he came to the phone in the visiting area. The baby stretched his arms out to him. But they were separated by a sheet of bulletproof glass and had to communicate over the phone.

"What happened to you? Why did you do it? I nearly went crazy when I discovered he was gone," Ellen said to him. "I thought he'd been kidnapped by someone who snuck into my parents' house." There were tears in her eyes as she said it, and he could see how upset she was. He hadn't thought of that when he took Scott. He had left her a note, but she said she hadn't found it for several hours. He had left it on the piano in her parents' living room on his way out, and no one ever looked there.

"I don't know. I think I went crazy for a minute. Everything went so wrong with us. We got married and our parents were on our backs all the time. I thought it was going to be exciting and romantic and fun, and instead you bitched at me all the time. All of a sudden, you didn't like my friends, I drank too much, I couldn't smoke weed in the house, my job wasn't good enough, I didn't make enough money."

She winced when he said it, and couldn't deny it. It was all true. He'd been twenty-three years old and she was twenty-two. She had thought that marriage would make him grow up and he'd be more like her father. Instead she saw how immature he was. He wanted to go out with his friends every night, or have them hang around and mess up their apartment, which he never cleaned up. And all he wanted to do with them was go to concerts or get drunk or stoned.

"And then you got pregnant, and it all got worse. You were sick all the time, you talked about the baby all the time, and I had to be a father. And when you had him, you never let me near him. Your parents pay for everything, so they think they own us. And mine never help us, which I agree is shitty of them. And he screams a lot." Robert nodded toward his son. "You nurse him all the time, so I can never feed him or get near you. I thought it was going to be wonderful, but it's been miserable. Your parents constantly say how irresponsible I am, as though I can't hear them. And I think we got separated because they told you to."

"We got separated because you *are* irresponsible. Look what you just did," she said and he hung his head in shame. But he'd been desperate and didn't know what else to do.

"I just thought if I could take him away for a while, we'd get to know each other, and I could get used to being a father without everyone breathing down my neck."

"Why Japan?"

"I saw it on the Internet, and it looked nice." He was as unrealistic as ever, but he wasn't a bad person. She had been in love with him in the beginning, but she had hated being married to him. And her parents were right. He was a kid. Even at twenty-five now, he was immature. She was ready to be a grown-up and take care of their baby. He had no idea what that meant, and he wanted to let his stoned friends play with him all the time, or put Scott in a backpack carrier and take him to a concert where everyone was smoking dope. It wasn't what she wanted for herself, and she hadn't realized how unready he was to become an adult. Having the baby had shown her that in spades. He had come to the delivery stoned, with two friends, and got upset when she told them to leave. She knew he loved the baby, but he didn't really know what that meant.

"He threw up all over some woman on the plane," he said and laughed about it.

"He had an earache and the stomach flu when you took him, and you didn't take his antibiotics with you." She sounded like an adult and he didn't, because he wasn't one. He wasn't a criminal or a kidnapper. He was just a stupid kid. But their son needed a father and not another child. "And you could have both been killed on that flight. When I called your mom she said there were brochures about Japan all over your room, but she wasn't worried."

"You called my mom?" He looked shocked.

"Of course. You stole our son."

"Was she pissed?"

"I don't know. She said you'd probably bring him back in a few days and he'd be fine. But what if he wasn't? If you had an accident with him, or went down on the plane? You'd break my heart."

"Yeah, mine too," he said glumly. She thought of all the things he didn't. She always assumed the worst. "Do you think we could ever start over again, Ellen? We were so happy in the beginning."

"We were kids in college with no responsibilities. It takes more than a wedding to make a marriage," she said sadly. He had been a big lesson for her, and her parents had warned her, but she didn't want to listen. "And what do you suggest we do about him?" And she gestured to their child.

Robert looked blank for a minute as he thought about it. "We could leave him with your parents for a while. He likes them, and they're good with him." Listening to him was like being in fantasyland, and he wasn't even stoned. This was who he was.

"We can't go backward. We can't just hand our son off to someone else, and I don't want to. We can't start over for us. I can't do this again. I've hated the last two years too. You have to go away somewhere and grow up. And then you'll be good for someone else. Not for me. This has been a terrible experience for me," she said with tears in her eyes. "But you can start again with Scott, when you're ready to. I won't trust you alone with him again. I talked to my lawyer, and the court can appoint a monitor to be on visits with you, so he's safe. Until you can demonstrate that you're responsible." He didn't say anything and just nodded. It sounded horrible to him.

"I'm going to withdraw the parental abduction charges. And I'll drop the back child support. I know you can't pay it. My father said he'd help us. He's putting money aside for college for him anyway, and he'll give me some of that. But if you want to be Scott's father, you have to act like it," she said, staring at the man she had married who had turned out to be an overgrown boy. He acted like a teenager at twenty-five.

"Are you really going to withdraw the charges?" He looked happy about that as she nodded.

"And the child support. When you can afford it, you can start giving me money for him. I know you can't now anyway. You need a better job than a surf shop or bicycle shop or skateboard shop. You need a real job."

"I'm not ready for a real job." He wasn't ready for life, and surely not for a wife and child. Ellen stood up then, and Robert looked at her sadly. "You really don't want us to try again?"

"No, I don't," she said firmly.

"We were great for a while." He smiled at her.

"No, we weren't. We were stupid kids and we never should have gotten married. But I'm glad we have Scott." She gazed tenderly at their baby, who gurgled at her. "Take care of yourself. And I'm not paying your way back to New York. You can figure that out. I'll take care of the rest."

"Maybe I'll stay here for a while. Everyone says San Francisco is cool." He looked excited about it as he stood up too.

"Do whatever you want," she said to him. After talking to him, she had no regrets. She was glad she had come. It had been her father's idea. He said they needed to talk to each other as two adults and figure out what they wanted. She knew now. She didn't want him. And she wondered when Scott would see him again. Robert was obviously in no hurry to go back and grow up.

She turned around and left then, and never looked back. An hour later, the charges had been dropped, and Robert was released from jail. He texted her one word, "Thanks." She was already at the airport, waiting for her flight back to New York. She had done what she came for. Robert left the jail a free man. He checked into a small hotel in the Haight and went out to buy some weed. The neighborhood looked like fun to him. He got there just as Ellen's plane took off for New York with their son.

* * *

Helen was surprised when Ben called her the day after the press conference to ask her how she was feeling.

"I'm okay." She was touched that he had called. "I must be getting old. I used to do triathlons. I still hurt all over after eight hours in the water."

"You could probably swim the English Channel in less. Are you kidding? You were in a life-and-death stressful situation, made a water landing with a commercial plane, saved all your passengers, got swept out to sea, and hung in for eight hours. I'm surprised you can stand up." She laughed at his description of it. "How are your kids doing?"

"Relieved. I think I scared them all to death. They can handle the plane coming down better than my disappearing and being lost at sea for eight hours."

"Yeah. No wonder." He wasn't surprised.

"Do you have children?" She knew very little about him, and was curious. They had dealt with an emergency together but shared nothing about their personal lives. They'd had no reason to.

"I never had the courage, or the time. I was married twice, and both my wives said that my work isn't compatible with normal life between humans. I work a lot. So I stopped trying. Kids never fit into the picture. Once in a while, I regret it, but I don't think I'd have been good at it anyway."

"It's never too late," she said, smiling. "You might surprise yourself. Lots of men your age marry younger women and have kids."

"Now, that's a terrifying thought," he said and she laughed. He seemed like a kind man, and she thought it was too bad that he was alone.

"We're going to Disneyland next week." She changed the subject. "The kids don't know yet. I love it as much as they do."

"I've never been," he confessed. "It doesn't fit my image as a registered curmudgeon. I go to baseball games, and play pool in bars."

"Both my sons are in Little League," she said. "I'm thinking about coaching. I played softball in the Air Force, in a women's league. I have to be Mom and Dad now."

"That must be tough." He was sympathetic as he said it.

"Sometimes it is," she said honestly. "You do what you have to do. Things don't always turn out as you plan." He knew what had happened to their plans, when her husband was killed. But she seemed to be a normal, well-balanced person and was doing all right, and it was obvious how much she loved her kids.

"Well, don't forget about our dinner in New York. You look like you could use a decent meal. You probably never eat."

She was on the thin side, and always had been. "I eat. We eat a lot of pizza and burgers at our house, and barbecue on the weekends. Jack used to do that. I'm actually a lousy cook."

"But a great pilot. You can't do everything."

"You can tell my kids that."

"Have fun in Disneyland."

She suddenly wondered if he was still in California, and asked him.

"Actually, I am. The chief out here wanted to talk to me about something. I'm going back tomorrow. He's a nice guy."

She wished him a good trip back, and forgot about the call after they hung up. She had to take her oldest son to his baseball game in an hour. Life was back to normal. It was hard to believe that two days before she had been fighting to save the plane and had nearly died. And now she was driving to Little League games. Life was indeed very strange.

Tom Birney picked up Catherine promptly at seven o'clock at the Four Seasons just as he had told her he would. He had made a reservation at The Sea, with French and Japanese cuisine. She was wearing a pale blue dress the color of her eyes, with a trench coat over it. She managed to look both businesslike and sexy all at once. And she was wearing high-heeled shoes similar to the ones he had noticed on the plane.

"Nice shoes," he complimented her. "Manfredo Bizarro?" he asked, trying to remember the name she had told him.

"I think you mean 'Manolo Blahnik.' And no, these aren't, unfortunately. But I like 'Manfredo Bizarro.'"

"I'm not up on women's fashion," he confessed, and they settled down at their table and ordered wine, before they looked at the menu. "How did the interview go?" He was curious to know, and she seemed very pleased, so he suspected it had gone well.

She glanced at him conspiratorially, and it struck him how beautiful she was. "I got the job," she whispered and beamed at him. "I think they felt sorry for me because of what happened on the flight out, so I got the sympathy vote. But whatever the reason, I got it, and it's just what I wanted. I'm moving out here in a month. They're going to let me use a company apartment until I find one. It's perfect," she said happily, as she sipped her wine.

"Congratulations, I'm pleased for you." He had news of his own in that department, and shared it with her after they ordered dinner. "I have a new job too. Or actually, an old job. Or a new job with my old company."

"That sounds confusing," she laughed at him.

"I gave notice where I'm working a while back, after some personal disagreements with the CEO. Our egos got involved, so I think I may have been a little hasty in my decision. I had a bad case of ruffled feathers. In any case, I met with our CEO today. We both apologized and I'm going to stay. I'm really pleased about it. They've added some new features to my old job and enhanced it with a component I really like, which will mean more travel between our East and West Coast offices, and more autonomy and authority. So I'm staying where I am. I'd always loved the company until our disagreement, and I'm proud to work for them."

"Well, that sounds interesting. After our conversation on the plane, I thought I was going to move here just in time for you to go back to New York." She was happy that he wasn't, and that his job brought him to San Francisco often.

"It could have been Atlanta, or Houston, I've been setting up interviews there too. I have a grown son who lives in Chicago, and I was considering moving there. He's my only child and he works hard, so I don't see him much. But I won't be moving there now. I'll be in San Francisco and New York. I'll just have to visit him more often. And actually, I have meetings in New York for my company on Monday. When are you going back again?"

She looked horrified at the thought. "After the flight out here, I think I'd rather walk. I'd take the train, but I have to get back." She didn't look happy about it.

"I could fly with you on Sunday, so you wouldn't have to fly alone. You can have three champagnes when we board, sleep for two hours, have three more, and we'll be there, and I can carry you off the plane if you can't walk."

"Very funny. The champagne really helps."

"Listen, after the flight on Wednesday, you're entitled to do whatever you need to, to get there. But seriously, do you want me to fly with you?"

She thought about it and nodded. "Actually, I do. Would you mind?"

"Of course not. I'd enjoy it—that's why I suggested it. We can play Scrabble or cards, or watch movies."

"Or send each other emails," she said, smiling. And then she looked serious for a moment. "I'm happy you'll still be coming out here often, and didn't quit."

"I'm pleased too. Being in the same city definitely has some possibilities. Do you have friends out here?"

She shook her head. "Not a soul. I was ready for something new. I was doing the same old things in New York. I was bored with my job. It seemed like the right time to make a change."

"I'll introduce you to some people. I have a lot of friends here. Do you play tennis?"

"Not in a long time. I'm a workaholic," she admitted. "But maybe that needs to change a little too."

"I work a lot too, and the enhancement to my job will increase that, but at least it's doing what I love." Their dinners came then, and they talked about their work. He said he'd help her find an apartment, and she was looking forward to flying back with him, without a crisis happening. It seemed like a good beginning, and a first step toward her new life.

He took her back to the hotel at ten-thirty, and told her he'd pick her up at noon the next day. He was going to drive her around the area and show her the sights.

"I've already had a good look at the Golden Gate Bridge. We can skip that," she said wryly.

"I wasn't planning to include it on the tour," he said seriously. He wasn't sure that he would be able to see it in the same way himself after what had happened. "We'll do something else." She had given him her flight number at dinner, so he could make his reservation for Sunday to fly with her. "See you tomorrow," he said, as she waved and walked back into the hotel, while he watched her. Meeting her had been an interesting turn of events, and if anyone asked down the line how they met, they could always say that they had been on a plane that crashed. It was different at least. And he liked how courageous she was, starting a new life and a new job in a new city. She was a gutsy woman, and she made him feel gutsy too. He liked her, a lot, right down to the Manfredo Bizarro shoes, or whatever they were called.

Chapter Fifteen

Helen went to Connor's memorial service. It was held at a small Episcopal church in Marin, near where he'd lived. His children had flown in for it and organized everything. The flowers in the church were beautiful. The soloist at the service sang "Amazing Grace," and after the memorial, they were sending his body to be buried in the family plot in Illinois, where one of his daughters lived and his children had grown up. His late wife was buried there too, and it seemed like the right place for him to be, not in a lonely cemetery in California. They had held the service there so that his friends could attend, and there were about a hundred people in the church. He and his wife had lived in Marin County for a long time and had loved it there. They had moved to California, Helen learned, when their kids grew up.

It was a somber event, given the way he'd died, and she was relieved that she and her children were going to Disneyland that weekend, which would take her mind off the fallen pilot who had died on her watch. She felt guilty about it, since he had been trying to help her when Jason shot him. The whole thing was still so hard to stomach and to accept. She was touched by how gracious Connor's children had been to her about it. They knew it wasn't her fault. But she felt bad about it anyway, and knew it would haunt her forever.

The trip to Disneyland was a big success, and they stayed three days. They did everything all three kids wanted to do, including all the scary rides and roller coasters the boys loved. She and Lally waited outside for them, and went on all the rides in Fantasyland for her and bought her a Cinderella costume at the gift shop, complete with plastic "glass" slippers. The weather was gorgeous in L.A., and the lines weren't too long. It would be busier once school let out, but she had taken them out of school for two days before it ended for the summer for a special treat, so the park wasn't too crowded. They had invited Helen's father to join them, but he'd opted for a quiet weekend at home instead.

In June, she went back to work. It was hard getting back into the routine again after a month of leisure, doing nothing other than following her kids around, driving them to Little League games, taking them to movies on weekends, having their friends over for slumber parties, and riding bikes with them around Petaluma. They all complained when she went back to work.

She was flying A321s again, and her first day back at work was the hardest, remembering what had happened the last time she'd flown. The crew members all knew about it, but the passengers didn't realize that she was the pilot who had flown under the Golden Gate Bridge and landed on the water.

By sheer luck, Joel was on her first flight to New York, back from his honeymoon in Tahiti, the color of coffee with a deep tan, and showing off his wedding band to the flight attendants he knew. He gave Helen a big hug when she came on board, and served her himself for the entire trip. She had a very pleasant copilot that day whom she'd flown with several times before. Everything was perfect. When she got to the hotel in New York, she wondered if she should call Ben for the dinner he had mentioned, or if it had just been social talk.

She had nothing to do that night, and Joel was seeing friends for dinner, so she couldn't have dinner with him, and it was a beautiful spring night. In the end, she called Ben when she got to the hotel. He was still in his office, and startled to hear from her. She told him she was on a quick turnaround and going back to San Francisco the next day.

"You don't give a guy much notice, do you?" he complained. "How about dinner at eight o'clock? I'll pick you up at your hotel." He had tickets to a Yankees game that night, but didn't tell her. He walked into Amanda's office and handed them to her. "Go. Learn something. Take a friend." They'd been getting along much better for the past month, and had found a secret mutual respect for each other, though he never admitted it to her. But he told everyone else how smart she was, and it got back to her.

Ben drove into the city straight from work, after making a reservation at his favorite steak restaurant near Helen's hotel. They could walk to it, so he put his car in a garage.

He was in the lobby at the appointed time, and she came downstairs quickly, wearing jeans and a red sweater. She looked young and more relaxed than in her uniform. He took off his tie and stuffed it in his pocket the minute he saw her. The place he took her to had a cozy, old-fashioned atmosphere, half English pub and half New York bar. It had a pool table. He liked to play sometimes, and he challenged her to a game before dinner, when she said she used to play a lot in the Air Force. She beat him squarely, and he was a good sport about it, and said they'd have to play again after dinner, when hopefully she'd be tired and relaxed enough to take the edge off her game. She didn't drink at all since she was flying in the morning, and they talked a lot. He was an interesting person, and his years with Homeland Security, the Justice Department before that, and as a police detective when he was younger had been busy and exciting. He had come up through the ranks, and surprised her when they finished the meal and he told her he had a new job.

"After all that, you're leaving Homeland Security?"

"Not exactly. Moment of madness. I'm moving. I had a bad case a couple of months ago and figured I needed a change to get it out of my head."

"I know about those," she said quietly.

"Alan Wexler, the San Francisco chief, is retiring. Since he credits me for helping to save the Golden Gate Bridge, he offered the job to me as a favor. I thought it was a crazy idea at first, but then I didn't." He had talked to Mildred Stern, and she liked the idea for him, but he didn't tell Helen that. He thought she'd think he was weird or neurotic if she knew he'd seen a shrink, which Mildred told him was an antiquated theory. Crazy people are the only ones who don't see a shrink, she'd told him, watch out for them. "They've got some good people out there, and it's a smaller office. Maybe a little less pressure, which would be nice. And the truth is, I don't have any personal ties here. I don't have kids, I don't have a girlfriend, I've been divorced for a long time. I have some friends and my job. I can always come back here if I want to, but I kind of like the idea of California for a change."

"That's why Jack and I wanted to move there, and my father retired there. Nice quality of life. And in my case, good for the kids. In yours, maybe you'll miss the big city."

He shook his head when she said it. "As long as they have a baseball stadium, I'll be happy. And they have a good team out there."

She knew all about that. "My sons love to go too. They're big Giants fans. So you took it?"

He nodded, looking a little stunned himself. "I did. About two weeks ago. I almost called you for advice, but I figured you have enough on your hands."

"So when are you moving out?"

"In six weeks. They have an apartment I can use for a while, in kind of a lousy neighborhood, but I don't care. I think I want to live in the country, like Marin County or something. I took a look around when I was there."

She was smiling as he said it, and thought it was brave of him and sounded exciting. Moving to a new city wasn't easy, but he didn't have schools to worry about, or kids, or all that went with it. "That sounds great, Ben," she said, looking genuinely enthusiastic, and with that, he challenged her to another game of pool, since they'd finished dinner. This time he beat her. He tried to coax her into another game. He was enjoying her company too much to leave, and the evening had flown for both of them.

"I can't. I have to get up at four-thirty to make my plane, and I'll be a mess if I don't get some sleep," although she hadn't slept well for the past month anyway, but it was getting better. "There's a great bar in Petaluma where I live, with a pool table. I'll take you there."

"I'd like that," he said, looking down at her. She was exactly the kind of woman he was attracted to, quiet, honest, gutsy, fun to be with, smart, real. He hadn't met anyone like her in a long time, and wasn't sure he would again. "Dinner again next time you're here?" he asked her hesitantly.

"Sure," she made it easy. She could sense what he was asking her. "You'll have to come to one of our barbecue nights, and meet my kids." She was letting him know she liked him in answer to his unspoken question.

"Maybe I could take you all to a baseball game sometime."

She laughed at the suggestion. "We're a pretty rowdy group, and I'm as bad as they are."

"I think I can take it." They sounded like good kids to him, and she was a good woman. He had realized afterward that he had liked her when he heard her on the satcom when he was warning her about Jason Andrews. And he realized how much he cared about her when he saw her land the plane under the bridge, and do everything she could to keep it floating until everyone was out. And then she'd disappeared and he'd been terrified she was dead. When they finally pulled her out of the water in the harness, and she looked like a drowned rat, he had never seen a more beautiful sight in his life, and he wanted to know her better. "I really enjoyed dinner to-night," he said, smiling at her.

"You won't for long," she said confidently. "I'm not letting you beat me at pool again. I think I was tired."

"Yeah, whatever, sore loser. You had a headache, right?"

"Exactly." They were both good players, and he knew that was going to be fun too. He liked everything about her so far.

"When are you coming back here again?" he asked, trying to sound casual about it.

"Twice a week for the next month," she answered, and he was pleased.

"Good, pool and dinner." He was smiling at the idea.

"You're going to be tired of me before you ever come to California," she warned him. She'd had a nice time too.

"I doubt that."

"You know what they say about Air Force pilots. They're pretty dull."

He laughed out loud at what she said. "Captain Smith, if there is one thing no one is ever going to say about you, it's that you're dull. You're the most exciting woman I've ever met," and she could see he meant it.

"Flattery will not induce me to let you win at pool," she said. "Although I'll admit, it's a nice touch."

"Go get some sleep, and call me the next time you're coming back. And try to give me more than two hours' notice. I gave up a Yankees game for you tonight," but he looked like he had no re-grets.

She was instantly embarrassed. "I'm really sorry," she said sincerely.

"Don't be. I had a better time with you. Good night." He kissed her lightly on the cheek and she walked back into the hotel. Ben walked down the street to the garage whistling. It turned out that the move to California was not such a crazy idea after all.

Chapter Sixteen

The notice came to each of them on the first of October. Helen had had no inkling of it whatsoever, or who would have recommended her for it. She had been invited to an award ceremony in Washington, D.C., on the fifteenth of November, where she was to be given a Presidential Medal of Honor for bravery above and beyond the call of duty. It was the highest and most prestigious personal military decoration, normally given to members of the armed forces. They were giving it to her after her years of service.

She didn't know who to ask or tell about it, other than her father, and when Ben came to dinner with her and the kids that night, as he did often now, she tried beating around the bush about it, because she didn't want to hurt his feelings or make him feel left out.

"Why? Are you getting some kind of award?" he asked her, with a look of innocent surprise.

"No, well . . . actually I heard about it, but nobody has said anything to me," she said and he laughed at her.

"Helen Smith, you are a terrible liar. It's the Presidential Medal of Honor, and they're giving me the Presidential Medal of Freedom," which was the highest civilian award, for his contribution to the security and national interests of the United States, "so you don't have to be polite about it. I'll call around tomorrow and see who else is getting it. My guess is it's everyone who was involved in the Golden Gate Bridge rescue caper."

"Oh." She felt much better when he said that. "I didn't want you to feel bad about it," she said, and he kissed her while the children were out of the room. They knew that their mother and Ben were dating, but she didn't think they needed to see the details or the evidence of it at their ages. But they were crazy about him, and he was enjoying them too. He took the boys to sports games a lot, and had dinner with them several times a week.

The next day, he had the whole list for her. She was getting an award, and so were Ben; Phil, the head of the New York office of Homeland Security; Alan, the head of the San Francisco office at the time it happened; Tom Birney; Dave Lee, the head of airport security at JFK; Bernice Adams, the TSA agent; Connor Gray was receiving it posthumously; and the entire flight crew that day, Joel, Nancy, Bobbie, Jennifer, and the others. Helen was getting the Medal of Honor, and all the others were getting the Medal of Freedom.

"Wow, I think we should go," Helen said, studying the list. They hadn't left any of the key players out, which made her feel better about it. She didn't want to be singled out, and she hadn't been. Saving the passengers had been a team effort.

"Of course we should go, and take the kids," he said. "They should see you get it."

"And you," she reminded him. She had invited her father to go as well. He was very proud of her and so were her kids.

Helen made flight and hotel reservations for them the next day. Ben was flying with them, but she thought he should still have his own hotel room, just for the sake of appearances for the kids, although Ben thought they had figured it out over the summer—the boys anyway, since they were older than Lally.

Ben and her father got along well too. They had played golf together several times, and wanted to go to Giants spring training, and were going to take the boys.

Helen saw Joel on a flight a week later, and he said that he and Kevin were going to Washington too. The whole thing was very exciting, and her kids could hardly wait to meet the president, since he would be giving them the medals himself. Oliver was going to write about it as a project for school.

Tom called Catherine at the office as soon as he got the invitation, and asked her to go as his date. Things were going well between them, and they both loved their jobs. They were spending almost every weekend together, since he spent most of them in San Francisco, and at least two full weeks a month.

They had gone to Chicago for a weekend, and she'd met his son. It was the kind of relationship they had both wanted and never found till now.

And when Bernice opened the envelope, she sat and held it in her hands for a long time. She picked Toby up from school, and when they got home, she told him.

"Remember when you said you wanted to go to Washington and meet the president of the United States?"

"Yeah." He nodded.

"Do you still want to?" Toby nodded and she hugged him tight. "Well, he's going to give me a medal for the thing I did about the postcard and the bad guy who wanted to hurt the bridge. And you're coming with me." He was the most important person in her life.

She had started a new job in September, at a Wall Street law firm, just like she had promised him. She had graduated from law school and taken the bar exam that summer, and she was waiting for the results. They had taken her on as a junior lawyer in the meantime, for more money than she'd ever dreamed of. She had left TSA in August, and Denise had wished her luck. There was a farewell lunch for her, and Bernice had been stunned when Denise hugged her when she left and Della cried.

"Can I have a medal too?" Toby asked her.

"You can have mine," she promised him. "And we've got to get you a suit to go to Washington, and I need a new dress." It was the most exciting thing that had ever happened to her. A presidential medal, for her contribution to security and the national interests. She was smiling from ear to ear, just thinking about it.

The sky was gray the morning of the award ceremony, but none of them cared, as they arrived separately at the entrance to the White

House, showed their identification, said what state they were from, and a smiling guard said, "Welcome to the White House!"

The ceremony was to be held in the Blue Room, on the State Floor, which was used for greeting important dignitaries. It was a beautiful oval room, with a blue oval rug, blue drapes, and uphol-stered antiques. It had a view of the South Lawn, and was perfect for an occasion such as this.

Catherine had come with Tom Birney as his date. She was living in Palo Alto, and Tom was planning to move in over the holidays. Ben was happy to see Phil and find out what was happening in New York. He introduced him to everyone, and it was like old home week when Dave Lee showed up from the airport. The whole flight crew was there, Joel with Kevin, Bobbie and Annette, and Jennifer, the chief purser on the flight, and the other flight attendant in first class. They had gotten everybody out that day. Helen was startled and pleased to see Nancy seven months pregnant, and Peter had come with her with their newly adopted daughter from Beijing, whom they had named Jade. And Connor Gray's children were there with his grandchildren, huddled in a corner, looking somber but proud. Helen's children were so excited for her they could hardly contain themselves as they asked when it was going to start. And she introduced her father and Ben to everyone. She had bought new suits for the boys, and Lally a new pink dress, and she had bought a white suit that was the most expensive outfit she'd ever owned, and Ben beamed whenever he looked at her.

The last one to arrive was Bernice Adams, looking very stylish in a red dress and a black coat, with black suede high heels, her hair freshly done in a bun, and her son, Toby, in a black velvet suit. She went over to talk to Ben, whom she recognized, and he introduced her to Helen and her children. Lally and Toby were the same age.

"It's an honor to meet you," Bernice said to Helen, looking awe-struck for a minute.

"You're the one who saved us. If you hadn't called about the post-card, the bridge and the plane would have gone down. It all started with *you,* so we're all thrilled to meet you. Are you still with TSA?" Helen asked her, and Bernice smiled a wide ivory smile.

"I graduated from law school in June and took the bar last sum-mer. I'm working for Harper, Steinman, and Coles," she said proudly.

"Good job!" Helen said, duly impressed. "That's terrific!" She loved stories of women who had fought their way up from the bot-tom and made it.

The president came in a few minutes later and addressed all of them, and said how much they deserved the medals he was about to give them. "You saved a national landmark, and your passengers' lives. We will owe you a debt forever. And you serve as an example to us all. Each one of you is a hero."

He handed out the medals to each of them then, shook their hands, and spoke to them for a few minutes, and he wished Nancy luck with the baby and she thanked him. It wasn't due till January but she looked like she was going to pop any minute. He spent a little more time with Helen. She had worn all her military medals on her new white suit, and he added the presidential medal on it. She already had the Air Force Cross and the Air Force Distinguished Service Medal from her tours of duty as an Air Force pilot. They were two of the highest medals the military gave.

"We're very proud of you, Captain. We're proud of all of you," he said addressing the group, and especially the children. "It's very important for all of us to try to be heroes in our daily lives."

As he said it, Helen knew again that it wasn't something you tried to do. It was something that happened to you, an accident of circumstance, and you became a hero without ever meaning to. It was what had happened to all of them. They had gotten up in the morning and had gone to work, never thinking that anything different was going to happen to them. And then it had. They were all accidental heroes, no matter what the medal said, but brave men and women nonetheless.

THE CAST

CREATIVITY. AMBITION. FRIENDSHIP.

Living in New York, Kait Whittier is a successful writer. With her children grown up and dotted around the globe, she finds herself looking for distractions from her empty nest. Always inspired by the many brilliant, independent women in her life, Kait dreams up the concept for a TV show. Kait's life is transformed by the success of the show and the relationships she forms with the star-studded cast. It's not long before Kait's new friendships become an extended family, supporting her through the tragedies, pitfalls and romances in life that make Kait her own leading lady.

Available for pre-order

PURE HEART. PURE STEEL.